The Flames of Albiyon

by Jean Z. Menzies

Music, when soft voices die,
Vibrates in the memory—
Odours, when sweet violets sicken,
Live within the sense they quicken.

Rose leaves, when the rose is dead,
Are heaped for the belovèd's bed;
And so thy thoughts, when thou art gone,
Love itself shall slumber on.

Percy Bysshe Shelley, 1821

For my dad.
I wish you had been able to read this novel
because without you it would never have existed.

Prologue

From the records of parliamentary member Lady Isla II of Baile

In this, the 100th Spring of the People's Democratic Parliament, the realm of Albiyon remains relatively peaceful. New measures to provide for the welfare of Albiyans were passed this spring to an overall positive reception. A small increase in tax of 1% has been levied against the wealthiest of our citizens; this will fund investments into new modes of transport between rural areas, as well as more secure storage facilities to preserve food and other necessities during winter in those regions where trade is more difficult during the colder months. This motion, which was passed with a 70% majority met with some resistance from the self-titled Traditionalist lobby group, with the support of parliamentary members Lord Tristan and Lady Mirin, but their objections were not enough to quell its support among the populace.

In more disturbing news the town of Invergorm has raised concerns around the water supply that comes from Loch Gorm. A local group has been collecting complaints from residents who have noted a metallic taste in their wells and springs, because of which they have petitioned parliament with a request to send a magician or witch to purify the water. The first attempt at such a clean-up was conducted last week, but Madam Willowherb was unable to solve the problem.

She has instead added her voice to those of the concerned citizens who do not wish to remain in Invergorm if this problem persists, out of concern for their health. As Loch Gorm is a major reservoir, parliament is putting serious resources into solving this issue. In the meantime, I can only hope it does not worsen; residents have already appealed for temporary housing while investigations go on, and although many of us in parliament feel they are entitled to what they ask for, nothing is ever as quick as one would like it to be in these situations.

Chapter One
The Egg

There really was no way she could ignore it. Countless pairs of eyes had already turned from across the room to look in her direction. Heads raised from the maps they were studying, books were placed face down to mark the reader's place, and bodies swivelled where they stood. Adairia meanwhile was torn between mortification and horror. As she stood there, mouth agape, the rag she held in her hand slipped between her fingers and onto the marble floor. Aghast, she watched the fracture spread, new lines spiralling outward from the original fissure in an ominous embrace; the noise the first crack made had reverberated throughout the otherwise silent room, impossibly loud. Finally, it seemed to pause in its tracks, ceasing to spread any further, and Adairia felt she could tear her eyes away for long enough to gaze around the cavernous chamber. Without exception, everyone's eyes were fixed firmly in her direction. Expressions of shock, confusion, and even anger stared back at her. There was no fleeing now.

*

It had been midmorning in Eòlas when Adairia reached the marble gallery. She had been hard at work since five that morning, scrubbing floors, polishing pedestals, and replacing books that had wandered from their appropriate shelves. Once she finished dusting this last room, she reminded herself, she would finally be free to enjoy a well-earned midday meal and perhaps some light reading of her own. At the beginning of each month the university's domestic tasks were divided up between its residents. The foundling children raised with the support of the university were welcome to continue to live on institution grounds once they were legally adults, however, they were each required to pitch in their share. In order to receive room and board, they were responsible for the same tasks as any employee would be: from cleaning to cooking; caring for the horses and other animals on site; repairing anything that might need a little restoration; as well as serving as messengers for the various academics who worked there full-time. Adairia had never been much good at cooking or mending broken wagons, but she had a fixating nature that made her an excellent gardener and cleaner.

That month Adairia had been tasked with keeping the third floor of the university's attached museum neat and tidy. Each of the grand rooms that made up the building were known colloquially by the material their walls were made from. Just moments before she had left behind the now spotless limestone chamber for its more glamorous marble neighbour, and this had been the last room on her rounds for the morning. The gallery itself was a cavernous, circular room that could be seen jutting out from the rest of the building by any observer stationed outside. It had a specially-built ceiling made of thinly formed rose quartz that cast a pinkish hue over the marble walls and floors. There were various tables and chairs dotted around the room haphazardly; some adorned with maps and larger reference volumes, while others remained empty and waiting. These were accompanied by various plinths and glass cabinets that bordered the space. This is where the museum displayed some of its most impressive artefacts: the armour and shield of the legendary King Leith; a larger than human size gilt mirror that let the gazer look upon the face of the person they missed most; the red-velvet clothed diary of the university's founder, bound shut by magic and unopened for centuries; as well as an enormous, fossilised dragon's egg, the dazzling orange surface of which had been perfectly smooth up until six seconds ago.

Adairia would swear she had not touched the thing, not even with her cloth - she knew better than that. All she had done was gone to wipe down the front of its pedestal like every other time she had cleaned this room. As soon as her hand touched the base, however, she had heard that sickening crack. Horrified, she leapt to her feet and watched with bated breath as the damage she would surely be blamed for unfolded. Not until the fracture finally ceased to spread, was she able to catch her breath. *Maybe it was not that bad? Of course, it was bad, but not as bad as a splintered pile of rubble and some fossilised infant dragon bones. Maybe she was not about to be thrown out of the university for the destruction of a priceless historical artefact? Maybe?*

It was at that moment that she felt a hand on her shoulder. Turning her head a fraction to the right, Adairia found herself staring at the slightly watery brown eyes and coarse braided grey beard of Cyril, one of the senior academics at the university. He stood about three inches taller than Adairia, looking down at her ever so slightly, concern plastered across his features.

'You best come with me.' He whispered gesturing to the archway at the back of the hall, which Adairia knew led to a narrow flight of stairs. 'I'll take you to the chancellor's rooms.'

Together they walked to the exit. Cyril marched in front

while Adairia trailed behind staring fixedly ahead, afraid of what she would see if she caught anyone else's eye. It was not until they were halfway up the winding stone staircase that she blurted out the words she had been holding in since the moment she had withdrawn her hand from the plinth.

'I didn't touch it, I swear it.' She hesitated before blundering on. 'I mean I touched the plaque, but I didn't touch the egg. I would never touch… it's just it was on the rota… and I've cleaned it countless times before…' She trailed off when Cyril paused just long enough to turn and look woefully back at her.

'I'm not sure that makes a difference.' Cyril sighed and without any further elucidation turned back around and continued up the stairs. Adairia was not sure what else she could say at this point so she trudged behind him, hitching the skirts of her dress up so she would not trip and break her neck on top of everything else. *That was about all she needed.*

At the top of the stairs was a short corridor, no longer than a few paces, just enough space for a life size portrait to hang on one wall bearing the face of the university's founder, Caledon, in a heavy gold frame. Cyril reached the door at the end of the corridor first and rapped the knocker lightly against the wood. They did not have to wait long, as a split second later the door swung open to frame the figure of a tall woman who at first glance might have passed for her early seventies - although Adairia knew she was well past ninety - with long white hair, brown skin, and an imposing wooden staff held in one hand like a walking stick. This was the university's chancellor.

'Cyril! We've been waiting on you to get started.' She exclaimed. 'Come on then.' She moved back into the room slightly to allow Cyril past, and it was at this moment that she caught sight of Adairia standing a little way behind him, reluctant to stray far from the steps she had just ascended. The chancellor's voice immediately took on a more serious tone. 'What's going on?' She asked, looking between Cyril and this unexpected guest.

'I think we best come in and I can tell everyone at the same time.' Cyril motioned for Adairia to follow as he stepped into the room; *well, what choice did she have?*

*

'It what!' A short figure exclaimed from his perch on a round footstool beside the fire, clearly echoing what everyone else in the room was thinking.

'It cracked,' Cyril repeated for the third time. It was at this point that Adairia felt she should chime in.

'I didn't touch it, really, only the base.' The chancellor turned to look at Adairia directly, her gaze assessing.

'We believe you,' she sighed, furling and unfurling her fingers around the staff in her hand.

'Do we?' The question came from the shorter figure again whose expression remained suspicious, if not downright incensed.

'Yes, Tronk, we do.' The chancellor spoke more firmly this time. 'Not that it matters.'

Adairia knew each of the figures in the room by name even if she had never exchanged more than a nod of greeting with some of them. The five individuals currently in the room with her were what made up the official University council, in charge of managing the centuries' old institution. There was Chancellor Aliya who had greeted them at the door. She was responsible for ensuring that every aspect of the university ran as smoothly as possible and had dedicated her life to doing so. The other council members effectively reported to her.

The short creature who was looking suspiciously at Adairia, arms folded across his chest, was Tronk, the Goblin representative. Goblins tended to live in the more remote mountainous regions of Albiyon, where the air was thinner and temperatures cooler. For that reason, Tronk was one of only a handful of goblins Adairia had ever encountered. The goblins were long-time keepers of knowledge. Many of the most famous scholars Adairia had read had been from their numbers. They hosted their own library built deep into the mountainside where they lived, full of ancient goblin literature that Adairia dreamed of one day visiting, but the journey was an arduous one for a human like herself. It was tradition therefore for one of them to act as liaison between their people and the university, and Tronk had served in this role for as long as Adairia could remember.

An observer may have taken the heavily muscled figure beside Tronk for a blacksmith or farm-labourer based on his thick limbs and imposing size. This, however, was Angus and he was the head-librarian. The middle-aged man, who had yet to speak up, was striking with his bright red curls, thick beard and piercing green eyes. When Adairia had been a child he had simply been another of the university's numerous library assistants, reporting to the previous head librarian, Morgana. When Morgana had retired a decade before, to travel beyond Albiyon's coastal borders and 'experience the world outside of this tiny island whilst she still had her libido intact' as she put it, Angus had been her natural successor.

Slightly behind Angus' armchair stood an ethereal figure; there was no other way to describe the Lady Mirin. As much as she attempted to stand back from the rest of the group, she was the most visible presence in the room. Her silver hair had a mind of its own, weaving through the air intermittently, and her pale skin almost shone with a pinkish hue. She reminded Adairia of silk. Everything about her appeared almost painfully delicate, yet Adairia knew she was both the most powerful and the oldest being in this room. She was the university's tie to the fair-folk who had once sat adjacent to the throne, and to this day continued to hold great sway over the way in which Albiyon was run. In fact, the Lady Mirin occupied one of the few remaining hereditary seats in the Albiyan parliament, it having been passed down to her by her father who had been one of the last king's closest advisors. It was also a not so well-kept secret that she had once vied for the position of chancellor herself.

Then of course, there was Cyril, a scholar in his seventies who oversaw the University's teaching department. As well as the foundling children who were raised there, the university also catered to the surrounding villages who did not have their own schoolmasters and offered any child the opportunity to be taught by some of the best minds in Albiyon. Cyril had been Adairia's own tutor growing up, and while he still ran a few classes here and there he was predominantly responsible for the school's organisation these days.

Adairia had never before appeared in front of the entire academic council at once. While she had grown up in the University, there was rarely cause for any foundling or day student to pay a visit to those in charge of the institution itself. Cyril was the only member she, or any of the others, had regular contact with over the years outside of casual encounters in hallways or study rooms. Now she felt each of their faces fixed on her. Unsure of where to look herself, she instead stared avidly at a silvery moth that was dancing on the windowpane

13

behind the Chancellor Aliya. *All because of that blasted egg.*

Cyril had explained to the room what had happened in the marble chamber as soon as they had closed the door behind them. Tronk had reacted the most violently while Angus had looked almost as alarmed by the tale. Aliya and Lady Mirin had been harder to read although Adairia was sure she had seen a trace of worry flicker across the chancellor's features for the briefest moment before disappearing again. None of which reassured her.

'Could this mean…?' Angus began before trailing off.

'It is waking up.' Mirin's voice was barely more than a whisper, but it held the attention of everyone in the room.

'I believe Lady Mirin is correct,' responded Aliya.

'Surely not because of this girl,' barked Tronk. 'She's nobody.' Adairia frowned but could not reasonably disagree so said nothing.

'That remains to be seen.' Aliya turned to address Adairia directly. 'Do you have any idea what we are talking about Adairia?'

'Yes chancellor, I think so…' she replied slowly, trying to keep her voice even, 'but you can't mean the egg is awake?'

'That is exactly what we mean.'

'But – but I thought it was a fossil? That's what we were always told.'

'As did we all, but fossilised eggs do not begin to crack of their own accord. If you weren't aware, it is notoriously difficult to tell a barren dragon's egg from one that holds a living creature within its shell. This egg has been in the University far longer than I have, and that is saying something. In fact, from what I recall, the original artefact entry suggests it has been contained within these walls for more than two centuries. Not

14

that that is any indication of age. It could have been held elsewhere for far longer. Nevertheless, for an egg to remain unhatched yet continue to hold the promise of life for even that long is unheard of. Naturally, therefore, it has long been assumed to be dead.' This last word hung in the air whilst the rest of the room processed the implication behind the chancellor's statement. 'It does appear, however, that our judgement, and that of the scholars before us, was too hasty.'

'So, I'm not in trouble?' Adairia responded hesitantly. There was a lot of information to take in at that moment, but she could not focus on any of it until she had clarified her own position in this room.

'Depends on how you look at it,' Tronk snorted, folding his arms across his small chest.

'You haven't done anything wrong, no.' said Aliya slowly. Adairia wanted to relax, but her body did not appear willing to assent to this request and she remained a tight knot of tension as everyone else in the room appeared to be waiting for someone else to speak. It was the Lady Mirin who broke the silence.

'A dragon has not been born in Albiyon in your lifetime, but I have witnessed their births in mine. Dragons do not rely on their mother's protection and their eggs can be abandoned soon after being laid. Instead, the infants wait inside their shell until they choose to bond with the first creature they feel drawn to. It is only then that they hatch.' She waited for this to sink in before continuing, 'I think I speak for everyone in this room when I say that, given the circumstances, we believe there is a strong possibility that you are the creature this dragon has chosen to bond with. It takes an entire cycle of the moon for an egg to fully hatch, however, so we cannot yet be certain.'

Adairia stared at the fae woman, blinking gormlessly, unable to speak.

'Perhaps it would be best to give Adairia some time to process what we have told her. It will also give us time to discuss how to deal with this situation as it stands.' Aliya stepped a little closer to Adairia, her expression sympathetic, before turning to address Cyril. 'May I suggest you show Adairia out and then return here with the egg Cyril.'

'Yes, of course.' He nodded solemnly and gently placed a hand on Adairia's shoulder. 'We'll send for you shortly, once we've talked things over. By then you will probably have some questions of your own.' Adairia nodded, unable to respond with words, and allowed Cyril to guide her back down the short hallway and away from the council. As soon as the door closed behind them the voices inside picked back up, and as Adairia and Cyril walked away she could make out the tell-tale sounds of an argument unfolding in hushed but animated tones.

Chapter Two
Adairia

The university gardens were rarely empty, but they were nevertheless the place that Adairia felt most at peace. She had always had an aptitude for gardening and growing vegetables. She found the hard work satisfying; you got what you put in, quite literally. She loved learning about different plants and adapting to their needs as she watched them bloom. It allowed her to apply her appetite for research to something tangible. Then, each year, when she came to harvest the results of her labour, she felt an unparalleled sense of pride and productivity. Dismissed from the chancellor's chambers and unsure of where else to go, it was only natural, therefore, that she found herself wandering into the gardens and picking up a trowel from the side of her little plot before starting to tug at the weeds.

It was one of the last few warm days before summer ended. Adairia could feel the heat of the unimpeded sun tickle her skin, but at the same time there was a crispness to the air that signalled the impending arrival of autumn. The allotments themselves were communally run, with all their produce being used to feed those under the care of the university. That had not stopped individuals from gradually claiming their own little plots and taking up responsibility for what grew in them though. Every turn of the season, Adairia's plot was inevitably one of the most flourishing, and more novice gardeners often asked her for advice on whatever they themselves were attempting to grow. Thankfully, however, no one seemed inclined to bother her this afternoon.

A dragon? There had not been tell of a new-born dragon in Adairia's lifetime, albeit twenty-seven years short. The last dragon hatching she was aware of had been sixty years ago, before even her parents had been born for all she knew. In principle she understood what the chancellor had told her, but the idea of an actual dragon still felt impossibly distant to her. Even if it were true, that the egg had begun the hatching process, she could not make herself feel in any way connected to the events that had set such a mammoth affair in motion. Perhaps that was telling. Perhaps her lack of draw to the dragon egg meant the council was wrong to suspect it was she whom the tiny creature wished to bond with. Or perhaps this numbness was simply the result of the shock she still felt at having witnessed the shell begin to crack in front of her this morning.

Sighing, Adairia brushed a lock of golden hair from in front of her eyes, managing to smear dirt across her forehead in the process. She had not exactly come prepared and had nothing on her that she could use to tie the thick mane of waves she sported out of the way. Not to mention she could feel the sun beating on her bare, freckled complexion, unshielded by her usual gardening hat. Exasperated, she plopped herself down on the edge of the upturned earth, head in her hands. *What if it were true? What if this dragon had bonded with her in the time she had spent cleaning the room it slept in?* She was not exactly sure how these things worked - not having read much about dragon lore - but she had certainly spent plenty of time in that room over her twenty plus years at the University. *Did she have any choice in this? Presumably these were the questions she was expected to bring back to the council when they called for her.* For now, she supposed all she could do was wait to find out exactly when that would be.

*

Like many of the children raised by the University she had been a resident there since she was a mere baby. There was an understanding in the realm that if someone gave birth but could not care for their child, they could leave the babe outside the doors to the university's chapel, and it would be taken care of. There had been the rare occasion when a mother or father had returned to claim their abandoned child months or years later when their circumstances had changed. Adairia, however, had gone her entire life thus far without word from her birth family, and it was something she tried not to dedicate a terrible amount of thought to.

Adairia had grown up surrounded by other parentless children, cared for by the scholars and other staff at the university. They were taught alongside all of the other children in Eòlas during the day, but in the evening, they ate, played, and slept alongside one another in their university dormitories. These children, and the adults who had taught and fed them, had been Adairia's family growing up. And while many of her fellows had left the university once they had turned eighteen, preferring to go off and start lives elsewhere in Eòlas or the wider Albiyon, she and her two closest friends had remained.

Morag was her oldest friend, both girls having been left as foundlings within a few months of one another and only a year apart in age. Morag was the older of the two, with dark skin, a head of thick, black spiral curls, and discerning amber eyes. She could usually be found in the dankest underground archives of the university, as far away from any other living creature as possible. Then there was Calder who had joined them when he was already seven years old. This was rare but not unheard of. Calder's parents had both died in a fire, leaving him with no other family to take him in. When he had arrived, the two young girls had already turned eight and nine, but they had become fast friends. He had grown into a short but solidly built young man with auburn hair and a well-developed tan, courtesy of hours spent working the land surrounding the University and tending to its animals.

If Adairia could count on anything, it was finding Calder outside come rain or shine. Too agitated even to garden, but not yet ready to go back inside, she decided to seek him out; perhaps some familiar company would help her straighten out the complicated tangle of threads her thoughts had become. Thankfully, she did not have to look long or far before she found him mucking out the pigsty nearest the gardens, a contented grin plastered on his face as he shooed away a curious piglet trying to get beneath his feet.

'There she is.' He called out when he saw her, raising a glove clad hand to wave her over.

'Aren't you done with your chores yet?' she teased, putting her hands on her hips and raising an eyebrow.

'Oh aye,' Calder chuckled, 'but the pigs needed tending and no one else was volunteering.' He bent down to tickle the persistent piglet under her chin. 'They're the only decent company in this place anyway.'

'You might be right.' Adairia nodded seriously, gazing down at a piglet who proceeded to trot over and sniff curiously at her dress between the wooden posts of its enclosure.

'How about you? I thought afternoons were for serious study. Or is that just an excuse Morag is using to avoid me?' he asked, taking a moment to relinquish his spade and walk over to her.

'I just… needed some fresh air… doing some thinking.' She was not sure what to tell him. If she explained what had happened this morning in the marble hall, in the chancellor's chambers, she would be accepting that it was not all a figment of her imagination. She would have to talk over all the possibilities and what they meant with Calder. It would all become very, very real. She did not have to mull it over for long, however, as Calder's next words broke through her reverie.

'Did you hear about what happened this morning?' he asked, and when she was only able to blink back at him, he continued. 'There's a rumour going around that the fossilised dragon's egg in the museum cracked. Duncan was here not fifteen minutes ago telling me that it'd been taken off public display by Cyril and a couple of men just this past hour.'

'Aye, I know.' Adairia sighed.

'Ken you, miss ahead-of-the-gossip,' laughed Calder. 'Did Duncan get to you first?'

'No, I was there.'

'You were what!' He exclaimed. 'And you didn't lead with this?'

'I was cleaning the base when it happened.'

'You were cleaning the… you mean you were the one that broke it.'

'I never touched it,' Adairia growled. 'I was wiping down the bloody pedestal when the damn thing started cracking.'

'Still…' Calder frowned.

'I know alright!' She was almost shouting by this point. She

21

was starting to feel an overwhelming heat rising through her body and a strong desire to run away and hide. 'The chancellor thinks it might have bonded with me, someway, somehow, but they can't be certain, not yet. It's another month before it hatches, which feels like tomorrow and years away at the same time. And honestly, they had me out of there that fast, I have no idea what's actually going on so don't ask me to explain anything...'

'Calm down Ads, just breath for a second ay?' Calder stared at her while she caught her breath, processing what she had said. Finally, after a few long moments he clapped his hands together. 'But this is brilliant news, Ads. There hasn't been a dragon birth in goodness knows how long. I would love to meet a dragon.' A look of blissful longing spread across his face as he spoke.

'Are you sure you weren't in the room this morning when the egg cracked? Maybe it wants to bond with you.'

'I wish! Dinnae look so dour faced, this could change your life.

'That's exactly what I'm afraid of.'

*

Adairia enjoyed her quiet life. She had Morag and Calder and was eternally grateful for their friendship. But she also loved the steady labour of gardening with its reliable results; walking the fields and rolling hills of Eòlas, preferably with a fascinating tome to occupy her mind when she paused to relax; or reading through the University's exhaustive library, which contained books that could not be found anywhere else in Albiyon. All she really wanted was to be a scholar. Adairia had not just been raised in this university, she had been raised by this university. Its spirit had seeped into her very being as she had grown into the woman she was today. It was the reason she had never left to seek new pastures elsewhere. She had walked every part of the grounds she had access to, yet they still captivated her. She had read through the library day after day, but it would be impossible to ever run out of books in this place. She had tended the earth that surrounded it, cleaned virtually every room or glass case she could reach. She knew when it had been founded, who its various chancellors had been over the centuries, and how the university had changed under their different styles of management. She had even dreamed one day of having her own name decorating the spine of the very same books that lined the university library's walls.

Not once when Adairia had imagined the path her life would take had it included gigantic, winged beasts with a mouth full of deadly weapons and the ability to cast a decent sized house into shadows. The number of facts she knew about dragon's in Albiyon could be counted on one hand. She knew that the legendary King Leith's wife had supposedly had a dragon companion whilst she was alive. She knew that her dragon egg had been acquired for the University Museum by one of Chancellor Aliya's predecessors more than two centuries ago. She knew that since then, it had sat undisturbed in its halls, a monument to a rare but important species that drew curious spectators from far and wide. She did not, however, know the first thing about actual dragons. *Hang on – her dragon egg? What was this nonsense? No, this was ridiculous, she wanted nothing to do with any possible dragons and she was going to tell the council exactly that.*

Chapter Three
Choices

Shortly after her conversation with Calder, Adairia found herself marching determinedly back up the narrow stairwell to the chancellor's rooms. On her way through the marble hall, she passed the plinth that mere hours ago she had been dusting contentedly, none the wiser, and sure enough the egg was gone. *Nothing to do with her*, she told herself firmly. Having had some time to think things over, she would now politely extricate herself from this entire situation. Someone else could have the thing, someone with more experience, who glowed at the possibility of becoming a dragon companion, someone like Calder. This is what she told herself. Still, it was impossible not to notice how her hands shook, and her feet were stomping perhaps a little harder than usual as she trudged up the stairs.

Adairia had expected to hear voices once she reached the short hallway that led to the chancellor's rooms, but everything was silent when she arrived on the landing. For some reason this only increased her level of agitation and she edged cautiously towards the door with her hand outstretched, but unsure of whether to knock or not. She was practically pressed up against the solid wood before she was able to deliver the most pathetic little rap of her fist against its surface. Nevertheless, it did the job.

'Come in,' came a muffled voice from within. Upon pushing open the door, Adairia found chancellor Aliya seated at her desk, the rest of the room empty of its earlier occupants.

'Adairia, welcome, I was wondering when you'd be back,' said the chancellor, looking up from the book she had evidently been reading before she had been interrupted. Her words made Adairia hesitate.

'I… I was waiting to be summoned, Cyril said…' She faltered, unsure if she had misunderstood her instructions.

'Yes, yes, you will be, the whole council will want to talk to you as one at some point I expect.' She stood up and walked round to the front of her desk. 'Would you like something hot to drink, a peppermint tea perhaps?' When Adairia said nothing, Aliya nodded. 'Yes, I think tea would be appropriate. Have a seat whilst I brew us up some cups.'

Adairia looked around for a moment before choosing to position herself on a cushioned window seat that looked out onto the University gardens. In the meantime, the chancellor boiled a pot of water in the fireplace and then poured it into two cups inside which she had already placed a few fresh peppermint leaves.

Adairia was better able to take in her surroundings on this second visit. The room was a mixture of study and sitting room: it hosted a large, ornate fireplace that featured a selection of woodland animals carved into its entablature; a worn but plush burgundy armchair accompanied by a small brocade sofa that had probably seen better days; a wall that was made up of precariously packed bookcases while to its right sat an imposing oak-wood desk; behind this was another door that presumably led to the rest of the chancellor's private chambers.

'Here we are.' Aliya handed Adairia a cup full of steaming

warm liquid; the feel of it in her hands instantly made her feel a little calmer than she had five seconds ago. The chancellor took her own cup and sat down on the armchair, which was the closest to the window seat.

'Cyril tells me you're quite the budding scholar yourself, a student of history I believe he said, agricultural?'

'Yes mam. I try at least.'

'An important discipline, yet often undervalued.' Adairia sipped her tea, starting to wonder why she had come here again. 'But you came to see me did you not. What would you like to discuss?'

'My egg,' Adairia managed to get out before catching herself, 'the dragon's egg I mean. I don't think I would make a suitable companion to a dragon. I would like to excuse myself from whatever you and the council have planned for the beast. I realise I may have played some part in creating these circumstances without realising it, but I don't wish to stake any claim on the creature. There is surely someone better suited to its care.' Chancellor Aliya smirked ever so slightly as she listened to these words rush forth from Adairia's mouth with barely a pause for breath.

'Yet you refer to it as your egg.'

'A slip of the tongue,' Adairia insisted. Aliya sighed.

'I'm afraid it's not quite that simple. You may be confused, even frightened, at the prospect of a future that involves a dragon. By the sounds of it, however, that is your future. What was it you said, you do not wish to claim the dragon? Well, I believe the dragon has claimed you my dear. That is why you have begun to think of it as a part of you, even in the slimmest manner. But that feeling will likely grow as the dragon's bond with you becomes deeper.'

'But this wasn't part of my plan. I never dreamed of dragons as a child. You said it yourself, I want to be a scholar.' Adairia's voice was flustered.

'And you think being bonded to a dragon will prevent you from fulfilling your dreams?'

'How could it not!' she exclaimed. 'A dragon can hardly curl up beneath my desk as I read for hours. Will it not require attention, demand my time from me when I should be conducting research?'

'Yes, I'm sure it will demand your time. But a dragon is not a pet. Life bonded to a dragon may perhaps expand your horizons rather than limit them.'

'I didn't want to expand my horizons.' Adairia huffed, she was starting to get annoyed now.

'Well, as much as we might desire to create neat little boxes in which our life can unfold according to plan, walls can always be knocked down. You are not the first person to have their circumstances suddenly change, and you will not be the last. You may even come to be grateful for this particular change.'

Adairia was unsure of how to respond to that. She wanted to scream. Were there no words that would get through to the woman that sat before her? She wanted to stamp her feet and demand someone remove this unwanted hurdle from her path. She did none of these things, however. Instead, she asked in small voice, '…what do I do?'.

'I think all any of us can do in these circumstances is wait.' *An honest but frustrating answer*, thought Adairia, who stared back down at the mug in her hands. The chancellor pressed on. 'In the meantime, my dear, we have the good fortune of those who possess warm tea and pleasant company. What shall we discuss? I myself would love to hear more about your research if you can spare the time. I so seldom get to do any of my own these days what with the demands of bureaucracy.'

'Well,' Adairia hesitated before latching on to the opening, 'I've been looking at the different crops specific to each area of Albiyon and the trade ties they cultivate. I'm working on a thesis that looks at the larger ties between communities that have arisen as a result of local agricultural variety.'

And from there, Adairia found herself discussing in detail the research she had been conducting for the past couple of years while the chancellor listened and offered up interesting titbits here and there. As they talked the sun passed slowly but surely over the university, and the woes of the day were pushed to the side for just a little while.

*

When Aliya had finally instructed her to shuffle off to bed, Adairia found herself staring dumbfounded at her ceiling for longer than she cared to admit. It was all very well for Aliya to tell her to sleep, but Adairia could not relax. Her mind whirred as she tossed and turned in her bed that night. She had to acknowledge there was an element of truth to what the chancellor had said. Not about the future, but about her feelings towards the egg. She had begun to feel that it was hers in the same way that she felt her toes were her own. This feeling had crept up on her gradually throughout the day, but it was undeniably there. *Adairia.* Her own name flashed through her mind. She was not sure where the thought had come from, but the effect it had on her was a surprisingly soothing one and it was not long after that she finally found slumber.

The next morning Adairia woke abruptly. Her sleep had been disturbed by unsettling dreams that faded with the first light of day. She had no desire to remain in her bed after such a tumultuous night, so hastily she dragged herself to the basin she used for washing and readied herself for the day. She chose a simple linen dress of forest green, the long sleeves of which clung tightly to her forearms before stopping a little above her wrist - practical. She then proceeded to tie her unruly hair back into a plait that fell to her waist, and gave herself a stern glance in the mirror. She was as prepared for the day as she would ever be.

Not having been instructed otherwise Adairia was prepared to return to her cleaning duties as normal that morning, but when she opened her door there lay a small white envelope on the floor outside her room. She picked it up, her name was printed on the paper, and opened it carefully. Inside was a note that simply read:

The council is ready to meet with you.

And so it was that Adairia made her way to the chancellor's chambers for the third time in less than twenty-four hours.

When she reached the familiar doorway, it was already ajar, so, rallying her nerves, she went ahead and pushed it fully open without waiting for an invitation. The entire council had returned to Chancellor Aliya's study and its members were perched around the room on the various seats available, much as they had been the day before. It was Cyril, however, who spotted her first, as his vantage from the window seat looked directly upon the doorway.

'Adairia, glad to see you got my letter. Come in, take a seat.' He gestured to her with a wrinkled hand.

Without a word Adairia conceded to sitting on a simple stool positioned the furthest distance from the rest of its companions. Nervously she gazed around the room, at the faces

29

now fixed on her. All five council members appeared to have been awake and alert for some time now. There was not a bleary eye amongst them; although, that was all their expressions shared. Cyril appeared genuinely concerned for Adairia and continued to nod in what she assumed was intended to be a reassuring way. Chancellor Aliya appeared at ease, yet an air of business hung about her, ready to take charge and get on with things. Tronk remained as watchful and suspicious as he had been yesterday while Angus looked almost giddy with excitement. The Lady Mirin may as well have worn a mask for all her face told Adairia of the fae's feelings.

'We have discussed the situation in detail since we met yesterday Adairia,' Chancellor Aliya started, 'and we have come to a consensus amongst the council.' Tronk sniffed haughtily but no one else made a sound. 'We have sent word to the closest dragon and his companion and requested their presence at the university. Their purpose here will be to aid both the dragon in its transition into the world, and if we are correct about your bonding, your transition to this new relationship.' Aliya paused to look at Adairia, apparently waiting for a response.

'Where is the egg now?' was the first thing that came out of her mouth when given the floor to speak.

'Ah yes.' The chancellor nodded at Cyril who walked behind the huge desk to an ornate wooden chest that sat against the back wall. Its surface was decorated with a carved pattern of knots, which had been painted over with bright primary colours. Cyril took out a key, slid it into the lock on the front of the chest and turned it. Upon being swung open, the lid revealed the egg within, nestled quite neatly in a chamber lined with purple velvet.

'You put it in a trunk!' Adairia exclaimed before she could stop herself.

'I can assure you, there is no place safer,' the chancellor responded. 'The chest is enchanted with a protection spell.'

'But what if it hatches whilst locked inside?' Concern bubbled up in Adairia unbidden and her eyes darted around the room to each member of the council in turn, finally landing on the raised eyebrow of the Lady Mirin.

'She has a point Aliya,' Mirin mused, flicking her wrist as though this were the most casual conversation she had participated in this week. 'Perhaps locking the egg away is ill advised.'

'No one needs to worry,' Aliya insisted. 'The spell isn't designed to keep something inside, only those without permission out. I wove it myself.' Her tone was light but final, ensuring no attempts at a second rebuttal.

Adairia. Again, she heard her own name float to the front of her mind as if being called to. More alert than she had been the night before, this time she recognised that the voice was not her own. She stood up abruptly and walked over to the open chest at Cyril's feet. Cautiously, she knelt down, placing her hands on the rim of the trunk, and peered in at the cracked surface of the egg.

'Hello,' she whispered tentatively. *What else did one say to an unborn baby dragon?* As soon as she had spoken, however, she felt warmth rush throughout her body. It was as if she was being wrapped in a blanket of the thickest, softest wool and her whole body seemed to relax in response.

'It spoke to me.' She sighed; her words directed towards no one in particular. As Adairia stood and turned back to the rest of the people in the room, she noted each pair of eyes was cast firmly in her direction. Cyril was positively grinning, and the chancellor nodded, the tiniest of smiles playing at the corner of her mouth.

'I think that wipes any remaining doubt we may have had that you and the creature were bonded from our minds.' And Adairia could not help but notice the head librarian nudge Tronk with his elbow, who simply harumphed in response. Aliya looked as though she were about to continue but the Lady Mirin spoke up once more.

'What did it say?' she asked, her tone remaining impassive.

'My name,' responded Adairia. 'It said my name.'

The fae woman said nothing further in response but continued to watch Adairia closely. Adairia's eyes, meanwhile, were fixed on the dragon egg. The smooth orange surface glistened in the sunlight peeking through the nearby window. No, it did more than glisten; the surface of the egg almost seemed to be in motion, shades of copper and gold rippling across the surface like gleaming smoke. The effect was hypnotic. She found herself unable to drag her eyes away until she heard Aliya cough meaningfully behind her.

'I think we have found the egg's guardian for its final stages of hatching in this case.' Adairia could hardly say no at this point, and her desire to do so was steadily dwindling. 'In the meantime, we will await the imminent arrival of our visitors, and perhaps Cyril or Angus can assist you in doing some pre-emptive research of your own. There must be plenty of dragon history in these musty old halls.' The chancellor smiled knowingly at Adairia who responded in kind; she had a lot of reading to do.

Extract from an Introduction to Dragons

There is no living being recorded that exceeds the size and weight a fully-grown dragon can attain. They are most notable for their scaled hide, un-feathered wings, and indestructible black claws. While some dragons can breathe fire, most are only capable of producing hot air, although this too has its uses. The females are usually larger whereas the male dragon's slighter build makes him a speedier flier. Dragons also come in a wide range of colours: see appendix three for an up-to-date list of recorded shades observed in the wild.

Chapter Four
Isla

'Her? Yes, that's her. She's the one who broke it? How did she do it? No, it's going to hatch. A new dragon? A new dragon! But who is she? What has she done? And the council have allowed it? Surely not. Really, a new dragon? How long has it been? How did it happen? Why her...'

Adairia really should have seen it coming, but she had been so wrapped up in her own unease to consider how the rest of the university inhabitants would react to the news of a new dragon companion in their midst. She could also understand. *Would she not be right there with them if it were someone else in her place?* Nevertheless, it stung to hear her name muttered scathingly by students and scholars she had barely exchanged a word with in the past; to have eyes follow her wherever she went in the university halls; to simultaneously become an object of curiosity and disdain amongst her peers. Sometimes, it turned out, whispers rang louder than screams, particularly in the usually peaceful library stacks. As much as Adairia craved her previous anonymity, knowledge of what had happened that morning, as well as her involvement, had spread throughout the university like wildfire, and there was no covering it up now.

'Ignore them,' was Morag's unfaltering response, but

Adairia could not help but squirm under their scrutiny. *Why her?* they wondered, and she wished she had an answer for them.

Meanwhile, Adairia's gratitude to her friends knew no bounds. Both Calder and Morag had rallied around her in the weeks following that fateful day; two better study companions she could not have asked for. Calder surprised everyone when he proved to already possess a store of knowledge concerning dragons. He loved all creatures, this was true, but he had always been more of a 'learn by doing' type and like the rest of them, he had never met a dragon in the flesh. Morag's exceptional research skills, meanwhile, would have been an asset to any project. She was after all considered somewhat of a prodigy by the university's alchemy department, and for good reason. They were each willing to give up an hour or two of their own days just to sit with Adairia in the library and pour over piles of books and scrolls that might contain even the smallest titbit of dragon lore. On more than one occasion Adairia often found herself pondering how she would ever pay them back but never once did they complain.

Otherwise, the next few weeks might have been like any other if it were not for the dramatic shift in research topic. Adairia completed her chores in the morning, then headed to the library to immerse herself in its tomes. She spent more time than ever before trailing behind Angus as he helped her in seeking out some of the more obscure volumes on dragons that the university held. The head librarian had a knack of knowing which books, despite being seemingly unrelated to their search, may contain useful information. Sometimes it was merely a sentence buried in an otherwise dry account of the illegal grain trade during the reign of Queen Torin, or immigration logs in

35

the year following the fall of the royal household. Adairia did not believe the flame haired man had read every word in the University's library, but he did seem to have a way of communicating with the manuscripts on the shelves that she could not put her finger on. When she finally asked him about it, he merely shrugged and tapped his right ear knowingly: 'You've got to use your ears as opposed to your eyes, nothing special about it'.

While Adairia worked, she often found herself glancing up from her books to find numerous pairs of eyes unabashedly trained on her. Each day was much the same for those first two weeks. They stared whilst she read. Some even went as far as to linger nearby and peer over her shoulder at whatever volume she had open. On one notable occasion, an unfortunate Duncan found himself the target of Morag's sharp tongue when he performed a mock curtsy while Adairia had been attempting to squeeze past him to reach a particular shelf he was obstructing. Despite everything, however, Adairia surprised herself as she gradually became more and more captivated by the subject at hand. There was one story in particular that she found herself returning to time and time again. The story of Prince Bayrd and his dragon Tearlach.

Adairia had known who Prince Bayrd was of course, any good historian would. A century ago, he had been next in line for the Albiyan throne until he had turned it down. The now defunct royal family of Albiyon had a long history of bonding with dragons. Some historians argued that there was something in their blood, a result of good breeding, that drew the majestic beasts even whilst still in the egg. Adairia could not help but scoff when she read these theories, knowing her own mundane origins. For whatever reason, however the dragon Tearlach had hatched to Bayrd when the princeling was barely five years old, and they had grown up as each other's constant companion.

Bayrd's father, Orlan, had been King at the time of Bayrd's birth but fell terribly ill before his son reached his tenth year. By the end, Orlan recognised no one at court except for his wife, and Bayrd's mother, Anna. The Queen had remained by her husband's bedside until his death, only to pass away less than twelve months later, so overcome by her grief. Bayrd had been barely thirteen years old, too young to take up his rightful place on his father's throne, let alone deal with the loss of both his parents. Instead, a council of regents was set up to rule until the prince was of age; a council that included his father's brother, Philip.

As he had grown up, Bayrd garnered a reputation as an unusual young man, particularly among the aristocracy; they felt he spent more time with the common people than was proper for a future King. He preferred to read than train for war and would disappear for days on end flying the length and breadth of Albiyon on the back of his dragon Tearlach. Some thought him irresponsible, others believed him thoughtless, and the council grew steadily more suspicious of his escapades. They were wrong to think Bayrd more concerned with himself than his kingdom, however, as he would long be remembered for his selflessness after his death.

On the first day of spring, and the Prince's twentieth birthday, Bayrd had requested a meeting with his council. They gathered in the throne room with no inclination of what their future King could possibly have asked to meet with them about. It was to everyone's surprise when he declared, 'I wish to turn down the crown'. Most of the council members were torn between horror and suspicion, while a couple quickly resigned themselves to the situation and began to ask themselves who was next in line for the throne. 'You wish to give up your throne to your cousin?' demanded Bayrd's uncle, the previous King's brother, who spoke of his own son. No one could have anticipated the young Prince's response. 'No, sir, I plan to demolish the monarchy.' One or two of the men in the room snorted in disbelief, but Bayrd's uncle narrowed his eyes in anger. 'Impossible', he shouted, but Bayrd did not balk. The Prince who wished to be a prince no longer had made up his mind.

That would have been the end of the story if the council had accepted Bayrd's decision, along with the rest of the nobles. As these things go, however, it would not be so simple. There was uproar among the upper echelons of the Albiyan citizen body; anyone who had the vaguest hope of claiming the throne, whether tenth or fiftieth or one-hundredth in line, objected to Bayrd's plans. To their gall, however, the Prince had forseen this reaction. In all the time he had spent away from the castle and its court, he had been with his people. He had made good friends amongst the inhabitants of Albiyon, those willing and able to rally the disparate groups of the country in solidarity with their cause. Men and women united behind their Prince in order to dethrone him and free themselves from the inequality of monarchy.

Yet, it would not be an easy battle to win, and Albiyon fell into civil war. The ordinary people had the numbers, but the nobles had the wealth. Bayrd and Tearlach did not back down despite countless bribes by council members who thought they could convince the Prince to return to his throne. The pair flew across the country from north to south, east to west assisting in the resistance effort. Tearlach's mighty form became the symbol of the revolution and the people of Albiyon cheered whenever he flew overhead. With the support of the country's farmers, craftspeople, teachers and even some of the University scholars, Bayrd's dream came to fruition. The monarchy was overturned, and the first Albiyan parliament was formed with representatives of all its inhabitants, not just a few.

There was an illustration of the resistance movement's flag in one of the books Angus had found for Adairia in the library, which she often found herself staring at. It depicted a huge purple dragon in flight, its wings fully extended and head pointing purposefully forward. Now and then she even ran her fingers across the drawing wondering what her own dragon would look like, what colour it would be. She had continued to receive intermittent communications from the creature, always simply her name, but for whatever reason these sporadic reminders of its existence provided her with a sense of comfort each time they came.

'Don't you think it's time for a break?' Morag's voice broke through Adairia's revery on one such occasion.

'I never thought I'd hear you of all people suggest such a thing.' She grinned but Morag simply rolled her eyes.

'Calder tells me you haven't visited your garden plot in almost a week, that's not like you.'

'Well, as you very well know, I've been kind of busy.'

'I know this is a big shock Adairia, that it's going to be a big change, but you can't burn out yet. Relax for an afternoon, the books will still be here when you return.'

*

Adairia had eventually conceded that perhaps it would be wise to heed Morag's words, so the next morning she did not head straight to the library once she had completed her chores. Instead, she made her way to her beloved gardens. The weather was starting to turn, and she had some tending to do in order to prepare her plot for the colder months. She also found that there was something rather reinvigorating about the brisk

39

breeze against her skin when she started walking through the courtyard and away from the main building. It helped to clear her head and make her feel a little more like herself again.

Adairia was revelling in this sensation, as well as the prospect of some good manual labour, when she approached the wooden fence surrounding the gardens. Her good mood was interrupted, however, when she spotted a man she did not recognise standing in the middle of her potatoes. She could only see him from behind as he bent down to examine the dirt at his feet, but his clothes were a dead giveaway; this man did not belong here. No one came to do a bit of gardening in such finery. He wore expensive leather riding boots and tight-fitting trousers trimmed with red satin along the seams. His long coat was also a vivid shade of scarlet and made of a thick wool well suited to this time of year. To polish off the look, his head was adorned with a wide brimmed hat embellished with gold thread.

'Excuse me, sir,' Adairia called out, half running up towards him. 'Can I help you?' She was about to politely request he extricate himself from the patch of vegetables he was trampling when he turned around and stopped her in her tracks. It was a woman.

'Ah, would I be correct in assuming you are Adairia then?' The woman removed her hat with a flourish revealing bright ginger hair that she had tightly braided in a crown around her head, although a few corkscrew curls had begun their escape.

'Um, yes, that's me.' Adairia felt her cheeks grow hot as a deep blush spread across her face. 'I'm so sorry, I didn't realise…' she trailed off. Thankfully the stranger only chuckled.

'Don't worry about it. I'm Isla, pleased to meet you.' To Adairia's relief, Isla extricated herself from the vegetable plot and stepped onto the path where the blonde woman stood, offering an outstretched hand. Adairia shook the hand, a little bemused.

'Were you looking for me?' she asked the stranger with a name.

'Of course.' Isla smiled before faltering. 'I take it my letter didn't make it here before me then. I sent a response to the chancellor's request shortly before I left, but I guess the messenger's horse wasn't quite fast enough to beat us.' She paused briefly before continuing on at a speed difficult to keep up with. 'I'm Lady Isla, companion to Tearlach the dragon. You are the woman who has recently bonded with the new hatchling, yes?' At the word dragon Adairia looked around them, startled, searching for the beast.

'Oh no,' Isla grinned cottoning on to Adairia's train of thought, 'I told him to go find himself some dinner. He was looking a little too longingly at those pigs in the sty back there. It was one of the young men tending to the animals there that said I might find you here.'

'I see,' replied Adairia, chewing her bottom lip.

'Well, I am at your service, Adairia. It's always exciting news to have a new dragon hatch and I'm here to make sure this transition is as easy as possible for you and the dragonling.'

'You've been through this yourself then? A dragon hatching that is.' Adairia was immediately keen to hear about Isla's experience now that the opportunity to ask questions had been opened to her.

'Alas, this is the one thing I can't directly relate to you and your beast in.' Isla sighed. 'Tearlach was my great grandfather's dragon first. He was the one who the young dragon bonded to whilst in his shell. As I'm sure you're aware, a dragon's lifespan far outstretches that of a human. After my grandfather's death he went into a kind of hibernation. He slept for nigh on fifty years waiting for a new companion that he could bond with. To my extraordinary honour it was me that Tearlach chose. We have been bonded since I was barely one year old.'

'You mean, you mean…' Adairia spluttered, 'the dragon you talk of is the same Tearlach who was bonded to Prince Bayrd? You're the great granddaughter of Prince Bayrd?'

'I am indeed.'

Chapter Five
The Dragon

It was getting chilly and Adairia was finding it difficult to separate from the anxiety over her vegetable patch long enough to formulate any coherent questions for Isla. For the safety of her produce, she suggested that they return to the main building for tea. On their way she stopped a young boy running late to his afternoon classes and asked him to tell Cyril that the Lady Isla had arrived. Adairia indicated that they would be in the kitchens and trusted the boy to carry the message to his teacher.

Once they had both settled on wooden benches in one of the quieter areas of the kitchens, with appropriately warm drinks, Adairia finally felt herself easing back down to earth. If she had known a fortnight ago that she would be confronted with surprise after surprise over the following weeks, she mused, she probably would never have left her room in the first place. As both women sipped at their cups, Adairia took a closer look at Isla. The young woman could hardly be more than a year or two older than her. Freckles swarmed a nose that barely protruded from her face, and slightly crooked front teeth tugged on a bottom lip that was especially full. Her dark green eyes were particularly piercing and, whether it was the casual way she splayed herself on the bench or the openness of her smile, there was something undeniably inviting about her demeanour.

'So, have you always lived here?' Isla queried, breaking the silence.

'Yes,' Adairia replied, 'I was left here as a baby.'

'Ah yes, one of the foundlings raised by the university. It must have been nice growing up surrounded by so many other children.'

'You don't have any brothers or sisters?' Adairia found herself asking, beginning to ease into the conversation. She found herself drawn to Isla's easy confidence, she seemed completely relaxed even in unfamiliar surroundings.

'No, my mother died in childbirth and my father never remarried. But I always had Tearlach as a companion.' She smiled fondly.

'What's it like, being bonded to a dragon?'

'I don't particularly remember what it's like not to be bonded to Tearlach,' Isla pondered. 'But I can tell you that he is a constant comfort to me, as I am to him. We share everything, and we are never far from one another,' she tapped the side of her head, 'bodily and mentally. We are family.'

'Surely that can get tiresome?' Adairia frowned, considering the prospect of having another creature so attuned to her every thought and desire.

'On the contrary, it is like having a physical manifestation of the best parts of yourself. He offers me consolation when he feels I need it, lending me his own mind so that my thoughts feel less cramped. I can offer him strength when he is tired and needs another to tend to his aches and pains. We are able to find solutions to our problems much more quickly together than we would be able to alone. I don't know what I would do without him actually.' Adairia had to admit that something about that did sound quite nice; but more than that, it was the expression on Isla's face that made her words sound so convincing. It was one of pure serenity.

'There you are!' A new voice interrupted this exchange, and Adairia turned in her seat to find herself looking at a windswept Cyril. His robes were tangled around his legs and tiny droplets of perspiration decorated his dark complexion. He was an old man after all. 'I'm so sorry no one was here to properly greet you Lady Isla, we had no warning of your arrival. I am Cyril, it was I who wrote to you on behalf of the chancellor. And I see you have met Adairia! Good, good.'

'There's absolutely nothing to apologise for, I fear I got ahead of myself, or my correspondents at least.' Isla chuckled, standing to greet Cyril with a jovial shake of the hand.

'Well, I've sent someone to prepare a room for you none the less. Your journey here was a long one so please take this opportunity to rest whilst it is available.'

'Thank you, Cyril, I think I have little more energy left in me.' She turned and winked at Adairia, who was not sure how to respond so simply blinked perplexedly back at her. 'Although I did want to ask if you might have a larger covered space available, a barn or outhouse not currently in use, that my companion may sleep in tonight?'

'Ah yes of course, I will ask around and find somewhere appropriate.'

'Wonderful, as I believe he is nearly finished with his dinner.' She turned back to Adairia. 'Perhaps you would like to be introduced?'

*

They trekked back out across the University grounds together for the second time that day, their group now numbering three.

This time they walked out beyond the gardens to the wild grounds lined by densely packed clusters of pine trees that marked the beginning of the northern woods. The massive mound that was Tearlach the dragon was visible from a mile away. As they approached, Adairia could not help but take note of the smattering of broken bones dotted throughout the grass surrounding the beast, presumably the remnants of his afternoon meal.

The dragon himself was an impressive sight. Adairia had never observed a living creature so large before. His height and girth were impossibly imposing, adorned with heavy set wings tipped with sharp black spikes folded against his sides; his hide was coated in gleaming purple scales, just as the stories had told; and his eyes were a vibrant shade of yellow that appeared to swim with the same smoke-like motion that she had noticed on her own dragon's egg. It was clear from his body language that Cyril was intimidated by Tearlach's presence as much as she was. He hung back the furthest from their small group, his mouth not quite fully closed, giving him the appearance of a dazed goldfish. Isla, on the other hand, might have been equal in size to the dragon. She bounded up to him, slapping his right foreleg with her hand and beaming at the two humans.

'This is Tearlach.'

The sound that followed Isla's words took Adairia aback. 'It is a pleasure to meet you both.' The dragon's voice vibrated throughout her body. Despite her many encounters with the various different species of Albiyon, she had heard nothing comparable in her lifetime. Uncertain what she should do next she opted to give a short bow in the hope of showing the creature her respect.

'I am Adairia. It is an honour to meet you Tearlach.'

'And I am Cyril.'

Tearlach nodded at each of them in turn and then turned his gaze back upon Adairia. 'You are the new caraid bheag?' he asked, the effect of his voice equally as disconcerting the second time around. Adairia wondered if it was something you ever grew used to. She also wondered what the dragon was talking about. Isla must have picked up on her confusion, however, and chuckled that joyful laugh that seemed to follow her everywhere.

'It's what the dragons call those they bond to. It means little friend, although most of us feel caraid does just fine.' To Adairia's horror, she actually poked her tongue out at the gigantic beast.

'In that case I suppose I am, although my dragon has not yet hatched.' Adairia nodded up at the dragon.

'But it speaks to you?' Tearlach responded.

'Only my name,' she answered sheepishly, but the dragon nodded in approval.

At this point Cyril chimed in. 'I better have someone find you some appropriate accommodation to spend the night. Is there anything else we can do for you while you are here? I expect the chancellor will want to meet with you both in the morning, but you've had a long day so please for now, take some time to rest.'

'Tearlach generally fends for himself, but I know I would greatly appreciate a small meal that I could eat in my room this evening if that's alright with you? As you say, it has been a long day and I'd like to get up early tomorrow morning,' Isla replied.

'Certainly.' Cyril turned to Adairia. 'Perhaps you could show Lady Isla where to find everything she wants. A room has been made up on the same corridor as your own so you should have no trouble in finding it. I should probably go and inform the rest of the council that our guests have arrived and see to that roof for Tearlach while I'm at it.'

'Of course.' Adairia assented and with that Cyril gave a quick bow to the dragon before hurrying off.

'I hope you don't mind if we leave you so soon friend.' Isla had turned her attention back to Tearlach who gazed down at her affectionately.

'Not at all. There's plenty excitement ahead, I too should get some rest.' He turned to Adairia, 'It was a pleasure to meet you caraid bheag. I look forward to meeting your dragon when they hatch.'

'Thank you,' was all she could think to say in response, but she managed to raise a smile from her lips at the same time.

*

That night Adairia found sleep difficult to come by. Her mind was abuzz with competing thoughts and her body was on high alert. After she had taken Isla back to the kitchens to fix a meal for that evening and they had located her room two doors down from her own, Adairia had bid her new acquaintance goodnight. Before she departed, however, Isla had asked if Adairia would take her to see the dragon egg in the morning and promised to be awake bright and early when she said she would.

'Tearlach is not the only dragon I have met, but I have never seen one hatch before,' she had said, the excitement evident in her voice. 'And don't forget, I'm here for you. Whatever you need. Don't hesitate to ask me anything, I'm sure it's a lot to take in.' She clasped Adairia's hand in her own and smiled kindly.

'Thank you, truly,' Adairia had replied in earnest. And she

had meant it. She could already sense that Isla and Tearlach's presence here would be invaluable in the coming days. Despite this, she was unable to drift off with any ease. Isla, Tearlach, they were not just words in a book. They were real and they were here. The purple dragon with his swirling eyes, sharp talons and gigantic wings was a reminder that her new research topic was not going to remain on the page for very much longer.

Chapter Six

Friends

The next day Adairia awoke, bleary eyed, after only a few hours of interrupted sleep. When she went to wash herself, she could not help but note the dark circles that rimmed the blue eyes peering back at her from the small looking glass that sat beside her basin. Thoughtfully, she ran a hand along the square line of her jaw and over the small dimple in the centre of her chin. A small, irritating part of her felt a flurry of nerves when she remembered Isla's effortless appearance and perfectly fitted attire from the day before. What had the other woman thought of her?

As it turned out, she need not have worried. When Adairia knocked on Isla's door to see if her guest would like to accompany her to breakfast it took a few minutes before it opened. When it did, it was immediately evident that it had taken Adairia's knock to wake the sleeping woman that stood there. Isla was still in her nightgown, her hair, now loose, hung in a mass of tangled curls and her eyes were crusted with sleep. Adairia had to admit she was somewhat taken aback.

'I'm so sorry,' she apologised. 'I was going to ask if you'd like to come to breakfast? There are communal meals provided in the main dining hall. But I didn't mean to wake you!'

'No, no, I'm sorry.' Isla's voice was hoarse. 'As you have

discovered, I'm not usually much of a morning person. Late mornings and late nights, that's me. If you don't mind waiting just one moment though, I'm sure I can make myself presentable for breakfast, well, as presentable as I'm going to get before warm food.'

Isla closed the door again and Adairia listened as a cacophony of sounds came from inside the room. It sounded as if Isla's hair was putting up a literal fight, one that included throwing her across the room. After a few short minutes the sounds ceased, and Isla flung the door to her room back open. She certainly worked fast. Her hair was scraped back into a long braid, and she wore another blouse and trouser pairing. This time each item was in a shade of dark green and accompanied by a matching waistcoat that remained unbuttoned. She still looked groggy but there was a smile on her face as they both set off to the dining hall.

*

Breakfast was excruciating. As soon as they had entered the dining hall, Adairia heard her name being called from across the room. Calder and Morag were seated across from one another at one of the many tables dotted across the hall and Calder was waving at her frantically, practically bouncing out of his seat. She shrugged her shoulders and gave Isla a sheepish grin before they headed over to sit next to Adairia's oldest friends.

'Mornin'!' Calder called gleefully as they approached. Adairia took the seat beside him whilst Isla sat down beside Morag. 'Hi there, remember me.' Calder added, waving his hand at Isla directly.

'Of course,' Isla smiled, 'we met yesterday when I was in search of your friend here.' She gestured towards Adairia.

'Didn't tell me you were a dragon companion though, did you?'

'Why would she have to tell you that?' Adairia demanded but Calder only shrugged. 'Lady Isla, this is Calder,' she sighed, 'and this is Morag.'

'Isla is fine, really.' She turned to shake Morag's hand on her left and smiled at Calder. 'Very pleased to meet you.'

'You missed the crier this morning.' Morag informed Adairia

'Dammit, I completely forgot they were visiting today. Any important news?'

The criers usually came once a week, varying depending on which member of their guild was passing through Eòlas on their travels up and down the country. Adairia rarely missed their visits. It was the easiest way to keep up to date with whatever was happening outside of their local area, especially when you were not a frequent traveller yourself.

'Apparently there was a riot in Drewr,' Calder answered seriously.

'He didn't use the word riot,' Morag scowled. 'He said a fight broke out between a rally of Purists and some other locals.' Purists were the most extreme faction of the Traditionalists, and they believed strongly in what they described as the purity of Albiyon itself. Their numbers were small, but every now and then you heard about an incident like this where they took to the streets to voice their prejudice.

'Sounds like a riot to me.' Calder shrugged returning to his tea.

'This isn't the first time the Drewrian Purists have caused a stir in the past few months.' It was Isla that offered up this titbit. 'They've been active enough that representatives from parliament have had to attempt a reconciliation in person already.' Of course, Adairia reminded herself, Isla herself was a member of parliament. As a descendent of the royal line, she had been guaranteed her seat since birth.

'Why now though?' asked Adairia, curious if Isla would have any bonus information the crier had not.

'Drewr has been hit badly by recent grain shortages this past harvest. Although the parliament has made efforts to get emergency supplies to them from our stores, the purists are arguing that if there were not so many mouths to feed there would not be a problem.'

'And let me guess,' scowled Adairia, 'the mouths they'd like to be rid of are the same ones they were railing against before the grain shortage?'

'One and the same,' sighed Isla, who looked drained at the mere mention of the topic.

'Why don't we get some food?' Adairia suggested, changing the subject, and indicating the buffet spread across the back wall.

Once they had filled their bowls with porridge, mixed with honey and cinnamon, and grabbed a couple cups of tea, they settled back down at the table alongside Morag and Calder who were halfway through their own meals. For the next thirty minutes, Calder badgered Isla with questions about dragons. *What did they eat? For how long could they fly? What were their temperaments like?* Even asking how many teeth they had. Eventually Isla conceded to introducing the young man to Tearlach, so that he could ask the dragon himself.

Morag remained reasonably quiet throughout the whole encounter, which was not uncommon, but occasionally Adairia would catch her rolling her eyes in her direction and smirking

53

at Calder's aggressive enthusiasm. After half an hour of this, however, a small child of around ten came running up to their table. She stood there awkwardly for a moment, staring at them silently with her hands behind her back.

'Can we help?' Adairia asked kindly.

'Please miss, the chancellor wants to see Lady Isla in her chambers. Professor Cyril told me to fetch her before class started and show her the way.'

'Well thank you for coming to find me,' Isla responded. 'I suppose I better come now then, wouldn't want you being late to class.' She smiled and rose from her chair.

'We'll see you the night for the festivities though, won't we?' Calder insisted, to which Adairia slapped her own forehead. *How could she have forgotten?* Today marked the autumnal equinox, when they paid their thanks for the past year's harvest; it was usually one of Adairia's favourite celebrations, but in the excitement of Isla's arrival it had completely slipped her mind.

'I forgot to tell you.' She explained. 'The university always builds a bonfire for the harvest festival. It's usually a lot of fun if you'd like to come with us?' She was not sure why exactly, but she felt her nerves spike in the second she had to wait for Isla's response.

'That sounds wonderful! I love a party.' Isla winked at Adairia, who to her embarrassment blushed in response. 'I'll see you all later then.' And with that she waved goodbye allowing her guide to lead the way.

'You know she's descended from Prince Bayrd,' Morag suddenly proffered up to the group.

'Aye, she mentioned.' Adairia nodded, chewing on the remnants of her meal.

'I didn't,' Calder said surprised.

'You don't know anything,' Morag scoffed.

'They've set the dragon up in the empty barn on the west side of the grounds apparently. I know that much,' Calder added, narrowing his eyes at Morag who simply stuck out her tongue in return.

*

After they had all finished eating and Morag and Calder had hurried off to their separate morning duties, Adairia contemplated her day. This was her day off, and with Isla visiting the chancellor she had the entire morning to herself. What had Calder said? Tearlach had spent last night in the previously empty barn to the west of the main building. Would it be inappropriate for her to visit him without Isla present? Surely not, he was his own creature after all. And once the idea had formed in her mind, she found it difficult to assuage.

With no one to stop her, Adairia headed off in the direction of the dragon's makeshift chambers. She had wrapped her maroon shawl around her shoulders in preparation for the increased chill in the air. Her golden waves were left loose that morning and they were swept up in the wind as she walked, but she did not mind; the breeze was invigorating. Once she arrived outside the barn, however, she hesitated. Should she knock? Thankfully her question was answered for her.

'Come in caraid bheag.' Tearlach's words rippled through her, and she shivered at the unexpected sensation. Stepping forward, she slid one of the heavy double doors open just enough for her to squeeze between the opening she had created. There sat Tearlach, his tail wrapped around his body and his head resting on his front legs, his dazzling eyes looking straight at her. She swallowed deeply, still intimidated by his gigantic size for all she had met him the day before. The dragon spoke first.

'This is a pleasant surprise.'

'I hope you don't mind.' Adairia hesitated. 'How did you know I was outside?'

'You smell.' There was a glint in the dragon's eye that made her wonder if he was teasing her. 'All humans do, that is. We dragons have a greatly developed sense of smell. I recognised your scent from our meeting yesterday.'

'I see,' Adairia replied. There was still so much she did not know about dragons. But who better to ask than a dragon itself?

'You must have a lot of questions.' Tearlach pre-empted her train of thought.

'Yes… and no.' Adairia sighed. 'To be honest, I don't know what to ask, I don't know what I need to know. I've been reading, but most of the books in the library deal with dragon history; I haven't found anything written by a dragon or its companion yet.'

'Maybe you could write a book on the subject one day in that case,' Tearlach replied, but Adairia only snorted. 'I'm not surprised. Dragons and their companions usually pass on knowledge to one another orally. You should hear dragons sing of our own past, there is nothing more beautiful.' The dragon's joy quickly turned to sadness, however, as he spoke his next words. 'But there are not as many dragons in this world as there once was. Even I did not expect your egg to still hold a living dragon, it is particularly long for a dragonling to wait. You must be something special caraid bheag.'

'Why did it choose me though? That's what I don't understand.'

'Only your own dragon can answer that question to your

full satisfaction. I can only tell you in the most abstract sense. In you it must have sensed a kindred spirit. Like I did with Bayrd and then Isla. We are alike in the most essential ways. We are driven by the same passion for justice. It is not uncommon for such a spirit to run in families. You know no one in your own ancestry who shared a similar relationship with a dragon?' His question took Adairia aback.

'I don't know anything about my parents or my ancestors. I am an orphan.' Tearlach only nodded so she continued. 'Why now though? I have lived in this university for twenty-seven years. I have passed by that dragon's egg a thousand times.'

'You were ready,' he stated simply.

'I don't feel particularly ready for anything.' There was a flicker of anger building up in Adairia now. All of the dragon's answers were as frustrating as they were helpful, but he continued to speak without her prompting.

'This dragonling will be but a child when it is born. You should not expect a fully developed creature like me. As unfamiliar as you are with dragons, this creature is unfamiliar with humans, and more than that, the world. You will be responsible for helping it to understand the realm it is born into, as my first companion was for me. He may have been a child himself, but he was able to support me in my development as I was him.'

It was at this point they were interrupted. Isla, accompanied by the university's chancellor, had entered the barn through the gap in the door that Adairia had made. While Aliya simply smiled and wished Adairia a good morning, Isla clapped her hands together, grinning.

'Braw! I do hope you have both had a chance to get to know one another a little better,' she beamed.

57

'I think we have,' responded Tearlach, keeping his gleaming eyes fixed on Adairia's own.

Extract from An Introduction to Dragons

There are four known species of dragon. The cthonic, pyratic, aetherial, and hydratic. Both cthonic and hydratic types are believed to be extinct as a result of interbreeding with the two more dominant genera. The cthonic seems to have died out first, with the last known male specimen mentioned in records dating back more than nine hundred years, but no more of its kind have been registered since the drake's presumed death. No one is quite certain as to when the hydratic breed died out as they have notoriously been the most difficult species to keep track of, preferring to live deep underwater, away from most land-dwelling creatures. There are records of their kind existing as recently as four hundred years ago, however.

Chapter Seven
The Harvest Festival

The heat that filled Adairia's cheeks could have been the result of a variety of factors. The bonfire that university residents had spent the past few hours stoking had grown at least nine feet tall at this point in the evening, although it was being carefully managed all the while. The air that surrounded the flames shimmered in their warmth as music echoed from the four-person band that had set up nearby and people danced chaotically to their tunes. Then there was the wine. Adairia could not remember if this was her third or fourth cup of the night but when it tasted this fine how could she say no? Her flush may even have had something to do with the pretty red-head who was forced to sit so close to her on the rammed bench that their thighs were pressed up against one another's.

'Would you care to dance m'lady?' Calder had just returned from pestering the band to play his favourite jig and offered his outstretched arm to Morag who sat on Adairia's other side. She too was looking a little pink in the cheeks, and without a word clasped Calder's proffered hand in her own before they fled together to the makeshift dance floor.

'Are those two sweethearts then?' Isla's lips were so close to Adairia's ear when she spoke that it sent a shiver down her spine.

'I'm not sure.' She shrugged. 'I'm not sure they know either.' She saw the way Morag and Calder stared at each other when the other one was not looking. There was more than the friendship that she shared with either between them, but no one seemed willing to acknowledge it out loud. Yet.

'All in good time, ay.' Isla winked and Adairia chuckled. 'What about you?'

'What about me?' Adairia replied, her eyes focused on Calder and Morag's gambolling forms. Morag could not dance to save herself, but Calder made up for both of them with his enthusiasm.

'Do you have a sweetheart Adairia, dragon's companion?'

'Not me. There was a boy, well a man I should say, a few years ago but no one else since.'

Adairia's first and only romantic encounter had been a slow burner. He had been one of the other foundlings raised by the university. They had both been seventeen and he had taken to visiting her when she was gardening. He seemed curious to learn about the different vegetables and herbs she grew, always seeking out more details than she initially provided. Over time, she had found that she enjoyed his company and even his incessant questioning. The spring before she turned eighteen, they had attended the local Beltane celebrations to welcome the change of the season together. Afterwards he had accompanied her back to her room, and they had both shared their first gentle night in another person's arms. When their next summer came around, however, their time together came to an end. Unlike Adairia, he was not a scholar; he had dreamed of becoming a travelling musician whose songs would one day be recognised across Albiyon. So, with his fiddle under his arm, he had set off on his own adventure when they both turned nineteen.

'Not true love then?' Isla prodded.

'No,' Adairia smiled, 'it was nice while it lasted but it definitely wasn't love.' She paused for a moment, her mind catching on something. 'He had red hair too actually.' This made Isla laugh while Adairia blushed harder. *Goddess, she must be drunk*, thought Adairia, mentally berating herself. 'What about you?' she asked, trying to turn the subject back on Isla instead.

'No men in my past but a few women. No blondes though.' This made Adairia choke on her wine, which in turn caused Isla to hoot loudly and slap her thigh.

Were they flirting? Adairia found she did not mind the thought. In fact, she did not mind any of this. A stomach full of good food, a cup full of sweet wine, the pleasant sound of friendly conversation garbled by the buoyant melody played by the band all around. She might even go so far as to describe herself as relaxed; relaxed for the first time in a fortnight if that were possible. Sure, she had recently become responsible for an ancient dragon's egg and what lay inside, but that was exactly why Isla and Tearlach were here. They would help her through this, as would her friends. In that moment, none of it seemed quite as insurmountable as it had done only twenty-four hours ago. On the other hand, she had drunk quite a lot of wine.

Adairia! The voice rang in her mind. Adairia had grown accustomed to the sound of her own name slipping into her consciousness when the unhatched dragonling reached across their connection. What had always brought her comfort before, however, this time sent alarm bells ringing. She clasped a hand to her forehead shocked by the intensity of the feeling.

'What's wrong? What is it?' Isla's tone immediately grew serious as she caught sight of Adairia's expression.

'I don't know. I've never felt... it's the dragon, I think it's distressed.' She found herself gritting her teeth between words, unsettled by the physical sensation the voice had had on her.

'Come on.' Isla stood up abruptly, ready for action. 'I'll come with you and we'll have a look.' To which Adairia nodded and scrambled from her own seat.

*

Earlier in the day, Adairia had been able to show her visitors the dragon's egg for the first time. Adairia had escorted Isla and Aliya back up the winding stairs to the chancellor's chambers where the egg had continued to live for the past two weeks. The chancellor had assured Adairia that her rooms were protected by magic that alerted her to uninvited guests, and she had even put a small spell of her own on the trunk itself to prevent anyone other than the two of them from opening it and gaining access to the contents. 'You can never be too careful', she had added in a conspiratorial tone.

As Tearlach was too large to enter this wing of the University, he had stood outside the tower where he was able to crane his neck just high enough to peer into the opened window. Upon being shown the egg itself he had murmured his approval, complimenting the colour and shine of its shell.

'It looks healthy despite its long hibernation,' he commented.

Adairia had to admit to herself that the notion the dragon's long slumber may have affected its health had not occurred to her. The thought made her squirm with guilt. She was beginning to realise how grateful she really was for Tearlach's presence now that the day of its hatching grew closer. The surface of the egg itself had developed an increasing number of fractures since the last time she had set her eyes on it. They had spread out in fine lines from the initial crack down the centre and created an intricate pattern that somehow managed to only enhance its beauty.

'You don't have long to wait now,' said Aliya, 'a week at the most. It might be advisable to take the egg into your own possession at this point unless you want to hole up in here for the next few nights.' She smiled kindly.

'Will it be safe in my room?' Adairia asked, uncertain she could provide the same level of protection the chancellor offered the egg.

'You can of course take the chest with you; the magic will remain intact even outside of my presence. I would suggest you don't leave it alone for extended periods of time though. Once the hatching process begins, I hear it can happen quite quickly.' She looked at Tearlach who nodded his massive head outside the window so that it bobbed out of sight and then back again.

'Then yes of course,' agreed Adairia fervidly.

'I'll have it delivered to your rooms this afternoon in that case.' And so, it had been.

*

This was how, late that evening, while most of the university's occupants celebrated the autumnal equinox in its grounds, the two women found themselves heading back to Adairia's room on the fourth floor. It was immediately evident, even from a few feet away, that someone at least had paid her a visit as the door was ever so slightly ajar. Not sure what to expect, Adairia quickened her step, hastily pushing the door aside when she reached it and scanning the room.

To Adairia's surprise, nothing looked out of place. There was the trunk situated at the foot of her bed with a blanket half obscuring it, just as she had left it. Hurriedly she knelt down in front of it, dragging the fabric from it and prying open the lid. To her great relief, the egg lay snuggled safely inside the velvet interior, as captivating as ever although decorated with a few more cracks since this morning. She had not imagined it though. That cry for help she had felt reverberate through her entire being had been real. The anxiety she had felt upon hearing her name had not been entirely her own and it only relinquished her now as she sat, one hand hovering over the egg too afraid to touch the delicate surface. The creature inside had calmed only at her presence but she had no idea what had upset it in the first place.

'Adairia?' came Isla's voice from over her shoulder.

'It's alright, at least I think it is.' She continued to stare at the egg, unable to tear her eyes away.

'What about the door? Could you have forgotten to close it before you came downstairs?'

'No, absolutely not.' This Adairia was sure of.

Chapter Eight
Let's Go Flying

Isla had escorted Adairia to visit the chancellor the next morning and inform her of the previous night's events. There had not been much to tell, with nothing damaged or missing, but it felt important to tell someone with more authority what they suspected. Not that either of them knew exactly what that was. Adairia had convinced herself that some kids had decided to try and get a peek at the dragon's egg while all of the adults were distracted but Isla had encouraged her to err on the side of caution regardless. Aliya had assured them she would look into it but for now there was nothing more they could do.

'Take solace in the knowledge that very soon your dragonling will no longer be confined to their egg,' Aliya attempted to reassure her.

'Well, if your dragon's birth is nearly upon us then I think it's time to truly get an idea of what it means to be a dragon's companion,' Isla added, glancing at the chancellor before looking back at Adairia, the corner of her mouth twitching as if she were suppressing a grin.

'What, what does that mean?' Adairia stuttered.

'Only one way to find out.' Isla grabbed a hold of Adairia's hand and began to pull her towards the door. 'Thank you for your time chancellor Aliya.' She called back and the chancellor nodded at both of them, a smile playing on her own features as they exited her room.

Adairia was pulled down the stairs, through the university halls and out into the grounds by Isla until they turned a corner and found themselves standing beneath Tearlach's gigantic form.

'How would you like to go for a fly?' Isla asked a dumbfounded Adairia, gesturing to the dragon's massive form.

'Now? On Tearlach?' she choked out. 'I didn't realise anyone other than a dragon's companion could ride them.'

'It's completely up to the dragon and Tearlach has already told me that he would be honoured to take you on your first flight. Your dragon won't be big enough to carry you for months yet.'

'I don't mind waiting.' Adairia shifted between her feet nervously, although she could not decide whether it was fear or excitement that was beginning to course through her body.

'Honestly, it's much better to ride for the first time on an experienced dragon. Tearlach is a magnificent flyer.' Isla patted her companion's right forearm affectionately.

'I've no doubt he is, it's just…' Adairia trailed off staring up into Tearlach's watchful eyes.

'I'll be up there with you,' Isla added. 'Don't worry, I wouldn't leave you up there on your own for your first time in the air.' She stepped back to Adairia and flung an arm around her shoulder. 'What do you say Tearlach, time for a quick flight before dinner?'

'Step aboard,' the dragon rumbled and lowered himself down so that his body was as close to the ground as he could get it. Even then he seemed impossibly tall and Adairia could not imagine how she would climb up onto his back. This was going to be nothing like riding a horse.

'Just follow me,' Isla grinned. She approached one of Tearlach's rear legs and used the ridges between his hard scales to heave herself up by her hands until she had her feet secured between scales of their own. With awe-inspiring agility, she proceeded to clamber up his leg and swing herself up onto his back once she reached his haunch. There she remained, crouched down, with her arm outstretched. After a moment's pause Adairia realised Isla was holding out her hand to help her up. Taking a deep breath, she strode forward and placed her hands on the ridged surface of Tearlach's hide. It took her a few tries before she was able to find strong hand and footholds on his scales, but once she had she cautiously pulled herself up his leg. As she neared the ridge where his upper leg was folded against his body, she reached her hand out to grab a hold of Isla's outstretched one. With the red-head's help she managed to roll herself inelegantly onto the dragon's back beside the other woman. Adairia looked up at Isla, out of breath but smiling.

'I did it,' she said, exhilaration coursing through her limbs.

'And that's just the beginning,' Isla laughed. She moved forward on Tearlach's back so that she was seated between his enormous wings and grasped onto a couple of scales that protruded a little farther out from his back. 'Grab on to me from behind and don't let go.' At her words Adairia scurried to seat herself behind Isla, her arms wrapped around her waist and her legs draped either side of the dragon's body. She had no trouble understanding why Isla was always found dressed in trousers now. In order to spread her legs wide enough she had to hitch her skirt up so that her calves were exposed to the chilly air and it bunched around her waist and thighs. Thankfully, the scales between Tearlach's wings were smoother, however, more delicate, and soft against her bare flesh.

'Hold on tight,' growled the dragon and Adairia felt the muscles in his back tighten as his wings unfurled from his sides. She could feel it reverberate through her own body as he stretched his wings and drew them slowly through the air in preparation for flight. Then, with no further warning, he practically leapt forward on his front legs and began beating his wings furiously. Instead of landing on the ground, however, he continued to rise higher and higher from his launch site. Adairia's stomach dropped as she felt the air around her change. They were flying. She was flying. Her arms tightened around Isla's waist, and she pressed her body against the other woman's back. This only caused Isla to laugh loudly over the wind, a sound which Adairia could not help but mimic until they were both whooping and laughing astride the dragon's back.

'It never gets boring,' Isla called over the rushing wind that now encircled them. Adairia did not find that difficult to believe. She gazed around them as Tearlach soared farther from the main university building and across the grounds. She watched as they passed over the gardens and continued their ascent. They were approaching the woods that bordered the university, but the trees were growing increasingly smaller beneath them.

Adairia felt her plait lift up behind her as the wind grabbed at it playfully. Her cheeks tingled with the chill but she could not stop smiling. This was incredible. For all of her anxieties that she could fall out of the sky at any moment she never wanted to land. The world looked entirely different from her new vantage point. She was able to look down on the entire university as Tearlach circled back around the grounds. It was one thing to walk through a building, or look at a plan of its design, but it was quite another to see all of its interconnected annexes and pathways from above. There were people mulling around, some tending to their chores outside, even a few who were pointing up at Tearlach. Adairia could not make out any of their faces, however, as they were all too far away. And while part of her wanted to wave at whoever they were, she was still not confident enough to remove either of her arms from Isla's waist.

'This is incredible,' she shouted to no one in particular, leaning her head back so she could better feel the wind on her face. As things often are, however, it was over all too soon. Her stomach dropped again as she felt Tearlach begin his descent and experienced the strange the feeling of falling forward although she was firmly held in place by Isla's body. It had seemed so effortless when she had witnessed Tearlach landings from land, but she felt the impact of the earth in her own limbs as soon as they touched down. It was a momentary shock to be solidly upon the ground once more, even more so once she had climbed off the dragon's back and stood for a few seconds, her legs wobbling beneath her.

'How was that?' Isla asked as she followed suit and practically jumped from Tearlach's back with all the ease of someone who had been riding since they were a small child.

'Exhilarating,' Adairia had to admit.

'I've never met a dragon companion who couldn't handle it once they were up there. They must sense it in us.'

'Who would not love to fly?' Tearlach asked bemusedly.

'You would be surprised how many people prefer to keep their feet remaining firmly on the ground.' Isla laughed in

70

response and Adairia could not help but join in.

The dragon snorted at them both but there was no resentment in his eyes. He stretched out his legs, folded in his wings and curled up on the grassy field in which they had landed. Suddenly overcome by tiredness Adairia decided to follow suit, slumping onto her back while Isla proceeded to sit down beside her. For the next hour all three lay quietly next to one another and watched the sun move across the sky.

Chapter Nine
The Hatching

If Adairia had been overwhelmed conducting her dragon research in the library, the next few days pushed her nerves to their limits. She spent large portions of each day with Tearlach and Isla, who regaled her with tales of their lives and those of the other dragons in Albiyon. As far as anyone was aware there were five more dragons living in Albiyon apart from Tearlach. Four dragons lived alongside their companions as Tearlach and Isla did but there was also a fifth dragon who had gone into hibernation after his bond with his companion had been broken, and who had yet to reawaken. Once her egg hatched, Adairia's dragon would become the seventh dragon living in Albiyon, as well as the youngest.

Tearlach was, surprisingly, not the oldest dragon her two teachers knew. Of the five other dragons in Albiyon two were older. Asha was more than one hundred and fifty years old, and similarly bonded with her second human companion Ode, who had immigrated to Albiyon almost fifty years ago. There was also Tarin, who was a decade older than Tearlach. His companion was a fairy named Bar whose lifespan was much more in keeping with a dragon's than any humans ever could be. Of the other three the reclusive Dileas was the oldest, having hatched only a year after Tearlach. Greer, companion to the dwarf Magnus, was next at around sixty-five years of age, while the youngest dragon in Albiyon was Callan who, at not quite sixty, was already bonded to his second human companion just like Tearlach and Asha. Isla had promised Adairia that she would be able to meet all four of the other bonded dragons and their companions as soon as her own dragon was strong enough to travel.

'I have written to them all and they are simply awaiting my word to meet us at my home in the north of Albiyon,' she told her. 'They are all incredibly excited to meet you.' Adairia could only smile weakly in response. She appreciated Isla's enthusiasm and support, but the prospect of more dragons and their companions left her feeling more anxious than excited. Four more dragons might not seem like much in the grand scheme of Albiyon itself, but it added up to centuries more knowledge and experience than she could ever imagine having. What exactly would they think of her?

'You care too much about what other people think about you,' had been Morag's response when Adairia had shared her concerns with her friend one afternoon.

'That's because I actually aim to get on with people, Morag.' She stuck her tongue out in response, but Morag saw past the lightness of her tone and did not smile back.

'Adairia, I'm serious,' she insisted. 'I know you're going through a lot right now, but you can't let it overwhelm who you are. Just because you're unsure about your future doesn't mean you should be unsure of yourself.'

Adairia was touched by her friend's reassurances. Perhaps she was allowing herself to be subsumed by this unfamiliar new identity she had been allotted. She did not think she had been this anxious since her research application to the university six years ago. Her days were filled with as much joy and excitement as they were worry, but, good or bad, this blend of emotions did not offer her mind much respite. She was on constant alert, particularly as the egg's hatching grew nearer and nearer.

'The right people will always like you.' Morag continued after a moment. 'In fact, I can think of one other dragon companion who seems to like you quite a bit.' Adairia blushed.

'What do you mean by that?'

'You knew exactly what I mean by that.' Morag grinned, putting down the book she had been flipping through. 'Isla can't keep her eyes off you. She lights up when you enter a room. And I can say the same thing about you. You're so obvious.' She laughed. 'Are you going to do something about it or just pine away until you're grey?'

'This is rich.' Adairia scowled, embarrassed. 'When you've been avoiding being alone with Calder for months now.'

'I don't want to talk about that,' Morag responded sharply, her expression darkening.

'Morag, I love you,' Adairia softened her expression and reached out a hand to clasp her friend's fingers, 'we're sisters. You're right to warn me against letting my emotions overrun me but take my advice when I say, you need to stop pretending as though you don't have any emotions of your own.' Morag met Adairia's eyes but did not say anything in response. 'I'm here whenever you want to talk, you know, and so is Calder.' Adairia squeezed Morag's hand before letting it go again and picking up her own book from her lap.

*

After another hour or so of companiable reading, Adairia felt it was time to bid farewell to Morag and head back to her chambers. It was getting late, and she had not checked in on the egg since that afternoon. Adairia now spent a lot of her time thinking about the egg. And not just when she was reading about dragons or discussing them with Isla or Tearlach; even when she was alone her mind would wander back to the shimmering shell that she now knew contained a living, breathing creature. Whenever this happened, she often had the sense that the dragon inside was similarly thinking of her, which, to her surprise, sent a warm sensation coursing through her body.

When Adairia slunk back into her room she found herself yawning loudly. Her energy had waned considerably since earlier in the day. Before allowing herself to flop down on her mattress, however, she took a quick peek in the trunk where the dragon's egg lay and found herself wishing it a goodnight in turn. It was now more riddled with cracks than ever before, but the sight did not concern her as it had once done. Reassured the hatchling was safe, Adairia crawled beneath her tousled quilt, more content than she had been for days, and fell asleep within minutes.

*

Adairia awoke with a start after but a couple of hours of respite. She immediately suspected that not enough time had passed for morning to be upon them from her groggy state. Dragging herself from her comfortable duvet and peering through her bedroom curtains, she quickly confirmed it was still pitch-black outside. That was when she heard the noise. It could almost have been a mouse it was so faint; a mixture of crackling and squelching reached her ears from the centre of the room, the exact spot where the dragon's trunk was situated.

Adairia almost tripped over her own feet as she scrambled

to reach the chest. Sure enough, upon lifting the lid, she saw something that sent a shiver through her limbs. The egg, so solid looking before, was warping before her eyes. The cracks in the shell were spreading and growing wider, held together with what looked like thin layers of glistening skin. Adairia froze for a moment, mesmerised by what she was watching. She then made a rapid decision. Sprinting from her room, unwilling to leave the egg alone for more than a few seconds, she rushed to Isla's chamber a few doors down from her own. Banging on the door with as much strength as she could muster, she did not let her arm fall back to her side until it lurched open. The red-headed woman stood in its frame dressed in her white nightgown and hair spiralling out in all directions; in the dim light of the candle she held, it looked as though her head was adorned by a crown of flames.

'What's going on?' she stammered, rubbing her eyes wearily.

'It's hatching!' Adairia practically screamed. At these words, any residual remnants of sleep fell away from Isla's face.

'Great goddess, come on then!' She kept a hold of her candle in one hand and grabbed a hold of Adairia's sleeve in her other. Both women rushed along the few metres between their doors and back inside Adairia's room.

Adairia had left the lid to the chest open and fell down onto her knees at its side as soon as she entered the room. She was quickly followed by Isla who could not suppress an excited squeal from escaping her lips upon catching site of what lay within. The egg continued to bulge and crack before them; with each second that passed the spaces between each fragment of shell grew wider and the jelly like substance that held them together grew thinner. The gel was not completely transparent

76

but there was evidently something stretching and moving inside the egg. *Something? A dragon!* Adairia could feel her heart pounding in her chest as she attempted to keep her breathing steady. She took a second to tear her eyes away from the egg to look imploringly at Isla who sat hunched at her side. The red-head attempted a reassuring smile and put her right hand over Adairia's left in an attempt to ground her.

As both women turned back to the egg the first sliver of skin-like glue between the shards of shell split and the edge of something dark, rusty brown poked out from the gap. Then it happened again and this time it was clear to all eyes watching that a foot now poked out from mass of shell and slime. Adairia lifted her hand to cover her mouth as she gasped aloud. Next came another foot, followed by the tip of a wing, then another, until finally the entire egg collapsed as the bulbous head of a baby dragon pushed its way free of its confines.

The creature's eyes remained closed while its face and body were coated in the gelatinous substance that must have kept it alive within the egg all those many years. It was clearly awake, however, as it opened and close its mouth slowly, stretching its neck out and pulling it back in, seemingly testing its new environment. Then she heard it again. *Adairia.* Her name sounded in her own mind, but less sure than it had done in the past. The small voice that spoke the word sounded hesitant and unsure, and it filled her heart with empathy.

'Yes, it's me, Adairia,' she said out loud, hoping the tiny dragon would understand her. Slowly she watched as it peeled apart its eyelids and looked up at her with sparkling green eyes. Instinctively she reached out her hand but paused before she came into contact with the creature's flesh. The dragon, however, took a wobbling step forward and pushed its nose up against her outstretched palm. It rubbed its face along her skin and its nostrils flared as if it were inhaling her scent.

In response, Adairia cupped her hand and stroked the dragons crown tentatively. It was sticky, and a little bit gross she had to admit, but the dragon responded by closing its eyes again and making a rumbling noise of satisfaction that she found hard to resist. The spell was broken, however, when Isla's voice chimed in from her left-hand side.

'Would you like the basin to wash her?'

'Her?' Adairia asked, astonished by this revelation.

'Aye, the males are born with sharp ridges all along their tails but hers is as smooth as snakeskin,' Isla explained. Adairia took this in and then nodded her assent.

'Thank you, there's a basin full of water and some cloth just there.' She pointed towards her own washing station and Isla lifted herself from the floor to fetch it over.

*

Isla sat silently on the floor beside Adairia as the young woman nervously wrung out the wet cloth she had been brought. Adairia proceeded to wipe the dragon down gingerly, beginning with its face. At first touch of the flannel the creature flinched, but when it grasped what was happening it began to lean into her hand with its entire body. Steadily, Adairia washed the dragon of all of the fluids and slime that it had been coated in until its scales glistened. The dull shade of brown it had appeared at first glance faded to reveal a bright orange hide that resembled the colour of burning embers in a fireplace. When she finally drew the cloth away and dumped it back into the basin now full of grimy water the dragon let out a little crooning sound as if it missed her touch and she found herself smiling down at it.

'She's beautiful,' whispered Isla and Adairia nodded, not taking her eyes off the tiny dragonling.

Now that its cleaning had ceased the dragon took a few shaky steps towards Adairia and tentatively rubbed its muzzle against her folded knees. In response she reached down and stroked its head gently. Almost simultaneously dragon and companion opened their mouths wide and let out competing yawns. Isla had to stifle a giggle at the sight of them both.

'Think you can manage without me until morning?' she asked.

'Aye, I think we could both do with some sleep,' Adairia replied.

'Well, rest up, Tearlach will be desperate to meet this wee one first thing tomorrow.' Adairia smiled and nodded at Isla's words. The red headed woman gave the blonde haired one a brief affectionate stroke of the hair and left the new friends alone in Adairia's room for the rest of the night. She was equally exhausted herself.

Extract from an Introduction to Dragons

The first dragon known to have settled in Albiyon went by the name of Cartimandua. She was a female of the species and immigrated to the country in the second year of King Leith I's reign. She was companion to Queen Isolde, wife of King Leith. Her hide is usually depicted as scarlet in the art from this period. The dragon herself outlived her companion but nowhere is her own death documented in the sources. We are therefore unable to confirm what age she lived to be.

Chapter Ten

Fia

Too exhausted to lift herself into her bed, Adairia had fallen asleep on the floor where she sat, a blanket draped across herself and the new-born dragon. After Isla had left them, the small creature had curled up in her lap and nodded off almost immediately; Adairia could only imagine how draining it was being born. A few hours later, she was woken by the shifting and rustling of the blanket around her caused by the stirring dragonling attempting to escape its confines. Instinctively Adairia wrapped her arms around the creature to still it, and let it know she was there.

'Shh, shh, I'm here.' Adairia stroked the dragon's head, and in return it rubbed its muzzle against her arm. 'Good morning.' She replied.

The sun had evidently already risen in the sky and was peeking through the gaps in her curtains. Delicately she lifted the dragon from her lap and set it on the floor so she could stand and open the curtains to let the light stream fully into the room. As she gathered herself up and went to fetch some clothes to swap out for her night gown, the baby dragon waddled around the room sniffing at her furniture and various knick-knacks. She watched it closely as she pulled a simple blue dress over her head and jumped when it started gnawing at one of her bedposts curiously. Before she had a chance to run over and tear it away, however, it was retching disgustedly, presumably not a fan of wood for breakfast.

'S'pose you want some food, you've still not had anything to eat since you hatched,' Adairia spoke out loud.

Whether it had fully comprehended her words or not she could not be sure, but the dragon immediately ran over to her upon hearing her voice and circled her feet happily. It was at that point there came a knock at her door. Adairia could not suppress her surprise when she dragged it open and found Isla standing there, fully dressed and seemingly wide awake.

'You're up,' was her disorientated response, to which Isla laughed.

'Don't look so shocked. It's almost lunchtime after all,' she replied jovially. She proceeded to proffer up a buttered roll seemingly from thin air, which Adairia took gratefully.

'It is?' Adairia exclaimed. She never slept this late. 'I had no idea. We just woke up.'

'Well, you probably needed a lie in after last night. But no more lazing around, Tearlach is on the verge of barging into the university himself and I don't think that staircase was made for a fully-grown dragon. Let's take our new friend to meet him.'

*

After watching the dragonling stumble treacherously down the first couple of steps on the main staircase Adairia had thought it safer to scoop her up and carry her the rest of the way. She made no complaints but craned her neck over Adairia's arms, continuously sniffing the air as they walked, and their surroundings changed.

Along their journey they crossed paths with Morag in the entrance lobby of the university. She was carrying a precarious looking stack of books in both her arms and had a distracted expression upon her face. Hearing Adairia call out her name, however, she did pause long enough to lower her arms so she could peek over the top of her miniature library. Morag beheld the creature in her friend's arms curiously but made no noise of surprise upon seeing a baby dragon inside the university halls.

'I saw Morag and Calder at breakfast this morning and told them what happened last night,' Isla chimed in, answering Adairia's unasked question.

'I see,' Adairia responded, somewhat perturbed at having been denied the joy of announcing their news herself. Pushing her momentary indigitation to the side, however, she held the dragon up a little higher to provide Morag with a better look. It inhaled deeply upon being confronted by the stranger but made no other movement. 'This is her then.

'Does she have a name?' Morag asked casually, eyeing up the dragon as if it were a vaguely interesting scroll that had landed on her desk.

'Uh, no, actually,' replied Adairia. 'How… how are dragons usually named?' She turned to Isla.

'If their mother is around, she might name them, but more often than not it's their original companion. She's too little to name herself if that's what you're wondering.' Isla winked.

Adairia nodded but said nothing. The thought had not occurred to her that she might be responsible for naming the tiny creature in her arms. It felt like an immense responsibility, although she felt she should be used to those cropping up unexpectedly by now.

'Well, I've got a lot of work to do. Aelish will be waiting for me,' Morag chimed in, referring to one of the senior university scholars as well as her personal tutor. Adairia was not particularly surprised that her best friend's routine could not be disrupted by anything so mundane as a new-born dragonling. She knew by now not to take it personally. 'But I'll see you this evening at dinner. Don't forget to find Calder at some point; he was practically drooling this morning when Isla told us your egg had hatched. He's desperate to meet the dragons, especially now that there are two of them.'

'Will do.' Adairia grinned. 'See you later.' As they parted ways, Isla waved goodbye on both of their behalfs while Adairia's hands were otherwise engaged.

*

'Knock, knock,' Isla called loudly through the open door to the barn causing Adairia to roll her eyes at the other woman.

As soon as they had come within ten feet of the outbuilding the baby dragon had begun to squirm in her arms; something had her excited and Adairia had to assume it was the smell of another dragon.

'Finally,' came Tearlach's deep voice as they entered his temporary accommodation. He stood before them clearly in a state of eager anticipation at their arrival. As soon as they stepped inside his eyes locked on the small creature in Adairia's arms. 'It has been so long since I've seen a dragon so young,' he sighed, taking a step forward.

'Isn't she bonny?' chirped Isla stepping closer to her dragon and patting one of his front legs with her hand in greeting.

'All dragons are beautiful,' growled Tearlach, although there was no real menace in his voice. 'There is no creature as majestic, and this wee one is proof of that.'

As Adairia stepped closer, Tearlach lowered his neck so that he was eye to eye with the dragonling. Next to this fully-grown dragon 'wee' seemed liked an understatement, but the babe was evidently not deterred by his size. She squirmed and stretched so that she could touch her own snout against his affectionately. In response, Tearlach bared his teeth, in what Adairia had to assume was the equivalent of a dragon smiling, and made a soft purring noise with his tongue. They all watched as the dragonling attempted to imitate him although the sound she emitted more closely resembled a gritty squeak. Tearlach nevertheless huffed kindly in response.

'You'll get the hang of it,' he said to the baby dragon and then turning his eyes to Adairia, 'what is her name?' Adairia had been thinking about this ever since their encounter with Morag in the university halls.

'I did wonder if she might suit Fia?' she replied looking down at the bundle in her arms.

'Flickering firelight,' murmured Isla.

'Aye, it's what I thought when I was washing her clean last night. The orange of her scales reminded me of flames.' She held the dragon up so she could look it directly in the eye. 'What do you think? Is Fia your name?' The dragon let out the same squeaky attempt at a purr that she had made seconds ago, and a rush of warmth flooded through Adairia's mind and body that she knew was a sign of the dragonling's approval. 'In that case, let me introduce you to Fia.' She turned the dragon back to face the other two. 'And these, Fia, are Tearlach and Isla. They are our friends.'

'Pleased to meet you Fia,' replied Isla who stretched out her hand to stroke the dragonling's head.

'I hope you've not forgotten your old friends Adairia,' came a man's voice from behind her. She turned to find Calder peeking his head through the open door, a nervous grin on his face. 'My apologies for interrupting you all. I just couldnie wait to meet the new bairn.' He shifted self-consciously in the doorway. Adairia laughed at his awkwardness and motioned for him to come in with a jerk of her head.

'Don't be daft, Calder, you're family. Come inside.' She turned back to the adult dragon. 'Tearlach this is my friend Calder, he has been excited to meet you since your arrival.' Tearlach bowed his head.

'Pleased to meet you Calder. Any friend of Adairia's is a friend of mine.' Calder's face went scarlet and he stumbled over his own greeting but Adairia was still pleased to see her worlds coming together, new and old.

'And this is Fia, Calder.' She held up her arms for Calder's inspection.

'Hello Fia,' Calder said in a hushed tone, his eyes gleaming. In response she burped loudly in his face making everyone in the barn burst into raucous laughter.

*

The next few days were strange indeed. Immediately after introducing Fia to Tearlach and Calder, Isla accompanied Adairia to the chancellor's chamber. The entire council were gathered in the small front room once again, apparently already well aware of Fia's birth. Adairia introduced the dragonling to each of them in turn and even allowed Aliya to hold her for a short time. They had all admired Fia's iridescent scales; even the goblin Tronk had grudgingly acknowledged his pleasure at meeting the first dragonling to be born in Albiyon in over sixty years. 'You're not so bad are you.' He had muttered patting her head. He instantly drew it back, however, when she attempted to nibble one of his fingers.

The experience of having a new-born dragon to look out for

reminded Adairia of what she thought it must be like to have a toddler. As soon as she put her down Fia would be running off in one direction or another and showed no indications of wariness when it came to approaching strangers. The dragonling even went so far as to, what Adairia imagined was meant to be playfully, bite Angus' ankle when he was stacking shelves in the library one afternoon. To her great relief the head-librarian only chuckled, responding to her profuse apologies by asserting that it was an honour.

'How many people could say they had been attacked by a dragon and survived?' he had laughed.

Communication between the two was limited at first. Dragons were not so different from other creatures in that they took time to fully master language and learn to talk. Fia was clearly picking up a few words here and there, other than Adairia's own name, and was using them intermittently to communicate with her companion but always via their telepathic connection. As yet, however, her vocabulary did not stretch much further than words to express her desire for food. When Adairia had asked Tearlach how long it took dragonlings to speak out loud he had told her it varied but usually around a month after they hatched; after all, he reminded her, they had much longer to develop inside their eggs than a human baby did inside its mother's belly. He had then gone on to mutter something to himself about the idiocy of humans exposing their infants to the elements whilst still so weak and underdeveloped, which had made Isla laugh riotously. 'He's got a point to be fair,' she had eventually managed to sputter out.

All in all, Fia's development seemed to be progressing along well. She had grown from the size of a puppy to a large cat in just two weeks, although she was a long way off flying yet. Still, Calder had noted that she would soon be overtaking the pigs in girth if she continued to grow at this rate.

Adairia could not mask the increasing sense of pride she felt whenever she looked at the fiery orange dragon. Their bond too, appeared to be strengthening with every day. She was becoming more and more aware of the nuances of Fia's moods and learning to communicate her own thoughts in feelings she could direct to the dragon's own consciousness. None of this made her feel any less out of her depth, however, as she continued to feel as if she were always one step behind when it came to learning the ins and outs of being a dragon's companion. The only difference now, was that the endless mental and physical education she was undergoing felt completely and utterly worth it.

Chapter Eleven
Parliamentary Business

'Fia, no!' Adairia made to leap after the dragonling in her panic but was stopped in her tracks by a booming voice.

'No, no, leave her, it's alright.' Tearlach chuckled and Adairia could have sworn she felt a tremor run through the earthen floor of the barn beneath her.

Fia was, at that moment, clambering frantically up the larger dragon's tail, using his body as a climbing frame. To her frustration the comparatively minuscule dragon had been having limited success using her tiny claws for leverage; she had thus resorted to grabbing a hold of one of the ridges along Tearlach's back with her teeth, much to Adairia's horror.

'I imagine you'd compare the sensation to a small insect bite; it is nothing to concern yourself with,' Tearlach assured her. 'We dragons are hardy creatures, it is only natural for Fia to be curious.'

Adairia, though, suspected there was more to Tearlach's forgiving nature. The way the older dragon looked at his young counterpart was touching. He had only known her for a few weeks, but he doted on her; they all did. The response to Fia's presence among Adairia's friends, old and new, had been heart-warming, and it made her glow with pride.

Unsurprisingly, Calder could not stay away. He was

regularly to be found showering the baby dragon with affection when not otherwise occupied; something Fia revelled in. Even Morag seemed to soften in her company. Without prompting, the usually stoic woman had gone so far as to whip up a calming lotion for Fia's scale loss, which were an unfortunate accompaniment to constant growth spurts. Adairia was overcome with gratitude for all of them.

Unfortunately, the gossip had not evaporated into thin air since Fia's birth. Adairia was unsurprised when she had continued to be the target of transparent stares and rude questions since the dragon's arrival. What had taken her aback, however, was the substantial increase in courtship offers from university residents she barely knew. One particularly self-assured graduate student had even turned up at the door to her room late one evening having apparently gotten the wrong impression from Adairia's polite but evasive response to his attempt at flirting earlier that day. Adairia's reaction to this surprise visit had been sure to leave him with no lingering doubts concerning her feelings, however. Minus the late-night drop-ins, hoever, Adairia could not find the energy to care any longer. A dragonling was no small commitment and Fia required every last drop of Adairia's attention. The role of companion to a new-born dragon would surely have sapped her dry, mentally and physically, if it were not for the help of Isla and Tearlach.

'Congratulations mighty one. You have reached the peak,' Tearlach hummed contentedly as Fia accomplished her mission to mount the larger dragon's scull. Equally happy with her success she made a noise that landed somewhere between a yelp and a bark and looked down at Adairia who waved up at her, a large grin plastered across her face. 'Such a fiery spirit, just like the colour of your scales wee one. Perhaps we have a new teine in our midst,' Tearlach added.

'A tiene? What's that?' Adairia inquired as she unfurled from her cross-legged position and stretched out her limps before her.

'It's the name the dragons use for pyratic dragons.' This response did not come from Tearlach but a new arrival who had entered through the half open barn doors.

'Isla!' Adairia smiled even more widely. 'There you are.'

'I think you mean pyratic is the name humans and other two-legs use for the tiene,' Tearlach huffed.

'You've got me there, friend. Sorry about that,' Isla conceded.

'A pyratic dragon?' Adairia asked, returning her gaze to Fia's slight form. 'Do you think so? How can you tell?'

'Well, no one can really, not yet. Only mothers know their hatchlings kind before they're mature enough to show any powers themselves,' Tearlach explained. 'Dragonlings typically take after one of their parents. Myself, I am from a long line of adhair on my mother's side, what you would call aethereal dragons.' Adairia thought it was just a hint of smugness that she could spy in the dragon's expression.

'Where have you been?' Adairia asked as Isla positioned herself on the ground next to the other woman.

'Ugh, I had a meeting with that...' Isla's cheeks turned red as she glanced at Adairia, 'with the Lady Mirin.' She finished.

'You don't need to shy away from profanity in front of me,' Adairia laughed.

'Oh, it's pointless anyway. She's just exhausting, not that she's alone,' Isla sighed.

'What were you meeting about, if I may ask?' Knowing that

Isla and the Lady Mirin knew each other from their shared posts in the Albiyan parliament Adairia could only assume it was on some sort of state business that they had met.

'We've talked already about the tainted water reserves in Invergorm?' Adairia nodded, prompting Isla to continue. 'Well, I received a letter yesterday informing me that the same thing is happening in Mathshire. They're both on the west coast but Mathshire gets its water from an entirely different loch. Whatever has infected the water isn't coming from one loch in particular, but we're still no closer to identifying what the cause is. And naturally no one wants to drink the water because who knows if there could be long term side effects.' Isla sighed. 'Another riot broke out like the one in Drewr, and this one was definitely a riot. Two lads broke into the bakery in broad daylight and tore up their storeroom before scrawling "back to the stable cuddie scum" across the front of the building. The owner is a centaur.' Isla added as an explanation.

Adairia gasped. While cuddie had traditionally been a term used to refer to donkeys, it had also been adopted by some as a particularly repulsive slur against the race of halflings who were part man, part horse. Centaurs were not native to Albiyon but ever since the coastal borders had opened up following the establishment of the Albiyan parliament some had chosen to emigrate from across the seas and make Albiyon their home.

'What's going to happen next?'

'Ah therein lies our problem,' Isla exhaled. 'Parliament is split. Myself, I'm on the side of those who wish to pour more resources into investigating the water pollution. And in the meantime, it might be worth distributing some of the central grain stores to those rural communities who are struggling. Or else we could relocate the families affected themselves, those

92

who are willing to move. We've all heard how meagre this year's harvest has been for much of the west coast and it must be related to the issues with the water reserves. It's too much of a coincidence not to be, right?' Isla looked at Adairia for validation.

'Well, shortfalls happen even in the best of times.' Adairia chewed her lip. 'It wouldn't be the first time a farmer had a bad year for crops.'

'Yes, but a whole swathe of farms in the same area the water has been contaminated?'

'I mean it does seem worthy of investigation. Surely the rest of parliament support you in that?'

'There are those members who believe our time and money would be better spent investing in an increased guard in those towns were there has been unrest.' Isla gritted her teeth. 'The Lady Mirin among them.'

Adairia was surprised by this. Since the dissolution of the monarchy Albiyon had been a land where an official guard existed only in the barest capacity. She was aware from the literature she had read that this was not the case for other realms across the sea but based too on these, the idea of increased sentinels did not sit well with her.

'Surely there are better ways?' Adairia insisted.

'That is what I hoped to convince the Lady Mirin of. I thought that if I could take the opportunity while I'm here to talk to her in person she would be more amenable to my point of view. But apparently, she's still pining after the good old days where the peasants did what they were told. She's old enough to have lived during the very end of Bayrd's father's reign you know?'

'I'd assumed,' Adairia nodded. 'Well perhaps you can

convince some of the other members of parliament instead?'

'We'll try, but the Lady Mirin holds a lot of sway.' Isla's expression looked grim as she stared down at the dirt floor; Adairia could not think what else to do but put an arm round her friend and let her lean against her shoulder for a little while. Her own mind, meanwhile, was racing with this new information.

Chapter Twelve

Sleep

'And how is Fia?' Aliya asked handing over a cup of warm tea to Adairia. They both glanced at the dragonling who was curled up beside the chancellor's fireplace, absorbing its heat.

'She seems well,' Adairia replied, 'constantly curious about her new surroundings.'

'I've heard nothing but good things from everyone who speaks of meeting her,' Aliya smiled. 'And how are you?'

Adairia thought about the chancellor's question for a moment. *How was she?* She had barely had time to check in on her own emotions since Fia's birth. *What word could possibly express those experiences that she had been through in the past few weeks and the effect they had had on her? Overwhelmed, terrified, excited, nervous, jubilant?* Nothing in her vocabulary felt adequate.

'Exhausted,' was the reply that she finally settled on

'I'd be concerned if you weren't,' Aliya smiled kindly, 'or at least concerned that you'd been making inappropriate use of the university's stock of herbs.' At the chancellor's words Adairia could not help but crack a small grin.

'It's a big responsibility, the care of another life,' she continued. 'You seem to be doing well considering how quickly this was all sprung on you.'

'I don't know what I would have done without Isla and Tearlach.'

'I hear from the Lady Isla that you plan to visit her home in the next few weeks?'

'Aye, it's about a fortnight now. We'll hopefully get to meet more dragons and their companions while we're there, but I wanted to wait until Fia was speaking out loud before we made the journey, make sure she's up to it you know.'

'It's a big adventure,' Aliya replied although Adairia suspected her words were regarding more than just the little dragon. 'You won't have travelled to the highlands before I suppose?'

'Never, I've never left Eòlas.'

It was true that Adairia had never ventured much farther than the villages that occupied the university's surroundings. She was not filled with wanderlust like some of her fellow foundlings had been. There were a handful of places, further afield, she had hoped to travel to someday, but she enjoyed the familiarity of home. She had to admit, however, that she was not dreading the thought of visiting Isla and Tearlach's home; in fact, the idea made her stomach flutter with a kind of nervous excitement. It was at that moment there came a soft knock at the door that made Adairia crane her neck over the back of her armchair.

'Come in,' called Aliya from her own seat and the door swung open to reveal Lady Mirin standing in the hallway beyond.

It did not seem to matter how many times Adairia encountered the fae woman these days, her ethereal appearance always left her feeling somewhat giddy. It was like staring directly at the sun only to close your eyes tightly and see dancing shapes and colours behind your eyelids; something about laying your eyes on her made the world sway slightly afterwards. She had read that the fae only got more dazzling as they aged, so Adairia could only imagine how old the Lady Mirin must be to affect her so.

'Ah Lady Mirin, I did not realise we had a meeting this afternoon. I was just checking in on Adairia and Fia here.' The chancellor gestured to the slumbering dragon on the rug.

'No, my apologies chancellor, we did not have a meeting arranged but I was hoping to speak to you further about the issue of university fees I mentioned yesterday,' replied Lady Mirin, bowing her head slightly in Adairia's direction. 'If you have company, however, I can return later when it is more convenient.'

'Oh, don't worry, I'm sure you've saved Adairia the pain of remaining cooped up inside with an old woman all day. Don't expect that you'll get me to reverse my earlier decision, however. I am not in the business of charging for education.' She turned to Adairia. 'You know you are always welcome to stop by if you have anything on your mind my dear.'

'Yes, of course, thank you,' Adairia nodded, setting her cup down on the small table beside her chair. The Lady Mirin meanwhile had approached the fireplace and stood peering down at Fia's sleeping form.

'She is well?' she asked Adairia without raising her gaze.

'Yes, thank you,' Adairia murmured, twisting her fingers behind her back. Before she could feel anymore awkward, however, the Lady Mirin flashed a smile that made Adairia lightheaded and she moved back from the dragon just far enough to allow the younger woman past.

Adairia shuffled over to Fia who remained sound asleep

and gave her ever growing form a little nudge in the hopes of waking her. When nothing happened, she grinned awkwardly at the two women, shrugging her shoulders ever so slightly. 'Looks like someone doesn't feel like walking today.' With that she scooped the dragonling up into her arms, wondering to herself how soon it would be until this was physically impossible. For her part, Fia continued to snooze on unaware of the world around her.

*

Fia slept unperturbed the entire journey from the chancellor's quarters to their room. Adairia could not help rolling her eyes when she set her down on the bed and she did not bat as much as an eyelid. Following suit, Adairia flopped down on the bed beside the dragonling and let out an elongated yawn. Since Fia had been born Cyril had excused her from her regular chores around the university. A small flicker of guilt remained in the back of Adairia's mind, for not contributing her part to the everyday running of her home, but she was not sure she would be much help at the moment anyway. One thing she had insisted on at least, was keeping up with the garden plot she tended, which was growing less demanding as the colder months approached. Even without her regular chores, however, she found herself exhausted as she peered up hazy eyed at the ceiling above her bed. So exhausted in fact, that she was asleep within minutes of laying her head down on the comfortable mattress.

Adairia's pleasant dreams were interrupted sometime later by an insistent knocking at the door to her room. Reluctantly, she pulled herself up into a sitting position on the edge of her bed and rubbed at her eyes groggily with her fists. When another insistent knock came at the door, she begrudgingly made her way to unlatch it from the inside and find out who had woken her up.

'Isla.' She said in surprise.

'You didn't turn up for dinner,' the red headed woman stated, her eyes narrowed. 'I was worried about you.' Adairia could hardly stifle a chuckle from escaping her lips.

'Sorry, Isla. I fell asleep, it's all just so draining you know.'

'No, I'm sorry. I shouldn't have jumped to any conclusions; I've just gotten used to eating our meals together I guess.' She laughed but it came out awkwardly and she turned her eyes down to stare at her feet instead of Adairia's face. Her expression perked up, however, when she drew something from inside her jerkin, wrapped in what looked like a napkin from the dining hall. 'I brought you some pudding. They had your favourite carrot cake this evening.' Adairia's eyes immediately lit up and she took the gift from Isla's hands.

'Thanks so much. I am a little hungry now you mention it, come in.' She stood out of the way so Isla could enter the room and close the door behind her.

'Calder and Morag were asking after you,' Isla said as she jumped up onto the bed next to Fia, stroking the dragon's neck with the palm of her hand. 'I can't decide if those two remind me of siblings or parents,' she snorted and Adairia laughed with her.

'They're family,' she replied, unwrapping her cake and taking a large bite of the rich sponge.

'This one must be exhausted too,' Isla noted as Fia remained undisturbed by her petting and continued to snooze on the quilt.

'Aye, she's been asleep longer than I have, since we visited the chancellor this morning.' She frowned at the dragonling.

'I'm surprised she hasn't woken up yet to be honest.'

'Fia.' Whispered Isla into the ear closest to her. 'It's time to get up.' She raised her voice slightly and repeated herself before giving the small beast an affectionate prod with one of her fingers. 'That is odd,' she muttered, as much to herself as to Adairia. She lent her head down to the dragon's muzzle before adding. 'She's definitely asleep.'

A previously unacknowledged sense of alarm started to insist on Adairia's attention.

'Fia,' she said in an authoritative tone. 'It's time to wake up.' She used both hands to tickle the dragon's body a little roughly in the hopes of waking her up. Her attempts were to no avail, however, and Fia simply rolled slightly further onto her side, still fast sleep. 'Is there something wrong with her?' Adairia's voice cracked as she spoke these last words, looking desperately at Isla.

'I don't know,' the other woman responded slowly. 'But I know who will. Let's take her to Tearlach.'

*

Adairia bundled up Fia all the more carefully this time and both women made haste to Tearlach's temporary home. Dusk was settling in, but when they turned the corner to the barn where they expected to find Tearlach, the dragon was already seated outside making spirited conversation with Calder. The young man sat on a low wall and although they were not close enough to hear what he was saying they could see him waving his arms around in the air animatedly, a smile on his face.

'Tearlach!' Called Isla, her pace increasing to a jog to reach him. The dragon turned his head at her voice and Calder's hands fell to his sides, their train of conversation broken. It was immediately clear to both man and dragon that there was something amiss with the two women as they approached. Their faces showed evident signs of worry and Adairia was swallowing deep breaths in attempt to keep herself calm.

'What's wrong?' Tearlach growled picking himself up so he stood on all fours.

'It's Fia,' replied Isla, regaining her composure as she reached the dragon. 'We don't know exactly but she's been asleep, or unconscious for most of the day and we can't wake her up.' Adairia came up behind Isla holding up the tiny dragon for Tearlach's inspection, her hands trembling. She could sense deep down that something was wrong. Ever since Isla had joined her in her chamber, she had been attempting to make a connection with the dragonling's mind like she had grown so used to, but to no avail.

'Put her down.' Tearlach spoke calmly sensing Adairia's increasing panic. She did as he instructed her and took two steps back, never moving her eyes from Fia's body.

Tearlach lowered himself back onto bended legs so that he sat as close to the ground as he possibly could and bent his neck so that he could examine Fia more closely. Calder had stood up from his perch on the nearby wall and was now standing next to Adairia silently, one hand on her shoulder. All three humans watched intently as Tearlach closed his eyes and inhaled deeply, taking in her scent whilst presumably attempting to connect with Fia's mind as Adairia had done. As she had learnt, all dragons were able to communicate with one another without speaking aloud, although they could only mimic this form of contact with other creatures they had explicitly bonded to.

'She's been poisoned.' Tearlach's voice was full of venom. At the dragon's words Isla gasped and Calder swore loudly.

'How do you know?' Adairia's voice cracked as she sunk to

101

her knees next to the dragonling.

'She reeks of it.'

'But she's still alive,' insisted Isla. 'What can we do?'

'I'm no expert but it is incredibly difficult to kill a dragon, even with the right poison. We are strong. Something has undeniably seeped its way into her system though; she needs a healer or someone well versed in herbs, but I don't know who here would be able to help.'

'Morag,' interjected Calder. 'I'll get Morag.' He squeezed Adairia's shoulder one last time and she attempted a grateful smile up at him before he sped off back to the University residences.

'Isla is right, Adairia,' Tearlach continued. 'She is still alive.'

'But for how long?' was all Adairia could say in response, tears beginning to build up in the corners of her eyes.

Extract from An Introduction to Dragons

A brood mare usually lays between four and six eggs in one clutch. It is unusual for more than one or two eggs to ever hatch, and on occasion an entire clutch will fossilise before any new dragons can be born. No one is exactly sure why the survival rate of unhatched eggs is so low. Even the dragons themselves have not passed comment on this phenomenon and accept it rather as the natural way of things. The dragoness herself will rarely lay another clutch until she has confirmed that all of the eggs she has previously laid have either hatched or fossilised. This is so that she can give her full attention to any possible dragonlings that may survive the process.

Although dragon eggs can survive in the wild, eggs that still retain the potential to hatch can be destroyed by predators or natural disasters so mothers will often guard their clutches closely. Many eggs, however, have been known to outlive their parents and still hatch unharmed. For this reason, it has become common practice for families with close ties to dragon kind, and whose numbers include existing dragon companions, to house any unhatched eggs while their future is still undetermined.

Chapter Thirteen
The First Dragon

None of them spoke as they waited for the return of Calder, hopefully accompanied by Morag and a plan of action. Isla and Tearlach would occasionally exchange glances with one another but Adairia was unable to tear her eyes away from Fia's unconscious form. She kept running her hand along the dragon's spine and muzzle, searching for any sign that Fia had stopped breathing. As they sat in the almost pitch black, with only the moon and stars to illuminate the sky, they finally heard the hurried foot-fall of more than one person approaching from the distance. Calder had returned, and he had brought Morag with him as promised

'Adairia!' she called as they both sped to their friend's side. 'Calder explained as much as he could to me. Fia has been poisoned?' It was unusual to see Morag look so harried; she was ordinarily so composed and single minded. But as Adairia looked up into the eyes of her oldest friend she saw the distress plain on her face.

'Tearlach is sure of it!' Adairia looked up at the larger of the two dragons who was staring down at them all.

'I can smell it on her,' he growled in corroboration.

'Can you give her something, something that will expel whatever it is?' Adairia asked desperately.

'Dragons can't ingest poison like we can, there's no point making her eat or drink anything to stop its effects.' For a moment Adairia was struck dumb by Morag's response, temporarily stunned by her friend's familiarity with dragon medicine more than anything else.

'How do you know that?' Morag rolled her eyes at Adairia's question.

'Mind, you weren't the only one reading those books in preparation for this wee one's arrival. Dragon's stomachs are lined with acids far stronger than anything found in our bodies. Almost any poison would have been redundant as soon as it hit her system from the inside.' It was clear that Adairia's panic was gradually growing throughout this lecture. Ever the empathic one, Calder took the opportunity to interrupt Morag's lesson.

'Morag!' he insisted. 'Tell her what you told me, about the bath.'

'Bath?' squeaked Adairia, nonplussed.

'Yes, sorry, sorry. It's far more likely she absorbed the poison through her skin and the fact that she is still breathing means it probably hasn't infiltrated too deep yet. The only thing I could think to do was bath her in the most common herbs we use to purge unknown toxins.'

'There's a trough full of water in my barn.' Tearlach offered. 'It should be big enough for Fia.'

*

Inside the barn Morag unfastened her satchel, which was full of small cloth bags and stoppered glass bottles that presumably contained the tools of her trade. Tearlach had guided them over to a substantial stone basin intended for cattle or the like, but that also served as the perfect drinking station for the enormous dragon. With striking efficiency, Morag pulled up the sleeve of her blouse and dipped an elbow in the water.

'It's too cold,' she muttered.

At Morag's words, Tearlach bent his head to the surface of the water and opened his mouth wide. No flames curled from between his teeth but the breath he let out caused the air in front of him to ripple and distort; the humans standing nearby could feel the heat it released across their exposed skin. Once he drew his head back, steam could be seen curling up from the water.

'Thank you.' Nodded Morag, pulling from her satchel a few choice containers, each containing a different herb. One by one she poured a portion of each ingredient into the trough and watched as the water undulated and absorbed the various colours of each newly added element. Once Morag had finished her task, she turned to Adairia and indicated with her arms that she should lower the dragonling into the concoction.

For a moment Adairia held Fia all the closer to her body, unwilling to let her go, but putting her trust in her oldest friend she stepped forward and gently submerged the unmoving body. Morag took her friends hands and showed her how to rub the dragon's skin in order to spread the now murky grey water between her scales. She then proceeded to use the fingers on her right hand to draw shapes in the air above the trough where Adairia bathed Fia. With each motion she outlined a different rune possessing different properties, the effect of which meant little to the rest of the group but their faith in Morag remained stalwart.

As she washed the still form of Fia in the healing bath Adairia was startled to feel something else between her fingers. Instead of just the water there was something thicker, more akin to slime running between her fingers. She stared in awe as something black seemed to seep from out of Fia's skin and into the trough. Adairia's breath caught in her throat as she swivelled her neck to stare at Morag, but her friend simply nodded at her to continue with the task. Encouraged, she did so with increased fervour.

After a few minutes had passed, the black sludge ceased to flow from Fia's body and it seemed as if nothing else would be added to the now black water. With encouragement from Morag, Adairia lifted the dragonling from the trough; her nerves made her skin itch, but she remained focused on her task. Carefully, she placed Fia in a swathe of fabric that Morag had provided and gently patted the still sleeping dragon dry.

It seemed no one was willing to break the silence, as if speaking before they knew whether the antidote had worked or not might affect its power. Isla did crouch down beside Adairia and Fia on the earthen ground of the barn while Calder caught Morag's eye questioningly, but she merely indicated with a nod of her head that he should keep his eyes on the dragonling in Adairia's arms.

Slowly but steadily the little dragon's jaw widened, revealing a mouth full of pointed teeth. Her lips curled back as she let out as large a yawn as was physically possible for such a small creature and peeled her eyelids back half-heartedly. Adairia let out a strangled noise that was half joy, half shock. As all of the tension abruptly fled from her body, she leaned forward to cup the dragon's jaw in her hands. Cautious of being too rough with their newly awakened friend she gently stroked the point beneath her chin and the dragon purred in approval.

'Thank you, Morag, thank you so much, I don't know how I'll ever be able to thank you enough.' She gasped, barely holding back the sobs from her voice.

'We're family Adairia. Fia too,' Morag replied, rolling her eyes at the woman on the floor, although a pleased smile quirked at the corner of her lips.

*

'You can't sleep?' Asked Isla later that night.

'No,' sighed Adairia.

'Neither can I.'

Both women lay huddled in Adairia's bed with Fia curled in the spot between them, equally awake but occasionally letting out loud yawns and shifting her position slightly. They had all waited a little longer in Tearlach's makeshift quarters in order to make absolutely sure that the antidote had taken full effect. Calder and Morag had been the first to leave when everything seemed safe once more, and shortly after bidding Tearlach goodnight Isla and Adairia had followed suit. The closer they had come to the University walls, however, Adairia had realised the extent to which her stomach was still tied in nervous knots. She did not want to be alone tonight, unable to relax or fully believe everything was well again. Upon expressing her anxieties to Isla the red-headed woman had offered to stay with both Adairia and Fia that night and keep them company. Isla had to admit that she too was shaken. Thus, the three of them found themselves resting against one another in Adairia's bed, unable to sleep.

'Talk to me.' Adairia murmured.

'Shall I tell you both a story?' Responded Isla.

'Yes, please.'

'Well, this is as much history as it is a story so listen closely.' Isla smiled.

'There once was a woman who did not even know herself how many years she had lived. She could not remember a life

108

any different from that which she experienced every passing day. She walked the land naked and unadorned, black hair curling down to the small of her back untamed and almost alive. She knew of no other creature like her although she was never entirely alone. The land was full of animals, some we still recognise today, others that have long since died out, and they provided her with some company. Not having ever spoken to another in a shared language before she didn't truly know what it meant to be lonely. She was satiated by the earth, warmed by the sun, and comforted by the soft grass. Nothing ever changed, why should it? That was, until one fateful day.'

'As she strolled through the meadows one late afternoon, she decided to explore the caves beneath the low hills that she had neglected for some time now. They were much darker than the rest of her surroundings, but their walls glittered with sparkling stones she could find nowhere else. The small beams of light that managed to peek through the mouth of the caves bounced off their surfaces to create a halo of greens and reds across the walls and ceiling; she loved to count how many she could spot while wandering the labyrinthine passages. One of the caves burrowed deep beneath the earth and led to a cavernous chamber that hosted a hidden lake. She loved to swim here and cool her skin on those days that it was particularly warm, sometimes diving down deep beneath the surface of the water and floating there for hours at a time. The lack of air in the depths of lake was of no concern, for this woman was what we would call a fairy, although different from the fae who walk among us today.'

'As she swam beneath the surface of the pool, she took in the various colours hidden in its depths. The dark green of the algae, the gleaming specks of gold embedded in the rocky walls, and the occasional silvery shoal of fish that passed by. All of it was familiar to her but no less pleasing because of it. She was struck, however, by the brilliant gleam of a round shape she had never noticed before, half buried in the sandy floor. Having no reason to practice caution she swam towards what she assumed was a particularly large gem and heaved it out of the ground. In her hands it appeared an iridescent shade of gold that refracted throughout the water. Intrigued, she brought her find back up to dry land with her to inspect it further. After thoroughly examining the oval shaped rock, she found it pleased her and she took it with her to her usual resting place under the shade of the trees.'

'Upon waking up the next day she found, to her surprise, that a crack had appeared on the exterior of the rock. Over the course of the next few rising and settings of the sun the number of cracks increased at a rapid pace, and she watched in fascination as the swirling surface of the stone transformed before her.'

'Is it..?' Adairia could not help herself from mumbling between stifled yawns.

'Wheesht and let me finish.' Smiled Isla patting her friend's dishevelled hair. 'As you have already guessed, the rock was in fact an egg. The woman had seen eggs hatch before, the reptiles and birds were usually born from their casings. This egg, however, was nothing like the ones she had seen before. As she stared on in awe, an unfamiliar creature broke free of the remnants of its confines. It was coated in a number of unknown fluids but beneath the slime she could see gleaming red eyes and startling gold scales that matched the colour the egg had originally been. This fae like being had just witnessed the birth of her first dragon.'

'The creature that sat before her was like nothing she had ever encountered before, and she felt an instant connection with the squirming form deep within herself that she could not explain. Struck by this unfamiliar feeling, she decided to take the burden of its care upon herself. With the passage of weeks, the dragonling grew larger and their connection became stronger. This continued to the point that they began to communicate with one another through their thoughts, and eventually aloud; gradually they found a shared language one another could understand.'

'As their bond grew so did the dragon's size, much to the woman's dismay. It grew larger than any other beast around them, even the elephants with their enormous bodies and powerful trunks. Along with its girth, its leathery wings expanded, and by mimicking the much smaller birds they met the dragon taught itself to fly. So close were they, it was never a question that when the dragon learnt to fly its companion would join it on its back to travel long distances, seeing more of the world than the fairy had ever seen alone.'

It was at this point that Adairia let out a snore that might have shaken the entire room. Isla smiled, pleased to have soothed the anxious woman's mind and help ease her into sleep, even if it did not reflect well on her story telling abilities.

'No worries, we'll finish it another time.' Giving the blonde woman's hair another stroke Isla settled in and closed her eyes, allowing sleep to take her too.

Chapter Fourteen
New Pastures

'I want to leave.'

Isla had barely opened her eyes when Adairia addressed her. Through the narrow window of her half-opened eyes, she could see the blonde woman sitting cross legged on the bed beside her scratching Fia's stomach, clearly having been awake for some time now. Isla did not open her mouth immediately, waiting until she had adjusted to the light streaming into the room before responding to Adairia's statement.

'Where?' She was groggy and unable to entirely comprehend what Adairia's words meant.

'Here, the University,' she sighed. 'I want to visit your home and meet the other dragons and their companions.'

'But I though you wanted to wait another couple of weeks before we headed up there.' Isla pulled herself up so that she was resting on one elbow and better able to look Adairia in the eye.

'I did.' Adairia paused before carrying on, ceasing to pet Fia who snorted and jumped off of the bed in search of water. 'For the first time in my life Isla, this place doesn't feel safe anymore. At least not for Fia. You know how difficult it is to poison a dragon, what happened yesterday can't have been an accident.'

Isla could not argue with this, she had thought the same

thing herself last night, as they had watched Morag work her magic on the sickly dragon. Instead, she sighed and nodded.

'Of course, we can travel up north as soon as you want.'

'Today,' insisted Adairia.

'Today?'

'Yes.'

It was clear that Adairia had made up her mind whilst the red-head had been asleep and there was nothing much left to discuss. In the short time they had spent together Isla had already learnt that Adairia did not rush into decisions haphazardly, but nor could she be easily swayed when she had made up her mind to do something. Once she had dragged herself from the bed, Isla departed the room to speak with Tearlach and check he would be fine to carry all three of them later that day. This left Adairia to inform the university council of the previous night's events before saying her goodbyes.

*

'So soon!' exclaimed Calder. He sat on the floor of Adairia's room scratching Fia's stomach whilst she nipped at his fingers playfully. Adairia was seated cross legged on her bed while Morag had sprawled across the only armchair in the room.

'Aye, I know but it just feels like time. We're living in a bubble here, Fia and I. I want to learn more about the other dragons and their companions. I think it'll be good for both of us.'

'When will you come back?' Calder asked.

'I don't know, I guess it depends on how things go.' Adairia stared in the direction of her window not looking at either of her friends. 'Don't worry though, as soon as Fia is flying we'll be back, and we can all go for a ride together.' She turned back, smiling at Calder whose face broke out in an excited grin.

113

'Who do you think was responsible for what happened last night?' Morag interjected, having remained otherwise silent throughout Adairia and Calder's exchange.

'I wish we knew. I talked with the chancellor this morning and informed her of what happened last night.' Adairia's shoulders sagged. 'She didn't have any answers either but assured me that she and the rest of the council would make a priority of looking into it.' She paused before adding. 'She also supported my decision to go up north with Isla and Tearlach for a wee while.'

'I don't think any one of us has been gone longer than a couple of weeks before,' Calder noted, his brow furrowing. 'You'll be missed lass.' To which Morag nodded in agreement.

'Just don't get up to anything exciting whilst I'm away.' Adairia winked, attempting to bring a little levity to their goodbye.

'Says the one who will be off riding dragons with beautiful women and meeting all sorts of new people. You'll return to us a new person.' Morag teased her friend.

'Don't be ridiculous. I am who I am and I'm not about to change anytime soon.' She purposefully ignored Morag's comment about her travelling companion, sensing a rising tide of embarrassment that she was not ready to unpack right now.

Despite her friends good-willed teasing she also felt the first sign of tears bubbling up and swiped aggressively at them with the back of one hand. As Adairia attempted to retain her composure, she felt Morag wrap her arms around her shoulders and slump down next to her on the bed, the mattress sinking ever so slightly under their combined weight. Grateful for the unexpected comfort Morag offered, she wrapped her own arms around her friend's waist in return and they hugged one another tightly.

Their embrace was interrupted a split second later by a third weight joining them on the bed and a hot nose pushing its way between their bodies in an attempt to burrow its way into their hug. Removing herself from Morag's arms Adairia bent over to give Fia a kiss on the muzzle, laughing at the little dragon's need to be included.

'I don't think Fia likes being left out much,' Calder laughed.

'Fia.'

Adairia blinked for a moment not sure if her ears were playing tricks on her, but that small, scratchy voice could not have come from anywhere else. Entranced she gaped down at the dragonling in her lap.

'She spoke out loud,' she continued to stare wide eyed at Fia who seemed unphased by the fuss.

'She said her own name,' added Calder.

'I think you might have a bit of a conceited wee dragon on your hands there Adairia,' Morag said darkly.

In unison, all three friends found themselves bursting into fits of giggles while Fia stared back at them this time utterly nonplussed by the humans' uproar.

*

'There they are,' nodded Tearlach making Isla swivel on the spot to look in the same direction.

In the distance she could see the four shapes of Adairia, Fia, Calder, and Morag walking towards them both. They stood in one of the open plains of grass situated not far from the barn where Tearlach had resided these past few weeks. Neither dragon nor companion had much in the way of luggage beside a small satchel swung across Isla's back; a pack that was one pair of trousers lighter than when she had arrived at the University.

Isla could observe even from a distance that Adairia had heeded her last piece of advice before she had left the young woman that morning. Instead of one of her usual heavy skirted dresses she wore a pair of thick woollen trousers that had previously been Isla's. This flight would not be like the short spins they had taken together around the University grounds and surrounding forests. They would be travelling for almost an entire day, perched on Tearlach's scaly back, and there was a reason Isla preferred trousers to skirts.

'I don't know how you can wear these everyday Isla,' called Adairia as she noticed the red-head taking in her new appearance. 'My skin feels trapped. I can't wait to get them off.' Isla chose not to tease Adairia on her choice of words, as the thought of the other woman riding a dragon, naked as the day she was born, briefly skipped through her head.

'Your skin will thank me when it's not blue from the cold air and rubbed raw from Tearlach's hide.' Adairia, however, only crossed her arms across her chest and rolled her eyes in response to Isla's words. Isla took the opportunity to turn Calder and Morag. 'It was a pleasure to meet you both.' She said, the sincerity evident in her voice.

'You too,' nodded Calder going in for a hug and clapping Isla emphatically on the back.

'Take care of our friend,' added Morag, although she smiled kindly as she spoke. No one standing in their small huddle truly thought Isla would do anything less, but Isla nodded all the same.

'Until we meet again.' She then proceeded to climb nimbly up Tearlach's leg and onto his back where she waited for

Adairia to follow.

'I love you both,' Adairia murmured as she gathered both her friends into her arms. 'Keep each other out of trouble.'

'Don't worry I'll keep an eye on Calder.' Morag nodded but Adairia turned to him herself and gestured towards Morag with her head.

'You know it's her I'm more worried about, right?' she asked and Calder chuckled loudly slinging his arm over Morag's shoulders.

'Nae need tae worry. We'll see you soon.'

With her goodbyes finalised Adairia proceeded to join Isla on Tearlach's back, although her ascension was slightly less elegant; the dragonling clinging on to her shoulder proved to be more trouble than aid. The enormous dragon himself looked down at the two humans left standing on the ground. He bent his head low in what must have counted as a dragon bow and both figures responded in kind.

'Bye!' yelled Adairia waving wildly with one arm whilst her other gripped Isla's waist. Her voice was drowned out, however, by the sound of Tearlach beating his wings against the air. Calder and Morag made sure to step well back from the dragon as it gathered momentum and watched in awe as he rose into the air before them. They both raised their own hands in turn to wave at their four friends as they climbed higher and higher into the air and gradually soared further and further away.

117

Chapter Fifteen
Baile

Though the university was out of sight, they had not yet left the boundaries of Eòlas before dusk settled over the group of travellers. Fortunately, it was a clear night, with not a cloud in the sky to obscure the various clusters of stars. Whilst keeping Fia fixed in her lap and an arm around Isla's waist, Adairia gazed down at the swathes of forest beneath them. In the dim evening light shed by the moon, the tops of the trees were an inky shade of navy blue; they stretched further than her eyes could discern, despite the speed at which they flew. Mesmerised by their surroundings she was startled when Fia started to keen and struggle in her arms. Looking down at the dragon tucked between herself and Isla, it hit Adairia that this was Fia's first time in the air. What with everything else going on she had completely neglected the significance of this occasion for the dragonling. Thankfully she could sense that it was excitement as opposed to fear that motivated Fia's struggle. Still, Adairia tried her hardest to settle her, so that she did not go tumbling from Tearlach's back.

'What's she up to?' asked Isla, turning to look over her shoulder.

'Got a restless traveller up there, have we?' rumbled Tearlach's voice over the whooshing air.

'Aye,' she called back. 'I think she fancies giving flying a shot herself.'

'This probably isn't the best time, or height, to try that for the first time,' chuckled the larger dragon. 'Hold on,' he added before opening his mouth once more, not to speak as Adairia expected, but to sing.

It was a sound unrecognisable to Adairia, completely unique. The music that rattled from between his teeth somehow managed to be harsh and gentle all at the same time. It made every nerve in her body stand on end and a shiver ripple down her spine. For Fia, however, it had quite the opposite effect. The dragonling settled down almost immediately, her eyes glassy. Then to Adairia's surprise, after a few moments she opened her own jaw and joined in with Tearlach's song. Together the melody they hummed filled the space all around them and travelled deep within Adairia's body. Goosebumps rose on her skin and her head filled with a dreamlike fog. It was hypnotic. This continued for a time until Adairia could finally see the outskirts of the forest that marked the edge of Eòlas. As their surroundings transformed, Tearlach let the music peter out, while Fia now sat calmly in Adairia's lap.

'What was that?' whispered Adairia in Isla's ear.

'Dragon song. It's supposed to mimic the sound that surrounded them in their eggs. They're born with the ability I believe. No other creature can mimic it.'

'It's beautiful,' Adairia replied, adding after a pause, 'and frightening.'

'A bit like dragons then ay.' She could not see the other woman's face, but Adairia could hear the smile in Isla's voice. Leaning forward she pressed her forehead against the the point between Isla's shoulder blades for a brief moment, before tilting

back and returning her gaze to the expansive landscape before
them once more. This would be the first time she had travelled
this far from Eòlas' borders, and she was bubbling with
anticipation.

*

She did not voice the thought out loud, but Adairia had to
begrudgingly concede to herself that she was glad she had
borrowed a pair of Isla's trousers. The longer they had spent in
the air the more wearisome it had become. She had never flown
for so long and she was ashamed to admit that the novelty had
worn off after the first couple of hours. The cool air that she had
found so refreshing at first was now biting at her skin insistently
and the muscles in her legs were screaming to be worked. There
was nothing she desired more at this point than to stand up and
walk whatever distance was left between them and Baile.
Thankfully, at least, after her initial excitement, Fia too seemed
to have lost interest in their situation and fallen asleep between
the two women's bodies. Adairia could not help but feel a
twinge of jealousy every time she glanced down at the snoring
dragonling in her lap.

As her discomfort grew almost unbearable and she was
tempted to request they paused their journey for a time,
Adairia's attention was instead grabbed by the changing
landscape before them. The seemingly endless expanse of trees
beneath them, which had done little but vary in density for
miles, was giving way almost entirely now. This was no small
clearing either, but a definite break in the forestry that spanned
the Albiyan landscape. Through her bleary, wind stung eyes,
which just a moment before had been so difficult to keep open,
Adairia spotted the flickering glow of lights that signalled to
her the presence of other living beings. It was too dark, and they

were still too high to make out the shape of any buildings, but the distribution of light suggested a great number of windows. She could not help but shudder at the idea of curling up next to a warm fire after so long in the air and eagerly straightened her back. Isla felt the other woman's position alter and smiled over her shoulder.

'Home is on the horizon,' she whispered. Adairia said nothing in response but gripped her companion more tightly around the waist in anticipation while a loud grumble of approval came from the dragon below.

*

Adairia was wobbly on her feet and had to lean against Tearlach's hind leg a soon as she dismounted from the dragon onto the soft grass. She had now flown a handful of times with Isla and Tearlach, although never for so long, yet she was evidently still unaccustomed to the transition from air to solid land. Isla on the other hand appeared unaffected. She was practically bouncing on the balls of her feet, her eyes full of glee.

'Welcome to Baile,' she raised her arms in the air to signal the imposing building behind her and Adairia stared over her friend's shoulder to take it in.

It remained dark outside, but a selection of lights cast a subtle glow across the stone face of the structure. It was a grand affair; multiple floors and towers adorning each corner while several of the windows were filled with intricate stained-glass images that Adairia could not make out the details of. Beyond the main house itself, a few small outhouses were just visible, as well as some animal paddocks that were currently empty. While Adairia had grown up in a building much larger than Baile that did not counter her awe. This small-scale castle was Isla's home.

'It's massive.' If she had not spent so much time with Isla these past few weeks, she would have shocked herself at her own rudeness but the two women had developed a bond that disregarded delicate etiquette for unabashed honesty. True to form Isla laughed aloud at Adairia's statement of fact.

'It was originally the royal family's summer palace but when Bayrd abdicated the throne he gave over the main castle to parliament and settled up here. My family have lived here ever since.' Conscious of the wariness on Adairia's features she continued, 'don't worry though, the walls and grounds are home to more than just descendants of the royal family. Whether visiting travellers or those who have settled in these parts, Baile is never empty. In fact, here comes one of our residents right now.'

Isla had turned to look over her shoulder and spotted a small, elderly woman, whose long white hair was wrapped in a blue kerchief that matched her dress, striding purposefully towards them from the main building. Turning from Adairia with a wide grin on her face Isla greeted the newcomer with a tight embrace.

'Jill! It's good to see you.'

'It's gid tae see ye too wee yin. But I didnae ken ye wid be back so soon,' the older woman replied. Adairia could not help but smirk at the tiny woman who was at least six inches shorter than Isla referring to her as 'wee yin'.

'Sorry, there wasn't time to send a message before we set out on our journey.' Isla hesitated. 'It was all quite unexpected.' The woman narrowed her eyes but made no comment. Instead, she looked past Isla to Adairia who stood awkwardly behind her, Fia at her feet.

'Well, you must be Adairia and Fia in that case, it's a

pleasure tae finally meet ye.' Adairia's immediate reaction was to turn to meet Isla's gaze and cast her a curious look.

'Ah yes, I sent Jill a few missives whilst I was staying at the university, just to update her on where I was you understand.' It was difficult to be certain in the gloom of the night but Adairia thought she saw a blush spread across Isla's cheeks. She simply nodded, however, and turned back to face Jill.

'Thank you, it's a pleasure to meet you too. Any friend of Isla's is a friend of ours. Sorry to have arrived so unexpectedly.' Adairia took Jill's proffered hand and smiled widely.

'Jill, would you mind showing Adairia and Fia to an available room whilst I get Tearlach settled back into his quarters.' Isla asked her friend before turning to Adairia. 'Sorry, do you mind, there's a building specifically built to accommodate dragons round the back of the main building, I can show it to you and Fia in the morning?'

'Not at all,' Adairia assured her. 'As long as it's not too much trouble?' She directed her question to Jill.

'You just follow me lass and I'll get ye both settled in. I imagine you're wabbit fae that ride.' With those words Jill spun on her heel, no less spritely despite her obvious age, and marched back towards the castle with Adairia and Fia in tow.

*

Adairia found herself constantly skipping to keep up with Jill once inside the castle walls. It was so easy to unconsciously cease mid-step and find herself enraptured by the various tapestries and paintings that adorned the halls. Occasionally Jill would offer up a brief explanation of who or what was depicted in the artist's rendition; it was clear to Adairia that this woman knew much of the history behind the previous residents of Isla's home. One painting grabbed her attention so fully that she was oblivious to the fact that Jill and Fia had turned the next corner without her. Thankfully they had noticed her absence and turned back to fetch her only to find her gawking at a framed picture of an elegant woman with jet black hair and ivory skin seated next to a majestic golden dragon.

'Ah that's King Leith's wife, Queen Isolde. She was the one who commissioned the building of this summer home.' Jill offered in hushed tones.

'She's beautiful,' Adairia whispered back.

'Aye, some say she was of the fair folk.' Jill's comment was not difficult for Adairia to believe; even in painted form there was something ethereal about this woman who stood so serenely next to her dragon. This was not, however, why she had found herself so immediately transfixed by the artist's work. Her instincts had told her there was something familiar about these two figures and as the three of them stood together in silence she realised why that was. This woman, Queen Isolde, and her dragon reminded Adairia of the mysterious creature from Isla's story.

Extract from An Introduction to Dragons

Dragon song has long been a matter of contention among scholars. No other race has successfully managed to mimic the sound or its physical effects using either voice or instrument. Some attribute its unique nature to the anatomy of dragons, who possess much stronger vocal cords than most creatures. Others meanwhile believe it is bound to their own natural magic and this is why it cannot be reproduced. While the effects of one fully grown dragon's song alone are minimal, some listeners have recounted experiencing full blown nausea or euphoria upon listening to dragons sing together for a prolonged period of time. The distinction between different dragons' sound is also indistinguishable to those who are not dragons themselves.

Chapter Sixteen
New Surroundings

After much dithering and dilly dallying in the hallways of Isla's family home, Jill eventually managed to persuade Adairia into an unoccupied bed chamber.

'Sorry it's no ready for anyone. Ah didnae ken you were on yer way or I'd 'av got it warmed it up for ye in advance.' Jill sighed stocking the half empty fireplace with more logs. 'Never mind, I'll get a fire started for yeh.'

'Oh, really it's alright, I can do it myself,' Adairia tried to assure the fussing woman. 'I don't want to put you out.' But before she could even attempt to take over from Jill the woman had bent down over the kindling, her arms outstretched, and flames burst forth without any preamble. Adairia quickly realised there was more to this resident than first met the eye. Jill, however, simply turned back around to face Adairia who must have been gawking because she chuckled amusedly.

'Right, well, I'll let ye and the wee yin get settled in and see if I can rustle something up for ye from the kitchen. I expect yer famished after that flight,' Adairia instinctively began to tell her not to go to any trouble on their account, but the older woman beat her to it. 'Wheesht, I'll no 'ave anyone telling me whit tae dae in mah ayne hame. If I want tae find ye something tae warm yer bones, then I will and there's nae arguing aboot it.' And with that Jill had spun on her heal and marched from the room, leaving Adairia and Fia alone for the first time that day.

Adairia had realised a few weeks ago now that she still considered herself to be alone even in the presence of the dragonling. Not that she could imagine feeling lonely in Fia's presence, but it was as though the dragon was a part of her these days. For all she was accustomed to Fia, however, she did not expect her to speak at that moment, at least not aloud.

'Where?' she simply asked, craning her neck up to look at Adairia from the thick carpeted floor of the room. For a few seconds all she could do was blink at her, taken aback at hearing the sound of her voice for a second time.

'This is Baile, the home of Isla and Tearlach,' Adairia replied, pulling herself together. Although the dragonling's verbal vocabulary remained limited, Adairia knew she understood every word that was said to her.

'Home,' was Fia's only response, repeating Adairia's words back to her and gazing around the room. After a moment, the fire evidently caught her eye; without preamble she padded towards the rug and laid out before its grate.

Meanwhile Adairia began to unload her meagre luggage into the large chest of drawers that adorned the wall facing the door. She had packed a few of her own dresses, not trusting Isla to own any, as well as the current book of dragonlore she was making her way through: *An Introduction to Dragons by J. Zacharski.* She was eager for Isla to show her the castle's library as soon as they had an opportunity. Given how strong a bond there had been between the royal family and dragon kind throughout the centuries she was certain it would be well stocked with relevant tomes she had not yet come across in the university.

Having unpacked Adairia thought she might sit alongside Fia for a short time and read aloud. This was a habit she had developed since her companion had joined her and Fia seemed to enjoy the sound of Adairia's voice even if she showed no interest in her words. Just as she had settled herself next to the fireplace with a cushion, however, there came a knock at the door.

'Come in,' she called, assuming Jill had returned. When she turned to look over her shoulder, however, it was Isla pushing the door open. She had abandoned her jacket somewhere along her journey and acquired a tray carrying two mugs of steaming hot liquid alongside a selection of biscuits.

'Mulled wine,' she grinned, catching Adairia's eye. 'Thought it would be a comfort after that journey. Ease those aching muscles and warm those shivering bones you know.' Adairia smiled in return, standing up to greet her friend.

'Thank you, really, I couldn't think of anything better right now.' She took the mugs off the tray and inhaled its heady scent deeply. 'Smell's delicious.'

'It better be.' Isla laughed. 'It's Jill's secret recipe. Won't tell me what spices she uses but I've never tasted anything else like it.' She took a long swig from her own mug and plonked herself down on the luxurious looking bed Adairia had yet to test. 'That's the stuff.' She exhaled.

'Make yourself at home,' Adairia teased, poking out her tongue.

'Don't mind if I do.'

Laughing Adairia seated herself next to Isla atop the beautifully embroidered quilt. Whomsoever had put their needle to this project had done an unparalleled job from what Adairia had seen. It seemed to depict every species of flower

128

she was familiar with, and some she was not, creating a luscious garden that more closely resembled a rainbow over the bed. Taking a sip from her own mug, she stifled a moan from escaping her lips. The warm liquid that slid down her throat was delightfully spicy and sweet at the same time, drinking it she felt immediately more relaxed.

'What did I tell you?' Isla said.

'We must get the recipe, even if we have to squirrel away in the kitchen somewhere and spy on her,' Adairia said quite seriously, which made Isla chuckle.

'You'll never get past that one.' She took a few more mouthfuls of her own wine. 'I'm glad to have you here Adairia.

'I'm glad to be here.' She agreed leaning her head on Isla's shoulder. 'It's beautiful. I can't wait to see it in the daylight.'

'In that case, you fit right in,' Isla replied, her voice a little more hesitant than usual, but Adairia just smiled up at her, completely contented.

*

The next morning Adairia found her body ached when she awoke. She had never flown for so long and her muscles were stiff and sore. Nor had she had a chance to change into her nightdress and still wore Isla's trousers and blouse. When she peeled her eyelids open she was surprised to see that Isla was already awake. She lay next to her in the bed where they had both fallen asleep, her eyes fixed on Adairia's. Adairia found herself blushing under her gaze and self-consciously wondering what she must look like. A moment later, however, she scolded herself for thinking anything of the sort; Isla would never judge her on how she looked.

'What are you frowning at?' Isla whispered, clearly watching Adairia's changing expression.

'Nothing.' She smiled back. 'Good morning.'

'Good morning indeed,' Isla agreed. 'How does breakfast sound?'

'Like you've seen into the very depths of my soul.'

'Then allow me to take you to the kitchen, my lady.'

Isla rolled out from the bed and gave an exaggerated bow, holding her hand out to Adairia. The other woman laughed and allowed herself to be pulled from the comfort of the sheets and pillows. Together they left the from the room with Fia in tow and headed down the hallway in a direction that Adairia had not travelled the night before.

Upon arriving in the kitchen, with its large windows that allowed the sun's light to stream into the room, they immediately spotted Jill stirring something over the stove. Beside her and standing on a small wooden stool in order to see the contents of the pot Jill tended, was a young girl who could be no older than ten. Her hair was a shade of deep mahogany and plaited around her head to form a crown. At their approach she turned around and squealed upon catching sight of Isla

'Isla,' she cried, rushing over to embrace the fully-grown woman around her waist. Isla laughed and hugged her back, hunching over slightly to do so.

'Adairia I'd like you to meet Flora, Jill's granddaughter.' The little girl let go of Isla and looked up at the stranger with no obvious signs of shyness.

'Hello Flora, it's lovely to meet you.' Adairia beamed down at her.

'It's nice to meet you too,' Flora agreed but quickly lost interest when she spotted who stood behind Adairia.

'Is that your dragon?' she asked in awe.

'Aye it is. Her name is Fia,' Adairia replied. 'I'm sure she'd like it if you introduced yourself.' With a little more caution, the little girl edged towards the dragon who watched her inquisitively.

'Hello Fia. I'm Flora.' She held her hand out to the dragon who responded by rubbing her muzzle against it and purring audibly. At this Flora turned her head to look back at her grandmother smiling broadly.

'You've made a new friend it seems.' Jill chuckled and turned her attention to the other two. 'Ye looking for some breakfast? I've just made a batch of porridge.' She lifted her wooden spoon from the pot in front of her and licked the tip tentatively. 'Aye it's ready if you'd like some.'

'More than anything,' Isla grinned. 'Thank you, Jill.'

All three of the adults sat down to eat at the long wooden table and benches whilst Flora and Fia went outside to play. Adairia had assured the little girl that it was alright when she had asked although her grandmother had insisted that she stay within site of the kitchen window. It was a morning unlike any Adairia had imagined for herself and she found she was quite pleased about it.

*

'I thought I'd write to the other dragons and their companions this morning and arrange a time that we can all gather here at Baile.' Isla had set down her spoon in her empty bowl and was rubbing her stomach contentedly as she spoke.

'How soon is that likely to be?' Adairia asked. She was equal parts eager and nervous to meet the other dragons and companions Isla had spoken of. It had been one thing to meet Tearlach and Isla for the first time and it was true that she was now more familiar with dragons themselves, but to be surrounded by those with so much more first-hand experience

131

than herself was daunting.

'I don't think it would be unfair to request their presence for three weeks' time, closer to the winter solstice, that should give them enough notice.' Adairia simply nodded. 'And in the meantime, I can show you round the house and its grounds, as well as introduce you to all of the other people currently in residence at Baile.' At this Adairia's smile brightened.

'That sounds wonderful.'

Chapter Seventeen
Settling In

Isla was as good as her word. She spent their first few days at Baile introducing Adairia to each of the permanent and temporary residents of her family home individually. There were travelling bards and druids who visited seasonally, entertaining the other inhabitants with songs and stories while making good use of the well-stocked library. Others like Jill had been born in the area and taken up residence in the palace during Isla or her parent's lifetimes. Baile was as much their home as it was the descendants of the royal family. Each member of the household contributed to its running, from tending the crops that supplied their own and some of the nearby settlement's food, as well as taking care of the everyday maintenance a building as old as this one required.

Adairia quickly learnt that the little girl Flora had lost her mother, Jill's daughter, to illness a few years earlier. Her father, however, lived alongside his daughter and mother-law lending a hand around the palace. He had injured his leg when he was younger due to an accident with a plough, which limited his ability to conduct manual labour, but had a knack for growing grains and vegetables as well as keeping the younger farmhands and residents organised in their tasks. He was a quiet man, with little to say but a short word of greeting here and there but Adairia found she took to him almost immediately – perhaps because they were both gardeners. Flora on the other hand was far more animated than her father. She was always in hot pursuit of her beloved grandmother wherever the older woman went and she endeared herself equally as quickly to both Adairia and Fia.

Not unlike life at the university, Adairia was expected to chip in as a tenant of Baile along with the others. Although she still desired time to herself most days to settle her mind, she found the communal spirit of Isla's home enlivening. And so too did Fia it seemed. The no longer quite so small dragon had hit a growth spurt shortly into their stay and was fast approaching the size of a large heifer. After a fortnight at Baile, Adairia could no longer lift her up in her arms and Tearlach joked that soon it would be she who would be being carried by Fia instead. The thought was more than a little unnerving.

Due to living in close quarters with Tearlach for so long most of the other inhabitants of Baile were at ease with the presence of another dragon. Flora in particular made fast friends with the dragon and when Adairia was occupied elsewhere, often studying with Isla in the library, she noted that the two of them could regularly be found playing together in the gardens, each one taking it in turn to chase the other until they were caught and the game reversed. Tearlach meanwhile was always close at hand to watch over the spirited youngsters.

The library itself was a sight to behold. Now, Adairia had grown up in a university, she was used to being surrounded by shelves upon shelves of books and scrolls but that did not diminish her excitement to find a new stock at her disposal. Unfortunately, however, and in contrast with the university library, there did not appear to be any discernible system of organisation. Books were arranged higgledy-piggledy between the shelves, according to no order Adairia could identify. Other papers still were piled in precarious towers throughout the room seemingly wherever their last reader had deigned to leave them. It was nevertheless a joy to rummage amongst them with Isla at her side; there were some useful few volumes that Isla had been able to ready at a single notice, those which she had evidently perused before, while others they came upon by mere chance as they perused the shelves.

Fia was not only growing in size but also in intellect. Although the two companions continued to regularly communicate through their thoughts, the dragon was talking aloud to anyone who would listen. She was, frankly put, a little immature, which was to be expected given her age, yet her increasing ability to speak made it all the more apparent. She demanded constant companionship and if it were not for Tearlach and the other residents of Baile, Adairia was not sure how she would have coped by herself. One strategy she had developed to keep the dragonling entertained was to read to her in the evenings from the books she brought back from the library. Some nights it would be just the two of them but on others Isla would join them and it was no longer unusual for the two women to fall asleep beside one another in Adairia's bed. It was one such night, when the three were settled together to read and drink in Adairia's chamber, that Isla brought up a subject she had been mulling on for a few days now.

'You know, I hate to say it to both of you, but soon Fia won't be able to fit through the doorframe to this room anymore.' Adairia was taken aback by Isla's statement. Glancing at Fia she could hardly see scope to argue with the other woman, but she had not considered the possibility of Fia leaving her bedroom

135

at any point. Of course, it made sense; Tearlach did not share Isla's room and Isla did not sleep alongside her dragon in his purpose-built quarters. Still, she had not spent a night apart from her own dragon since Fia had hatched. Whilst Adairia remained speechless it was Fia who spoke up.

'I think Isla is right Adairia.' She licked her lips, seeking out any lingering trace of her earlier meal. 'I had been wondering the same thing myself.'

'You wouldn't mind sleeping elsewhere?' Adairia asked, a little hurt by the ease with which Fia seemed to be taking this suggestion.

'You could read to me at night in the dragon's quarters with Tearlach instead. Isla too.' Fia said this as a frank statement of logic that forced a grin from Adairia's lips.

'I suppose I can.'

'I'm sure Tearlach would enjoy the company.' Isla smiled, pleased that her suggestion had not offended the young dragon. 'And when the others arrive, they will all be able to do a little bonding. You know, whinge about their companions out of earshot and what not.' Adairia swatted at Isla playfully.

'Fine then. Tomorrow we'll see what we can do but for tonight I think we'll manage just fine in here.'

Fia nodded and lowered her head back to the cushion she had previously been resting on and waited for Adairia to pick back up where they had left off in that evening's reading.

*

'Welcome to your new abode wee one.' Tearlach indicated the space around them by turning his neck this way and that.

'I'm not so wee these days,' Fia responded a little indignantly.

'No, you're not, but you've still got quite a bit of growing to do by my reckoning.' Tearlach bared his large teeth in a dragon's approximation of a grin.

'But I might be big enough to fly with Adairia soon?' These words were posed more as a question than a statement.

'I should think so. Once you've built up your strength enough to endure flying any distance with a passenger. It won't be long before we can all four of us fly alongside one another together. When our guests arrive, perhaps we can all show you how it's done out back.' Fia turned her own head to smile at Adairia who returned her expression gladly.

'I'm looking forward to meeting the other dragons once they arrive with their companions,' Fia continued as she settled down amidst a pile of larger than human sized cushions.

'They'll be equally excited to meet you, I'm sure.' Isla smiled. 'And you.' She directed these words to Adairia.

The dragon quarters themselves were deceptively simple from the outside. Although Tearlach had been the sole occupant until an hour before, they had clearly been built for a hoard of dragons to sleep comfortably at once. In appearance they resembled a large series of adjoining barns that encircled a grassy courtyard; on the inside, however, they were absent of the usual bales of hay and barrels of grain found in most outhouses. There were no walls or doors separating the structure into rooms though there were curtains hanging intermittently throughout the building to afford the dragons some privacy if desired. The floors themselves were sumptuously carpeted and piles of cushions, some larger than a human bed, scattered the ground at random. The walls too were elaborately decorated with thick tapestries that served both to retain heat in the cavernous structure and provide some pretty mesmerising decoration for its occupants. There seemed to have been no comfort spared for those dragons who found themselves occupants of Baile over the centuries since it had been built. It made sense when Adairia recalled that it was Queen Isolde and her dragon Cartimandua who had been responsible for its construction.

'This one depicts my original companion, Bayrd, and I at the founding of parliament.' Said Tearlach rather proudly as he nudged the tapestry above his own bedding with his nose. The image depicted a gleaming purple dragon that was unmistakably Tearlach himself standing alongside a red haired and heavily bearded, burley figure of a man that must have been Isla's great grandfather.

'Do you miss him?' Fia's question came as a surprise to Adairia who glanced towards Isla surreptitiously.

'I do, Fia.' Tearlach sighed. 'He was my best friend and my brother. We grew up together. Grief does not leave us, but we learn over time to smile more at those memories we still keep of that person than to wallow in their absence. We are the creatures we are because of them, for good or bad, and because of that their memory lives on.' Tearlach bent his head to rub his snout against Isla who wrapped her arm around his muzzle lovingly.

'Would you tell us a story about Bayrd, Tearlach, I always enjoy hearing tales of my great grandfather's life,' she requested.

'Oh yes, please do.' Adairia could not prevent the enthusiastic historian in her from sitting up straighter at the prospect of hearing history from a first-hand source. Fia too nodded eagerly.

'I would love to.'

Chapter Eighteen
Bayrd

Growing up, Prince Bayrd's closest friend, aside from his dragon Tearlach, was another young boy named Archie. Archie, or Archibald if you were his exasperated mother, was the local bladesmith's son. Bayrd's own father relied exclusively on Archie's to forge and mend his personal armoury and usually permitted his son to accompany him on his visits to the smithy. The two boys' friendship was an immediate one. Whilst their fathers talked, and on occasion drank a pint of ale together, they would run amuck outside, play fighting and climbing Tearlach's scaly form, much to the dragon's irritation. And, as they grew older, they remained steadfast friends. During the day Archie trained to take up his father's trade while Bayrd was educated in history and arbitration. In their spare time, however, they came together to discuss everything from pretty girls to their thoughts on that week's news.

The two boys were not jealous of their friendship, however, and were joined by Bayrd's cousin Alexander whenever he and his father visited the palace. Alexander's father was the King's younger brother, and according to Albiyan law this made Alexander next in line to the throne after Bayrd himself. He too was bonded to a dragon by the name of Dileas, a dark blue creature whose hide appeared almost black unless struck directly by the sun. The five of them, three boys and two dragons, made an agreeable cohort of companions and could easily lose track of numerous days and nights together. This was true both as children and as young adults.

When Bayrd's father and mother died soon after one another, leaving their teenage son an orphan and next in line for the throne, it was Archie's family the young prince turned to for support. The other boy's parents let him loiter around their home for days at a time, feeding him and treating him like one of their own. Even Archie's older sister, Faye, who until this point had treated the two younger boys like nuisances softened to him, allowing him to observe her as she worked on developing her own trade as a bookbinder.

Shortly after the passing of the king, Bayrd's uncle, Lord Philip, moved into the royal family's palace along with his son, so that he could steer the council of regents until Bayrd came of age. Despite the circumstances Alexander's move was met with great excitement from both Bayrd and Archie, who looked forward to being a more permanent band of three as they edged closer to adulthood.

The only tension that ever rose between them was the subject of Faye. The intelligent young girl who sometimes joined her brother and his friends in their late-night dialogues had over the years grown into an equally beautiful young woman – a combination that had not gone unnoticed by Bayrd or Alexander. Nor could either of the cousins successfully hide their fondness for Faye from Archie, who found the whole situation irritating by half. Both cousins, however, chose to resist the temptation to let the shared crush pit them against one another, for as long as that was possible.

As each boy became a young man, they had different

experiences of the world around them, and they often found themselves seated together around a table debating the issue of the day. For all that Archie's family had served the king, the smith himself had never bowed down to royalty; he had always treated Bayrd's father like any other customer. This attitude had extended to the prince, and Bayrd had grown up with an unfettered view of the Albiyon his subjects lived in. He often found himself frustrated by various inequalities he observed between the aristocracy and the working people of Albiyon. His disappointment was only compounded by his uncle's refusal to engage with him on the topic of reform.

'You're still too young to make any decisions, this is why the council exists,' Philip would tell him firmly before shaking him off.

Alexander, meanwhile, was less strong-willed than his cousin and often took for granted his own father's perspective on the world. His life had been one free of hardship and as far as experience had taught him, the system, as it was, worked well enough. In Bayrd and Archie's company, however, he often found himself challenged to examine those feelings of contentedness for the privilege they were. He was also free to ask questions his father would have never dreamed of entertaining. And, as philosophical conversations are wont to do, they gradually developed into discussion of action.

As each boy passed his seventeenth year in quick succession, they were welcomed into the taverns and ale houses dotted around the local area. There they found new talking companions and Bayrd was astonished to hear the men and women share their ideas with him freely. He had only ever listened in on the meetings of his father and his father's councillors, never expected to contribute even after the king had died. His tutors had taught him facts and tradition but never analysis. These ordinary Albiyans meanwhile, had issues and solutions based on experience, though they could rarely put them into practice thanks to their lack of voice in court. But nor were they content to remain unheard forever.

It did not take long before Bayrd found himself fully embroiled in revolutionary debate. Even after they had left the taverns, he stayed up well into the night with his two friends and the two dragons discussing politics. Sometimes they were joined by Faye, whose opinions and passion were as strong as any of the others he met with. It was these conversations that led him to a decision he had struggled with for many years – that was, to forfeit his impending coronation as king. But as the stories tell us, it was not enough for Bayrd to unburden himself of this role; he wanted to radically change the way that Albiyon was run, and he did not want to do it alone.

None of his friends required convincing. They were all seemingly in accord, whether human or dragon, and it was not long before prince Bayrd announced his abdication in favour of the founding of a democratic parliament. Reactions were split. Whilst he held the support of the majority of Albiyon's citizens, those with the greatest wealth, and oftentimes the greatest power, were not as happy to see the dismantling of the monarchy. As you well know, civil strife broke out between the two factions and the path to parliament was not a smooth one. The turmoil would eventually strike Bayrd himself at his very heart.

Between their talks of transformation Bayrd and Faye had only grown closer. One's feelings had developed beyond a childhood crush, while the other had watched the evolution of a kind and honourable man who was so much more than her brother's best friend. The two could do nothing to hide their feelings from each other, but Bayrd asked that they tread cautiously around Alexander in particular, worried his cousin would perceive the budding romance as a betrayal of their friendship. This was easier said than done; unbeknownst to either their flirtatious grins or playful whispers had not gone unnoticed.

Alexander loved his cousin and their mutual friend dearly. He admired both young men and their unshifting sense of what was right. He had always wished he too could mirror their internal strength. His was a different story though. His father was a harsh man. Younger sibling to the king of Albiyon, he had always resented his brother holding more power than him simply due to their order of birth. He had heaped these personal umbrages upon his son as he grew up, spewing diatribes about how Albiyon could flourish under the right ruler, one who wanted the job rather than one who was given it.

When Bayrd stepped down as heir to the throne Philip's immediate reaction was elation. This would mean that his son, Alexander, was next in line to be king of Albiyon. He had never much liked his nephew, always off gallivanting and neglecting his place at court. Nor had he enjoyed Bayrd's influence over his own child, but as the one-day future king he had thought it better to let Alexander ingratiate himself with his cousin than to keep them apart. Philip's delight was short-lived, however, when Bayrd revealed his plans to demolish the monarchy itself. In that moment he had immediately turned to look at his son who sat to his right. The boy, however, had turned his eyes away, instead choosing to stare at his feet. Alexander had known about this, it was clear, and Philip was furious.

But the old king's brother was not a man to simply concede

to others. Whilst Bayrd waged political war alongside those who were once his subjects, Philip turned on his son. He preyed on all the boy's insecurities, explouting his long-time subjugation to his father. He insisted that Bayrd was reckless, that the discord around them would never end until another king sat on the throne. He tried to convince him that this position was rightfully his and Bayrd would steal this from him with his self-serving arrogance.

'Was he truly content to be his cousin's lapdog when the country was in disarray? Did he wish to concede to Bayrd in this too?' As Philip was not unaware of all that went on in his son's life. For some time now Philip had watched as his son had admired from afar Archie's sister Faye, while it was her and Bayrd's relationship that developed into something more than friendship. Philip wheedled and cajoled his way into Alexander's fragile mind, pushing him to strike out against the abdicated prince. And Alexander had never been able to say no to his father.

As these things have a habit of doing, however, nothing unravelled as it was expected to. Too afraid to challenge Bayrd directly, and under the influence of his father, Alexander allowed his father to plan an assassination attempt with him as the bait. He had arranged to meet his cousin in the council chambers of the palace under the pretence of having some information regarding his father who had been barred from the castle. Instead of papers, however, he came armed with a sword.

Such a plot did not come easy to Alexander, and he waited anxiously, afraid he would not be able to follow through on his father's wishes. It was panic, therefore, that drove him to what he did next. As soon as the door swung open to reveal a man's figure standing in the hallway beyond, Alexander swung forward on impulse. As expected, his sword met soft flesh and sunk firmly into the stomach of his victim. Without hesitation, Alexander dropped the end of the sword he held and watched with horror as his friend Archie stared back in wide-eyed shock; his own hands were clasped around the hilt of the sword while blood seeped through his shirt. Mere seconds behind him came Bayrd who walked calmly down the corridor, momentarily unaware of what had taken place. He quickly realised something was wrong, however, when Archie fell to his knees in front of Alexander, and he immediately broke into a run.

Alexander made no attempt to flee or strike out at Bayrd himself. He watched in dismay as the light in their friend's eyes was extinguished, frozen to the spot. He wanted to scream, to turn back time, to beg for Archie's forgiveness, but he could not make a single noise. After a moment Bayrd turned his own eyes upon Alexander from the floor where he had slumped down next to the body of his fallen friend. Disbelief twined with disgust upon Bayrd's face as he took in his cousin, shaking uncontrollably, with blood on his hands.

Bayrd could not bring himself to push for Alexander's execution, but he realised neither he nor his father could go unpunished. With the support of those leaders of the revolution who would later take seats in the first parliament, the two men were exiled from Albiyon. Alexander's dragon Dileas had known nothing of the plot against Bayrd and was as shocked as Tearlach to discover what had happened. More than the events that had taken place, however, Dileas could not forgive Alexander for keeping such a secret from him. Perhaps if his companion had confided in him, he could have given him the confidence to reject his father's poisonous words. This broke the dragon's heart most of all.

Bayrd was under no illusion that Dileas was involved but everyone assumed that the dragon would nevertheless follow his companion into exile; it was practically unheard of for a dragon and their companion to separate once they were bonded. Dileas though, could not find it in himself to trust Alexander again, and without trust what relationship could they have?

Once it was clear Dileas did not intend to follow his companion, Bayrd offered him a home with himself and Tearlach. But despite their long friendship, Dileas could not bear the thought of living alongside the two only to be constantly reminded of what he himself had lost. Instead, he chose to live in seclusion, away from the companionship of others. Although it pained his friends, they could not begrudge him his choice and allowed him to depart from the palace and seek out a place of quiet isolation elsewhere in Albiyon.

*

When Tearlach had finished his story, Adairia found herself close to tears. When Isla had asked for a story of her great grandfather, she had not expected such sorrow. Of what she had read of their history, Bayrd and Tearlach's legacy had been one of triumph and liberation. This, however, was a tale of personal heartache, one that she thought few citizens of Albiyon probably knew.

'Adairia would never keep a secret from me, and I would never leave her,' interjected Fia now that the story was over.

'I am sure that you are right little one.' Tearlach turned to look at Isla. 'The idea seems impossible to me, but I was there, and I stood witness to these events.' He turned back to Fia. 'This is one of the responsibilities of dragons. We will live much longer than any of our companions, we will watch them die when there is nothing we can do, and we will have to live on. Within us they continue to live, however, when we remember them and share their stories with others. For those who leave their mark on us are never truly gone.'

Fia was silent but bowed her head to Tearlach's words and Adairia stroked her neck absentmindedly. She could hardly imagine Fia's life without her, but she supposed it would come just as Tearlach's had without Bayrd. She hoped there would be someone like Isla waiting in Fia's future as well.

'Cheer up.' Isla patted her shoulder comfortingly. 'It was not for naught. The monarchy was dismantled, the parliament was founded, and Bayrd and Faye eventually married.'

'She was your great grandmother?' Adairia asked.

'Where do you think I get this beguiling smile from?' And they all laughed despite themselves.

147

Extract from An Introduction to Dragons

The bonding process has been a topic of heavy debate throughout the centuries. The magic is elusive and neither dragon nor companion has been able to provide a satisfactory explanation for the event. The process appears to be an entirely organic one, a result of the dragon's own natural magic. The connection forms a psychic link between dragon and companion that allows them to speak freely with one another without fear of being overheard. This is the same technique dragons use to communicate with each other over long distances but one that cannot be replicated with unbonded creatures.

While bondings have occurred post and ante-hatching, never has the process been successfully manufactured despite attempts to choreograph partnerships in the past. This does not prevent dragons from creating new bonds once their previous companion has passed away, however, nor in rare circumstances from breaking their bond with a companion – an event that only appears to take place in the most extreme circumstances.

Chapter Nineteen
Embrace

After their time in the dragon quarters, Adairia and Isla had trudged back to the main building together. Adairia had been sad to leave Fia behind, but the dragon had reassured her with soothing words far beyond her age. Still, Adairia found herself twisting her hand into Isla's as they walked, seeking comfort and familiarity in her touch. She was not alone, she reminded herself.

'Will you stay with me tonight?' she asked in little more than a whisper.

'You need not ever ask me if I will stay with you Adairia.' Isla's mouth twitched in a smile that was different from her usual wide-faced grin.

Like two mischievous co-conspirators the two women stopped off in the kitchen on their return journey to beg some mulled wine from Jill who sat crocheting at the hearth. As she did on most nights, the older woman had a large pot of wine spiced and gently simmering on the stove for the castle's residents. Delighted with their bounty both women thanked Jill profusely for the mugs of her delicious brew. Together they snuck back to Adairia's room where the fire was already lit, and the curtains were drawn. It felt oddly empty to Adairia without Fia's lumbering presence. As she sat alone with Isla, each sipping their steaming cups, she felt something else in the quiet atmosphere that she had not had opportunity to explore before now.

The two women lay sprawled out on a pile of cushions by the fireplace, their knees just brushing one another's. There was a feeling of familiarity mingled with anticipation hanging in the air that made for a heady mix. Adairia let the smell of her wine wind up from the mug in her hands to tickle her nostrils. Sighing, she closed her eyes to revel in the warmth coursing through her body. She only opened them when Isla spoke for the first time since they had entered the room.

'Do you like it here?' She asked a little shyly, catching Adairia's eyes with her own. The blonde hesitated before responding. *Where exactly did Isla refer to? Baile, or here, by the fire, with her?*

'It feels… right.' She answered softly, settling on a response that suited both.

The red headed woman stretched out the hand she did not have clasped around her own mug and held it gently against Adairia's cheek. Adairia raised her own fingers in turn, holding the hand against her face and closing her eyes for a moment to savour the touch. Opening them again she gazed raptly at Isla's open features, searching for an answer to an unspoken question; then, leaning forward, Isla's palm still cupped to her skin, she covered the other woman's lips with her own.

Isla did not hesitate to respond in kind. With a steady hand she placed her mug on the ground beside them and raised her other hand to Adairia's neck. She answered the other woman's tentative kiss with an insistent one of her own, parting her lips and flicking her tongue along Adairia's bottom lip. Adairia found a small moan escaped her throat at the escalated contact and responded by offering up her own tongue to Isla's explorations. The dregs of their wine now abandoned, both women entwined their fingers in each other's hair, giving in to their persistent kisses. It was not long before Adairia leant back, still wrapped in Isla's arms, pulling the second woman down on top of her. She sucked and nibbled at Isla's lips as she felt the other woman's weight press down against her. Unconsciously she found herself raising her hips in an attempt to mould her body with Isla's, reacting fervently to the redhead's touch. The desire she had kept in check until this moment now overwhelmed her entirely.

In fact, Adairia could not prevent her hands from exploring beyond the soft curls atop Isla's head or strewn around her neck. Slowly at first, gaging Isla's response, she lowered one hand to her waist and then the other. She stroked along her spine with her fingertips and felt Isla's body shiver in anticipation of what was to come. In answer, Isla lowered her kisses to Adairia's jaw and then her neck making the flaxen haired woman gasp aloud. Adairia felt as Isla's deft tongue slipped out to stroke that sensitive bit of skin in the crook behind her earlobe, causing her pulse to increase markedly. Whilst Adairia's hands had slipped beneath the recently untucked fabric of Isla's blouse to stroke her back, Isla's own hands had moved to the laces at the front of her dress.

'May I?' Isla whispered into her still sensitive ear. All Adairia could do was nod impatiently.

Isla's fingers hastily unfastened the ties that held the front of Adairia's dress tight against her bodice, allowing her to push aside its sleeves and reveal lightly freckled shoulders. Bending her neck, she trailed her tongue along the other woman's collar bone and eagerly licked the sweat from her skin. Adairia felt

151

her own body rise insistently so she could push it harder against Isla's in her need for the other woman's touch. Encouraged, Isla pushed the fabric of her dress further down, exposing the curve of her rounded breasts and then the tips of her dark pink nipples; within seconds Isla had enthusiastically taken each between her lips in turn and gently tugged on them with her teeth, all the while staring Adairia directly in the eyes.

Not to be left out, Adairia forced Isla to part from her body for an excruciating second so that she could tug her blouse over her head and uncover her naked form beneath. Both in a state of half-undress she immediately pulled the red-head back down into another passionate embrace, locking their lips and revelling in the caress of Isla's breasts against her own. The groan that Isla emitted as she bucked against Adairia's leg, seeking out something more, only drove her wilder.

With their legs now entangled it took some fumbling to free each other of the remainder of their clothing, but they were not to be discouraged. Garments discarded, they trailed their hands across one another's thighs and hips, reaching between their legs once the other's cries grew too needy. They stroked and teased until neither of them could help but give in to wild abandon and grind fiercely against one another. Hands grasped flesh tightly while the sweat of both their bodies mingled. They kissed, licked, and bit in their frenzied need for release, found only after Isla compelled Adairia's body to still beneath her and took control. Needless to say, they never made it to the bed, but continued to indulge in one another with abandon for the rest of the night whilst the fire flickered beside them.

*

When Adairia opened her eyes to the first light of dawn peeking through the gaps in the bedroom curtains, she could feel the

152

steady inhale and exhale of Isla's chest beneath her ear. The fire had dwindled to little more than embers in the hearth and her uncovered skin goose-pimpled where it was not in contact with the other woman's body. Unwilling to move, however, she simply nestled more closely against Isla's soft breasts. The flesh of her stomach melded to Isla's thigh and she found herself absentmindedly tracing the silvery stretch marks that decorated them with her fingers. As Adairia's hands moved steadily across Isla's body, she heard a sigh escape the other woman's lips. Shifting her head slightly to peer up at Isla's face, she saw that she too was now awake, an indulgent smile tugging at her lips.

'I like sleeping in your room.' Isla's words made Adairia smile widely in return.

'I will never turn you away.' Then she paused for a moment struck by a thought. 'Although, I have never visited you in your room.'

'Yours is more comfortable,' Isla replied lifting her own hand to stroke Adairia's shoulder. Adairia found this statement a little surprising, she would have expected Isla to have the grandest room available in this old palace but she made no comment. 'In fact,' continued Isla, 'I think I shall remain right here all day, with you next to me.' This made Adairia laugh.

'I think we might get hungry at some point.' She pointed out.

'There is plenty here I can eat.' Isla's voice almost came out in a growl as she shifted underneath Adairia, flipping the blonde woman onto her back so that she leant over her, her hair creating a curtain around both their faces. She then promptly proceeded to lower her mouth to Adairia's neck and suck gently at its sensitive skin, occasionally nipping it with her teeth.

153

Adairia squirmed not uncomfortably beneath Isla, her heart thudding in her chest, suddenly far more awake than she had been mere seconds before. It was much to her vexation, therefore, when at that moment a loud knock came at the heavy wooden doors to her room.

'Adairia, Isla,' called a voice instantly recognisable as Jill's. 'Ye've got visitors.'

'Blast,' exclaimed Isla and raising her voice she shouted back. 'What are you haivering on about woman?'

'Dinnae you talk to me that way,' shouted Jill even louder. Rolling her eyes, Adairia pushed gently at Isla's chest, forcing the other woman from her.

'Sorry Jill,' she responded, giving Isla an exasperated look. 'Visitors? For both of us?'

'Aye, it was you two who invited all of these dragons and their companions to flock down upon Baile and eat us out of hoose and hame wis it no?' It did not take much to imagine Jill standing on the other side of the door arms crossed, scowling at the both of them through its wood.

'How could I forget,' Isla yelped excitedly, no longer unwilling to stand up. 'You'll finally meet the rest of our wee band.' She clasped Adairia's hands in her own and helped the other woman to her feet. Adairia just looked back at her dumbfounded. She too had momentarily forgotten there was anyone else in this world aside from herself and Isla.

'Ready?' beamed Isla.

'As I'll ever be,' Adairia replied, matching her grin with one of her own. 'Although I wish they could have given us another hour or two.

'Don't worry, I'm sure we can find those missing hours later tonight.' Isla winked in return.

'Right then, I'll tell them you're too busy canoodling shall ah,' interrupted Jill once more.

'We're coming dammit,' yelled Isla and at her words they listened as Jill's footsteps proceeded to march back down the hallway.

Hastily, Adairia changed into a clean dress whilst Isla slipped her discarded blouse and trousers from the previous day back on. When she watched Isla struggling with her heavily tangled hair, Adairia took the other woman by the shoulders and sat her down on the bed. Gradually, she unpicked the bird's nest with her fingers and smoothed the unruly curls into a tidy braid down the other woman's back. Once she was finished Isla took her hand and kissed it, holding it against her lips for a moment before standing back up and smoothing her hands down her creased shirt.

'Well, shall we?'

Adairia smiled back at Isla and stood to follow her out of the room. Silently, she trailed Isla down the corridor, presuming she knew where she was taking them. At first, they followed their usual route to the kitchen where most mornings they would head to retrieve themselves some breakfast, but they did not stop when they reached it. Instead, they exited out the back door and stepped onto the estate grounds. Isla confidently retraced their steps from the night before and led Adairia towards the dragon outhouses, from where tendrils of sound were already wafting their way to her ears.

Chapter Twenty
Dragons

The sight that met Adairia's eyes upon entering the dragons' quarters took her breath away. There stood Fia and Tearlach, gleaming orange and purple in turn, surrounded by a group of four more dragons and their companions: one gold, one darkest green, one pale pink, and another mahogany brown. Each varied in size, the gold and brown dragons outstripping even Tearlach in girth, a feat Adairia had previously thought impossible. Despite her recent growth spurt Fia appeared minuscule in comparison.

'Good morning friends,' Isla beamed, raising both her arms up in greeting as they entered the outhouse.

Tearlach responded with a rumble of approval that was mimicked by a couple of the other dragons, and all four of their companions stepped forward, wide grins splayed across their faces.

'There you are Isla. It is good to see you.' It was an older black woman who spoke first. Her tightly coiled curls were starting to show the first signs of grey and the thin lines around her eyes mapped years of laughter on her face.

'Ode!' Isla exclaimed. 'I have missed you the most.' She leant in to embrace the older woman who responded enthusiastically.

'And this must be young Fia's companion Adairia whom you wrote to us of.' The woman who had now been named as Ode stretched out an arm to Adairia who clasped it in her own. 'We have already met Fia here, she is a clever young dragon.' Ode's words caused Adairia to glow with pride as she glanced over at the dragonling.

'Thank you, Ode, it is a pleasure to meet you.'

'And this is Bar. They're the senior citizen of our small clan.' Ode laughed gesturing to a tall, lithe figure who had approached from behind her.

Adairia looked up into the face of a person who was undeniably fae. Their skin glowed iridescent and their hair was as silver as the most well-polished armour Adairia had laid eyes upon. They did not look a day over twenty, but she was well aware of how deceptive a fairy's appearance was when it came to gaging their age, so she took Ode at her word.

'Bar, an honour.' She offered the fairy a small bow, which was their preferred form of greeting and they returned the gesture in kind, bending low before her.

'The honour is all mine, caraid bheag to Fia, welcome to our fold.' Their voice was like honey.

'And I'm Aftab,' came a lyrical voice from a third figure who had bounded forward, plainly unwilling to be left for last.

This young man may not have been a fairy, but his beauty was surely unrivalled. His dark complexion had a natural radiance assuring any onlooker of his good health. Similarly, the loose black curls that fell to his ears and framed his face, were enviously lustrous. His cheeks managed to remain rounded whilst his jaw was hard and sculpted, and his wide smile showed rows of perfect, ivory teeth that could have charmed a snail out of its shell. Unlike Ode or Bar, he went straight in for a hug and wrapped his arms around Adairia before she knew what to do. When he released her, she looked down only to see that his right arm ended where her own elbow would have and his clothing had been expertly tailored to accommodate this. It was clear that he had caught her looking when he next spoke, shrugging and simply stating 'born this way'. His smile did not drop for a moment and Adairia found herself smiling back just as widely. His good cheer was infectious.

'Aftab, it is good to meet you.'

The final figure in their group was unquestionably a dwarf. His thick limbs and broad shoulders spoke of a man who had spent time underground, mining for minerals, and his unruly russet beard obscured half of his face. The eyes that peaked through, however, were kind and gently, a sparkling shade of blueish grey.

'Magnus, companion to Greer.' He stretched out a rough hand to shake one of hers, whilst indicated with his other the mahogany dragon behind him. She in turn bowed her head to Adairia who returned the gesture once she had been freed from Magnus' strong grip.

'I am pleased to meet you both,' she offered before turning her attention to the rest of the gathered dragons.

'I am Asha, caraid bheag,' spoke the largest dragon, her hide a brilliant gold. 'Ode is my companion.' Her voice had a soothing cadence that Adairia would not have associated with the deep grumbles she knew dragons to usually make.

'Tarin, companion to Bar,' added the dragon on her left whose own scales mimicked the leaves of an oak tree when seen in the gloom of night. Despite his size Adairia had no doubt he would be a difficult to spot if come across in the forest.

'Call me Callan.' The last dragon to introduce himself bared his teeth in what Adairia had now come to recognise as the dragon equivalent of a grin. 'It is so wonderful to meet Fia and her companion. None of us expected another dragon hatching to happen in most of our lifetimes. It's so exciting.' Adairia did not need to ask who Callan's companion was. If it were not made clear by process of elimination already, she would have guessed that the animated dragon before her, rattling of sentences without taking a breath in between, was bonded with the beaming Aftab.

'Everyone has been telling me all about their adventures together. They couldn't believe I have only been up in the air once, and on Tearlach's back.' Fia now pressed forward to rub her muzzle against Adairia's forehead as she stroked the dragon's neck in return. 'I cannot wait to fly Adairia.'

'Nor can I,' she smiled back, meaning it whole-heartedly.

*

Adairia had expected to be asking the dragons and their companions countless questions, but it was they who had the greater number of enquiries for her. They had all be shocked to hear of the poisoning incident, which Fia herself had informed them of before the two women's arrival. After Adairia had given them a run-down of what they knew thus far, as little as that was, they had each exclaimed in turn. The dragons in particular had made a series of particularly sinister noises, apparently of the opinion that an attack on any dragon was an attack on them all. Eventually, however, Isla insisted that it would be better to save their chatter for a proper dinner. She announced that they would host a formal feast, something they rarely had an excuse for these days she lamented. The visitors would join the rest of Baile's residents over a hearty meal and flagons of ale or goblets of wine depending on their preferences. And with that they were all flung into a day's worth of preparatory activities.

Adairia's services were swiftly enlisted by Jill in the kitchen. The old woman feigned irritation at the surprise dinner party but having spent enough time with her during her short stay Adairia knew Jill lived staunchly by the saying 'the more the merrier.' Whilst they were in the process of sculpting decorative pastries, they were joined by Magnus who was in search of a job to do. Without hesitation Jill had him sat down with a tray of dough and was instructing him in his task. As Magnus followed the older woman's instructions, Adairia was amazed to see his thick fingers deftly mould the edibles into intricate shapes; before her eyes each mouthful revealed itself to be a small swan, its wings folded against its side and its neck stretch languidly before it as if it were swimming through the air.

'These are bonny Magnus,' Adairia sighed wistfully, picking one up between two fingers to examine it.

'Och, 'av always enjoyed working wi' ma hands. Sculpting dough isnae tae different fae carving rock.' He looked a little bashful and carried on with his work without any further elucidation. Adairia wondered what more there was to learn about these strangers she had now found herself in the midst of.

'Dinnae just stand their dilly-dallying lassie, there's plenty else ye could be daeing tae lend a hand,' Jill called over from the fire she was stoking. 'I tell ye, springing us all wi' a last-minute feast might sound like fun...' Her mutters trailed away as she busied herself with her task and Adairia could not help but smile.

They spent the rest of the afternoon flitting between the

kitchen and the rest of the enormous estate. Bedrooms needed to be prepared for their guests; the formal dining room needed to be warmed and set for the evening; food needed to be cooked and drink needed to be fetched from the cellar. Cured meats from the stock that was kept in one of the underground chambers were even carted up for the dragons' suppers, no one expecting them to hunt for themselves after their long journeys. Baile was abuzz with people running from room to room and tasks often took twice as long as the newcomers stop to talk to familiar faces and strangers alike. Adairia, for her part, found herself engaged in a lengthy conversation with Ode who had wanted to ask after Aliya at the university; the chancellor and she, it turned out, were old friends. That was until Jill caught them and had them both scurrying in opposite directions, appropriately admonished.

After much work and numerous scoldings from Jill, everyone had gathered in the dining hall that evening, with its now blazing fire, ready to eat. Most everyone had changed their garb or tidied up for the occasion, taking the opportunity to dust off their finer clothing.

Adairia had dressed in the one formal dress she had packed when leaving the University, one of navy velvet. It had been a gift from Morag who was a much defter seamstress than she had ever been. Adairia had spied the fabric on one of their trips to the nearby market town and Morag had insisted on buying a roll for her birthday. It was a generous gift, but Morag had been adamant that a twenty-fifth birthday deserved a special dress. She had tailored it perfectly to Adairia's body although she had few occasions to wear it since the gift had been given. The neckline scooped low, the sleeves hanging off her shoulders, leaving them bare, and fanning out as they trailed down her arms. It clung tight to the swell of her chest before falling loose and billowing out around her legs and feet. Wearing it always made Adairia feel beautiful.

When Isla had knocked on her door to find out if she was ready to go Adairia had been surprised to find her standing in the hallway in a dress of her own. She had grown accustomed to seeing the red-head in trousers and blouses, but she could not deny that the sight of her in an emerald gown made her stomach flutter. The light refracted off the shimmering fabric encasing her body. The dress came up high enough to cover Isla's collarbone and was fitted tightly to her arms, chest, and waist. The skirt fell simply around her feet but was adorned with a high slit that exposed the knee and calf of her left leg.

'You look exquisite,' Adairia exhaled.

'So do you,' replied Isla, her eyes shining. 'I regret organising this feast now.' Her words made the other woman blush. 'M'lady.' She grinned as she took Adairia's hand in her own and they walked together to join the others already seated for dinner.

*

Dinner could be described as nothing less than a roaring success. The companions, who now numbered six, took their seats alongside the rest of Baile's residents. Jill, Flora, and her father Jackson were there, of course; a bard and minstrel who travelled together playing music and singing for their bread and butter treated them all to a duet about the heroics of Prince Bayrd and Tearlach; a quiet woman in her thirties called Lianne, who had moved to Baile with her three year old son two years ago after her husband had passed, sat next to Jackson and the two occasionally exchanged shy smiles with one another. In response to this last interaction Adairia spotted Flora catching

162

her grandmother's eye exchanging a cheeky wink, to which almost spat her drink back into her tankard as she chuckled silently. She herself was seated between Isla and Aftab, who sat to her left with Bar on his left in turn, while the other two dragon companions sat across from them on the other side of the table.

The food was delicious, and everyone cooed over Magnus' swan creations; if it were not for the coarse beard hiding most of his face Adairia could have sworn she had seen him blush. Aftab was a particularly good-humoured dinner companion; throughout the evening he regaled her with riveting stories of his and Callan's lives. The dragon had first hatched for his mother sixty years ago, but she had died ten years previously. It had seemed only natural that Callan would go on to bond with Aftab, who was his mother's son through and through and had grown up in the dragon's company.

Aftab smiled widely and laughed loudly, and it was difficult no to be infected by his joyful spirit. He could only be a few years Adairia's senior and seemed to get on well with all of the companions. He seemed particularly prone to teasing Bar who gave as good as they got. It was strange to see such an interaction between a human and a fairy Adairia thought. She had not met many fairies in her life as they were a reclusive race. Those she had, however, like the Lady Mirin, whilst graceful and softly spoken, were equally severe and aloof. Bar and Aftab, on the other hand, seemed to share something special between them.

As she chatted away to Aftab, Bar, Ode and Magnus she often found herself caressing the palm of Isla's hand under the table, or felt the other woman gently squeeze her thigh. They had reached a new level of closeness that made Adairia's heart flutter at every fleeting touch. Her life had changed so much in these past few months but nothing about meeting Isla had felt jarring or overwhelming. This woman who came into her life so swiftly had become her rock. She did not know what was next for her and Fia but she knew that whatever it was would include Isla and Tearlach; the fear that had filled her at first discovering her new fate had steadily been replaced by excitement as each week had passed.

'What're you thinking about?' Isla whispered into Adairia's ear.

'The future,' she whispered back.

'What does it look like?'

'Intense.' And she winked at Isla, who squeezed her hand in response.

Chapter Twenty-One
The Hot Springs

Despite their promises of delayed gratification, Adairia had found herself sapped by the day's activities. Meeting and talking to so many new dragons and their companions had been jubilant, but equally overwhelming for someone who had previously enjoyed their solitude. When it had been time to retire, therefore, Adairia had taken Isla's hand and explained that she would like to spend a little time alone, so perhaps it was best if they parted ways for the evening. A little nervous that Isla would feel rejected Adairia was relieved when the other woman simply smiled understandingly and pressed their foreheads together.

'Take all the time you need,' she had whispered.

The fact that it had been Adairia's decision, however, had not stopped her from waking in the night and reaching out for the red-head groggily only to feel disappointment when she felt the empty space in her bed.

After a night of interrupted sleep, Adairia had risen early and dressed herself in a comfortable woollen dress suitable for the chillier weather. She had spent enough time by herself; or she had at least had enough time without Isla she realised. The other woman would probably still be fast asleep in her own room if experience was anything to go by. *Why not take her a cup of tea in bed?* Adairia thought. She had never been to Isla's room herself, but Jill was happy to point her in its direction when she asked, although only after piling her with a stack of jam and bread to accompany two warm mugs of tea.

The room itself was in a part of the building where Adairia had rarely had cause to go. It was where, in the days of the monarchy, servants would have slept – a concept that was virtually redundant in Albiyon today. Most of the rooms, Isla had told her, had been converted over the years for purposes other than sleeping chambers. Adairia was surprised, therefore, to find herself knocking on one of the doors in this hallway expecting to find Isla's bedroom inside.

Upon hearing a croaky voice murmur 'come in' from behind the door Adairia pushed it open. Inside was a small room, much smaller than her own. The walls were bare and there was little decoration other than a simple fireplace on one wall. Isla was immediately visible sitting up in a single bed, half covered by her quilt and rubbing her eyes with her fists. As Adairia watched she let out a long yawn without covering her mouth; it was clear she had just woken up.

'Good morning,' smiled Adairia, walking over to sit on the edge of Isla's small bedframe and placing down her bounty on the side table.

'Good morning,' agreed Isla stretching out a hand to squeeze Adairia's before frowning. 'What brings you here?'

'I brought you breakfast!' Adairia chewed her bottom lip before adding, 'and I missed you,' to which Isla beamed.

'I could get used to this.' She swiped a hunk of bread from the pile and bit down enthusiastically as Adairia gazed around the chamber.

'I have to say, your room, um, it's a surprise.'

166

'Hmm?' Isla followed Adairia's gaze.

'It's rather…. stark?'

'Oh,' Isla replied, looking around her as if observing her surroundings for the first time. 'I see what you mean.'

'Is there a reason you sleep back here? It doesn't seem like anyone else uses these quarters for bedchambers.'

'I didn't always,' Isla responded slowly. 'I… you know my father passed away when I was nineteen?' Adairia nodded. 'Well, we were very close. He raised me, tutored me, did everything with me when I was growing up. After his death, his absence was more suffocating than being crammed into a crowd of people. Every corner of Baile reminded me that he was gone, and it made healing that much more difficult. I spent most of my time outside the building, but at night when I returned to my bedroom I rarely slept. When I did it was fitfully. So, I moved in here. No one had slept in these rooms for decades. It was, as you say, stark.' Isla gave a small smile. 'But simple was exactly what I needed, I felt at peace in this little room. Now, when I walk through Baile's halls my father's memory brings me joy, but I've grown to like my wee room all the same.'

'I understand.' Adairia returned the tight grip of Isla's hand still in hers.

'How're you feeling after last night?'

'Too exhausted to sleep apparently.' Adairia laughed, blowing an errant lock of hair from in front of her face.

'Here's an idea,' Isla lowered her voice conspiratorially, 'why don't I take you somewhere today? Somewhere secret. Just the two of us.'

'What about everyone else, wouldn't it be rude to scamper off just after they've gotten here?'

'Pfft, they'll all most likely be nursing headaches in bed well

167

into the afternoon and we'll be back for dinner.' Adairia did not think she could resist the grin that had spread across Isla's features.

'Alright but let me tell Fia first.' To which Isla jumped up, suddenly bubbling over with energy that had not been there moments before.

'You do that while I get dressed and grab us a couple of skins of water.'

'Can't I stay and watch first?' Adairia teased.

'No time, it'll take us at least an hour to walk there and I expect we'll just be getting undressed again anyway.'

Well, that sounded intriguing, thought Adairia.

*

Both women reconvened at the western edge of the Baile estate a short time later. Adairia had popped in on Fia and the other dragons only to find them all seated outside, entranced by a fire display courtesy of Greer. The magnificent mahogany dragon stood apart from the rest of the group as flames streamed from between her teeth and danced in the air. With a simple flick of her neck or widening of her jaw she was able to create a series of mesmerizing spirals and shapes that beguiled the onlooker. Adairia was momentarily tempted to join the rest of the dragons in the audience.

'Look at her control! Isn't she incredible?' Fia exhaled, her eyes fixed on the older dragon. 'She's a pyratic dragon. Maybe one day I will be able to do what she does.'

'Maybe,' Adairia had nodded, scratching the dragonling's neck fondly.

It was heartening if strange to see Fia surrounded by so many others of her kind at once. The sight reassured her that she would not be abandoning her companion if she took the

168

afternoon to go adventuring with Isla, to which the dragon agreed.

Thus, Adairia found herself journeying through the densely packed forest that bordered the palace grounds, Isla's hand in hers. After Adairia had grabbed at the other woman to prevent a near tumble over some surreptitious rocks neither had thought to let go. Now, Adairia held on tight to the warmth of Isla's skin against her own as she regarded their surroundings. Copper leaves carpeted the forest floor, leaving their previous hosts bare. The Alder trees, meanwhile, still dressed in full regalia, offered an intermittent canopy over their heads. Occasionally, Adairia heard a rustling from the undergrowth and turned to spot a rosy-tailed squirrel scurrying away from the interlopers. Isla had still provided no indication of where they were heading but Adairia found, to her surprise, that she was perfectly content not knowing. Eventually, after a hearty hike, the forestry began to thin out and Isla turned to Adairia with a mischievous grin on her face.

'What are you smirking about?' Adairia laughed. The air around them, she had noticed, was more humid now that they had reached slightly higher ground.

'You'll see,' Isla winked, dragging Adairia more insistently behind her.

A few moments later the trees finally parted to reveal a sight that took Adairia's breath away. Nestled among the thriving foliage was a pool of glimmering water. The small area of surrounding earth was dark and strewn with mossy rocks that created something of a border around the pool itself. Without the shade of the trees, the heat in the air was all the more palpable. When Adairia inhaled, she could taste the damp, warm air on her tongue.

'Hot springs?' She exhaled.

'Courtesy of Ben Losadh,' Isla explained.

'I hadn't realised we were so close to the mountain.' Adairia continued to marvel at the sight before her.

'Not that close, which is why these springs here are safe to bath in.' At which Isla unhooked her skin from her belt and began to pull her blouse over her head. 'You going to join me?' She grinned once she had freed her mass of curls from the garment.

'Just try and stop me.' Adairia laughed and began to strip off her own clothing in turn.

Isla was first to clamber into the warm water, having abandoned her attire at the edge of the pool, and Adairia could not help but pause in her own disrobing to watch the other woman as she did so. She was smaller on top than Adairia, with rounded hips and dimpled thighs that mesmerized Adairia as she descended into the water. Isla turned to stare over the edge of the pool as Adairia let her own slip drop to expose heavy breasts with nipples that had tightened in the exposed air, a fleshy stomach, and a thick thatch of golden-brown hair. Isla's eyes sparkled and she held out a hand in invitation.

Adairia took the proffered fingers and tentatively dipped her toes in the water. As she slid further down, submerging her body up to her shoulders, she let out a deep sigh and closed her eyes. The water washed over her, warming her to the core and unknotting the tension in her limbs. It was wonderful. She opened her eyes again to find Isla watching her closely, a small smile playing on her delectable lips. Adairia raised her free hand in the water to caress the other woman's hip lightly, trailing her fingers around so they ran across the crease where leg met body and feelt the hair there tickle her skin. She leaned in to take Isla's mouth in her own, groaning when the other woman sucked her bottom lip between her teeth.

'Would you like me to keep going?' Adairia whispered, glancing down between them to where her hand danced beneath the water.

'I think need you to would be more accurate,' Isla replied hoarsely, leaning her head back and letting her eyelids flutter shut.

'My wish is your command,' Adairia chuckled, kissing along Isla's exposed neck, and letting her fingers find the sensitive spot between her legs.

*

'You know, I still can't really believe I'm here, with you, with Fia and Tearlach.' Adairia was leaning against the side of the pool while Isla swam short laps back and forth in the water.

'You better believe it.' Isla stuck out her tongue, swimming up to wrap her arms around Adairia's waist and leaning her head against her chest.

'I was so frightened when Fia's egg started to crack,' She sighed.

'And now?' Isla asked, gazing up at her.

'Turns out frightening might not be such a bad thing.' Adairia smiled back. 'I can't imagine not be bonded with Fia now. I'm actually, dare I say it, glad she chose me that day in the library.'

'Well,' Isla grinned, 'not to sound selfish but I'm definitely glad she chose you.'

Extract from An Introduction to Dragons

Very few dragons mate for life. Generally speaking, both mares and stallions will breed with multiple partners across their lifetime. Despite this they remain a relatively rare race of creatures both historically and in current times. This is both as a result of long incubation periods and the number of eggs that never make it to maturity before fossilisation occurs.

As a species, dragons do not tend to live in hordes but are amiably disposed to each other when congregating. There are no recorded instances of serious dragon on dragon brutality that were not as a result of disputes that initially arose between companions. What this tells us of other species is less flattering, but I will not dwell on this topic here.

Chapter Twenty-Two
The Letter

The next few days at Baile were livelier than ever as Adairia got to know the other dragons and their companions better. Ode, she learned, had immigrated to Albiyon when she was in her twenties. Adairia was fascinated to hear that Asha's previous companion had not been a relative of Ode's. While she knew from her reading that this was objectively possible, she had not come across anyone yet for whom it was the case, in person or on page.

'Yes, my first caraid bheag was an Albiyan native like myself.' Asha had explained. 'Their name was Keir, but they passed away seventy years ago now. Human life spans are too fleeting.' She had nuzzled the head of her current companion at these words who had smiled kindly back at her.

'I am glad my caraid bheag is fae.' Tarin had nodded solemnly in response to their exchange.

'So, you were my age when you met Asha?' Adairia had asked, surprised and excited by this news.

'Thereabouts,' Ode had nodded. 'I know what it's like to have your whole world turned upside down when you least expect it. Asha saved me though. I was not a happy woman when we met, and she helped me find my way out of a dark place.'

It was incredible listening to various tales of the bonds shared by each dragon and their companion. Like Isla and Tearlach, they were all such consistent parts of each other's lives, they seemed to operate in perfect harmony. Callan and Aftab were able to talk animatedly about their shared love of Aftab's mother, Cyra, who had, in a sense, raised them both as the companion who had first awoken Callan's egg. Greer meanwhile loved to regale them proudly of Magnus' high rank among the dwarves, which made her companion blush profusely. Although dwarves were as much Albiyan citizens as any other race, they also had their own government to which various powers were devolved. Magnus himself occupied a seat in both assemblies as a dwarfish emissary.

After spending more time with them all it was obvious to see that Aftab and Bar were something more than friends. Adairia often noticed them touching each other in small but affectionate ways and exchanging meaningful glances. On one occasion, she was sure she even caught Bar wink at her when they had glanced between their and Aftab's clasped hands to Adairia and Isla's. Fia too was thriving from the company of other dragons. She had waxed lyrical about Greer's fire display to Adairia once the woman had returned from her trip the other day. Asha and Tarin meanwhile, had joined Tearlach in offering advice on flying to the eager dragonling. Although Fia seemed no closer to flight or breathing fire, she listened avidly to everything the older dragons had to tell her and revelled in their encouragement.

It was, Adairia had to admit, a blissful week. Their merrymaking was interrupted, however, when the postal carriage arrived one morning carrying an unexpected letter for Adairia. It was the first time she had received anything since

174

she had arrived at Baile. Immediately recognising the handwriting as Morag's she tore into the envelope, excited to hear from her friend:

Dear Adairia,

I hope all is well with you and Fia. It has barely been a month since we last saw you but both Calder and I miss you terribly. Is it not strange to think we have never been apart so long since coming into one another's company? I keep thinking to tell you of something ridiculous that Calder has either said or done and then remember you are too far away to load with such trivialities.

For that reason alone, you may have already gathered that I write to tell you of something more serious. The chancellor Aliya is gravely ill. Her sickness struck some two weeks after you left for Baile with Isla. At first no one thought anything of it, least of all the chancellor herself. We all fall ill occasionally. But as the days have passed whatever ails her has persisted, with each day looking bleaker and bleaker. None of the healers have been able to identify what is wrong but without appropriate treatment they are all sure whatever it is will eventually kill her.

To add insult to injury the chancellor's infirmity has sent the council into chaos. You would think four such learned people would be able to cope without one of their number, but they are at a loss without her input. Their bickering has escaped the privacy of their chambers and many of us have witnessed public arguments break out first-hand. Naturally their disunity spreads further discord throughout the university, and it does not feel like the same place you left anymore. You will better understand when you come home.

I do hope that you will return, for the chancellor has requested your and Isla's presence personally. Aelish has taken some of us off of our normal duties, myself included and appointed us as her attendants. She sleeps most of the day now but in one of her moments of lucidity she asked if I would send word to you. I'm sorry to write of this so abruptly but I want to get this letter out with tomorrow morning's post, and it is already late.

Despite the circumstances I hope we will see you soon.

Your sister,
Morag

Adairia? It was Fia; the dragon had immediately sensed her companion's growing distress as she had read the letter over her morning cup of tea, now forgotten on the table. *What is wrong Adairia?* She was still amongst the other dragons in their specially built accommodation, but distance was no barrier to such strong emotions between a dragon and their companion.

I received a letter from Morag. Adairia responded in kind. *She says the chancellor is on her death bed and the university is in disarray.* She hesitated before communicating her final thought. *She has asked that we return.* She held her breath as she waited for Fia to respond. *Then we must return.* The dragon's voice rung out in her mind.

It was at that moment that a fresh-faced Isla came in from inspecting a damaged chicken coop outside. Adairia's concern must have been plastered across her features as Isla frowned upon spotting the other woman's expression and raised a quizzical eyebrow. Adairia did not say anything but simply handed over the letter she was still clutching in her hand. Patiently, she watched as Isla scanned the words, her face falling as she took them in.

'This is terrible news.' She groaned looking back up to meet Adairia's eyes.

'Fia and I are going back.'

'Of course, Tearlach and I will come with you both.' Isla said without hesitation. 'We should let everyone else know the news. Ode is a good friend of Aliya's, after all. She might want to come with us.'

'Yes. You're right.' Adairia agreed. 'Let me see who I can find while you get something to eat, and we can all meet in the dragon quarters?' To which Isla nodded. 'See you shortly.' Adairia rose to leave, stopping only to take Isla's face in her hands and place a lingering kiss on her lips before exiting the room.

*

As it turned out, it was not difficult to hunt down the others. Adairia immediately headed to the dragon quarters and was unsurprised to find, along with the dragons, Ode and Magnus. Both were preparing Asha and Greer for late morning flights to stretch their wings and reacquaint themselves with the area surrounding Baile. They seemed pleased to see Adairia when she entered the outhouse, greeting her with jovial good mornings, which she hastily returned. Fia too was pleased to see her friend and bounded over to her before she had a chance to get further than two feet into the building. The dragon really was growing ever larger. She was now taller than Adairia and had to bend her neck ever so slightly to reach down and nudge her forehead.

'Hello to you too.' Smiled Adairia softly, rubbing the dragon's neck gently.

'I'm so sorry about chancellor Aliya Adairia.' Fia crooned. 'I wasn't sure what the plan was, so I haven't said anything to anyone else yet.'

'What's this about Aliya?' Ode had ceased from fussing over her own dragon when she had overheard Fia's words and was now turned to face Adairia.

'She's ill, I just received word from a friend at the university. I think we need to get everyone together.'

With the aid of their dragons, the missing companions were summoned to the bar and Adairia filled them in on the contents of Morag's letter. She informed them that she and Isla had every intention of flying to the university as soon as they could ready themselves, which meant later that day. To no one's surprise, Ode informed them that she too would fly to the university with Asha. As she pointed out, Fia was much larger than she had been last time all three had ridden together on Tearlach's back so it might be advisable to split their weight between the two older dragons and Asha was larger still than Tearlach. Aftab and Magnus, meanwhile, had offered up their apologies but neither would be travelling with them this time. Adairia understood but what she had not expected was that Bar too would request to accompany them south. She had no reason to refuse the fairy and thus their party became eight.

'I wish I could fly,' muttered Fia, once they had all agreed to the arrangements and dispersed for the time being.

'You will, soon, I'm sure.' Adairia consoled her, looking to Tearlach for affirmation.

'Your caraid bheag is right wee one. Your wings will continue to grow and soon no one will be able to keep you fastened to the earth. You just have to have a little patience. Human babies cannot even walk until they are almost one year old.' Tearlach snorted at his last statement and Fia looked shocked.

178

'Is that true?' She directed her question to Adairia who nodded. 'How terrible!' Fia was now shaking her head, evidently too appalled by the thought of waiting a year to walk to dwell any longer on her lack of flight.

Chapter Twenty-Three
Archives

'Hopefully she'll be awake just now, mornings are usually our safest bet.' Cyril whispered to Adairia and Isla as if his voice might travel through the door to the chancellor's chambers and worsen her ailment.

As Cyril slowly pushed the door open, all three peered into the room beyond. Although she had had some inkling of what to expect that did not stop Adairia inhaling sharply at the sight before her. The chancellor lay beneath a pile of thick blankets, her prone body propped up on a mountain of cushions. The whole effect made her appear even smaller than she had been since Adairia had last seen her. In just six weeks the woman's entire physique had altered. The arm that lay across the duvet was scrawny and limp; her eyes and cheeks were sunken into her once round face; and her pallor was ashen. She was, however, most definitely awake.

'I'm dying Cyril, not deaf.' She smiled weakly as they entered the room. Even her voice had lost the strength Adairia had grown familiar with. Cyril's brown skin on the other hand blushed deeply at her words and he stared self-consciously at his feet.

'Apologies Aliya,' Cyril muttered. 'Adairia and Isla arrived late last night.' The chancellor shifted her gaze to the two women standing beside Cyril.

'Adairia, Isla, it is good to see you, despite the circumstances.'

'Ode came with us. I know she would like to see you whenever its convenient.' Isla spoke first, moving forward so that she stood nearer the older woman. Adairia followed her, placing her hands on the back of a chair conveniently located next to the head of the bed.

'Right well, I'll leave you all be for now. I haven't been to the chapel to pray yet this morning. Would you like me to offer prayers for Aliya on your behalf while I'm there, Isla, Adairia?' Adairia nodded to Cyril who hurried from the room. Turning back to the chancellor she caught Aliya rolling her eyes.

'He prays for me every day in that chapel, but I haven't had the heart to tell him I don't even really believe in the gods.' These words made Isla chortle, but Adairia could not stop staring at the chancellor's deteriorated appearance. 'How was Baile Adairia?' Aliya continued, snapping her out of her daze.

'Good, it's been good.' How could she regale the chancellor with the joy she had experienced in Isla's home since leaving when Aliya lay before them so evidently close to death.

'And Fia?' The chancellor smiled. To this Adairia was able to answer more enthusiastically, how could she not?

'She is so much bigger, bigger even than me. Tearlach thinks it won't be long before she can fly now. But it's not just her size that has grown, so has her mind. She is so astute and curious.' Adairia sighed. 'I'm lucky to have her in my life.'

'A change of tune indeed.' The chancellor gave a small chuckle and Adairia blushed. 'Thank you for letting me know Ode is here with you, Isla. I would very much like to speak to her later if I am up to it. It has been many months since we last saw one another and letters are never quite the same as face-to-face conversations, are they?' Isla nodded before changing the subject.

'If you don't mind me asking Aliya, it seemed from Morag's letter at least that you had something more specific you wanted to talk to us about.'

'Yes, yes, you're right of course.' Aliya agreed and then turned her eyes back on Adairia. 'We haven't been able to make any progress on discovering where the poison that Fia absorbed came from.' Adairia nodded, unable to say anything but only tense her shoulders further. 'I am a scholar, however, and though I may be caught up in the admin of running the university these days I still know how to conduct a bit of research. Before I was bedridden, I managed to track down the archivist's log for Fia's egg. It came to the university long before my time of course. In fact, as it turns out, it was donated by your great, great, great grandfather Isla. Prince Bayrd's own grandfather, King Mactire. Although the egg itself long predates his time.' She gestured to the table by the window ledge where a large leather-bound book lay. 'Bring that here Isla.'

Isla did as the chancellor asked and heaved the book from its perch and brought it to the bed, which was no mean task. The book itself had evidently been well-cared for although it was impossible to entirely disguise its age. Growing up in the library aisles had given Adairia a good eye for book biding trends over the years and this book was surely at least two centuries old.

'Open it to where the ribbon marks.'

Following the chancellor's instructions Isla flipped the book open and presented it so that both women could read what was on the page. It was a list of items donated to the university over

182

the years, along with dates and any details the archivist felt were pertinent. After a brief scan of the page Adairia's eyes caught on the record Aliya was clearly interested in them reading:

Item	Benefactor	Date Acquired	Description
Fossilised Dragon's Egg	King Mactire II	The eleventh year of the reign of King Mactire II	Orange fossilised dragon's egg, presumed c.900 years old, product of the dragon Cartimandua companion to Queen Isolde, for more details see archive documents 1311a.

When Adairia looked up from the page she saw that Isla had already finished reading the entry and was now gazing at her intently.

'Fia's egg was lain by the first dragon in Albiyon,' she said, wide eyed.

'More than one thousand years! Her egg was unhatched for more than one thousand years! Is that normal?' Adairia croaked, looking between Isla and Aliya.

'I've never heard of such a long gestation period, but you'd be better to ask the other dragons,' Isla replied. 'What about these documents, though? What did they say?'

'Ah.' A sad expression fogged the chancellor's features. 'That is where the trail runs cold. I asked Angus to dig out the archive referred to but there was nothing there. Whatever documents or letters the archivist received along with the egg are gone.'

'Is that common?' Isla directed this question to Adairia.

'Things do get lost but it's rare that they can't be found again. Did Angus look elsewhere?'

'I had him and Cyril conduct a thorough search, but nothing appeared out of place,' sighed the chancellor.

'Do you think someone took them on purpose?' Adairia pressed.

'Ordinarily I wouldn't be so suspicious but what with Fia's poisoning the timing does seem odd.' Adairia and Isla exchanged nervous glances, disturbed by Aliya's words.

It was at that moment, however, that they were interrupted in their conversation by a knock at the door. As both women turned their heads, they saw the door swing gently open to reveal the Lady Mirin standing behind it.

'Lady Isla, Adairia, apologies for the interruption,' she offered with a bow of the head.

'Just Isla will do, Lady Mirin,' Isla responded briskly.

'Of course.' The fae woman smiled without offering the same courtesy. 'If it's not too much trouble I was hoping to talk to the chancellor about some university business whilst she is awake.' Isla and Adairia both turned to look enquiringly at the chancellor.

'That's fine.' Aliya nodded before turning her attention to her existing guests. 'Do take the book with you if you'd find it helpful. I'm sure we'll have a chance to speak again soon.' She put her hand on Adairia's and smiled consolingly. It felt wrong for the older woman to be offering her reassurance when it was the chancellor who was lying there so ill. Adairia, nevertheless, took comfort in her touch.

'Thank you,' she whispered as she got up from her seat to leave.

Both women nodded to Lady Mirin, departed the room, and hurried away as the door was closed firmly behind them.

*

'What are you thinking?' muttered Isla as they were traipsing down the winding staircase from the chancellor's rooms.

'That I'm so bloody sick of all of this,' responded Adairia grinding her teeth together.

'I'm sorry Adairia,' sighed Isla, squeezing her hand in her own.

'Don't be sorry Isla, just be here.' Adairia stopped on the steps and turned to face her friend and now, lover. She held her gaze silently for a moment before leaning in and kissing her. Their kiss began tender, but it quickly grew in eagerness as Isla's arms snaked around her neck and into her hair, melding their lips together as if they were one. They remained locked together like this until a cough broke through their embrace.

'We've been waiting for you.' It was Morag, her head peeking around the corner of the stairwell. A broad smile adorned her face and she winked at Adairia who had turned bright red at being caught kissing Isla in such a public space, and so profusely at that. 'You done?' She asked politely.

'For now,' Grinned Isla, taking Adairia's hand and leading them down the last few steps

Chapter Twenty-Four
The Lady Mirin

Adairia, Isla, Morag, and Calder, who had been waiting just outside the stairwell, relocated to one of the more comfortable communal reading rooms in the university that was otherwise unoccupied. The obligatory, if much appreciated, tight hugs and slaps on the back having been exchanged, all four friends were now spread across a selection of comfortable armchairs and sofas.

'How have you been?' Adairia asked eagerly. She had not had a chance to hunt down Morag and thank her for her letter between their arrival last night and their visit to the chancellor's chambers that morning.

'Oh, you know, bored senseless,' Morag responded jokingly. 'Calder never stops talking about pigs and slop. I've missed your conversation more than I can tell you.' Adairia laughed as Calder rolled his eyes from his seat beside Morag. They were both used to Morag's teasing and knew that behind it lay a deep affection for Calder that neither had yet seemed able to verbalise in the many years they had known one another. At least not in Adairia's presence.

'I can only imagine,' she replied in a tone of mock horror.

'Charming,' Calder sniffed.

'But how have you two been?' insisted Morag. 'How are Fia,

and Tearlach?'

'They're well,' smiled Adairia. 'We should all go down and see them later in fact.' To which Calder practically jumped out of his seat, his eyes shining.

'I heard that you four weren't the only dragons and companions to arrive during the night?' he probed eagerly, making all three women chuckle.

'No, Bar, Ode and their dragons Tarin and Asha travelled with us. Ode and Asha are old friends of the chancellor and wanted to visit her after hearing your news,' Isla said, her tone taking on a more sombre note. Morag nodded in turn.

'Well, you've both seen the chancellor now, what did she have to say?' Morag prodded.

In response, Adairia heaved the hefty tome the chancellor had entrusted to them onto the low table at their feet and flipped it back open to the page they had just been examining. Morag and Calder took it in turns to peer over and read the entry for themselves. Unsurprisingly, their immediate response was to ask after the documents referred to by the archivist and Adairia had to explain what the chancellor had told Isla and herself only moments before.

'So, someone has taken them on purpose?' Morag asked, frowning.

'Documents as old as that would never be lent out to someone, regardless of who they are. If someone wanted to study them, they would have to look over the originals in the scriptorium and make copies if necessary. So yes, the fact that they've been removed is suspicious. The chancellor seems to think so too.' Adairia answered, musing over the possibilities in her own head.

'This has got to be linked to Fia's poisoning right?' Calder offered up. 'It would be too much of a coincidence otherwise?'

'I guess.' Adairia sighed. 'It's all so overwhelming. And it only makes me more worried about her. She's my responsibility you know.'

'What're you going to tell her?' enquired Morag.

'The truth. There is nothing I would keep secret from her and she has more right to know than any of us,' Adairia stated matter-of-factly.

*

'So…' Fia paused thoughtfully, 'my mother was the first dragon in Albiyon? And she laid my egg a millennium or so ago?'

Adairia was silent as Fia processed her news out loud. Adairia had to confess to herself she had not even thought of the dragon Cartimandua as a mother in the same sense that humans might have parents. Nor had she ever considered that Fia may be as curious about her own parents as she once had been about hers. It seemed she had been remiss, however, as she observed Fia's reaction to this new information. The dragon had refused to sit down since Adairia had shown her the archivist's log and continued to pace up and down as she spoke.

Adairia had decided to talk to Fia alone first, given the personal nature of their discovery. She had excused herself from the groups' company after a few more tight hugs and headed to the same barn that had been Tearlach's accommodation on his last visit. This time, however, it had to house three fully grown dragons as well as Fia and the conditions were significantly less comfortable. Thankfully the other three were currently out hunting for wild animals to snack on in the nearby forest, providing Adairia and Fia with some privacy and room to breathe.

'Does that mean I am one thousand years old? That would

make me older than all of the other dragons we know.' Fia mused.

'I don't know if that's how it works. Were you conscious of your surroundings in the egg?' Adairia asked, curious now.

'The day my egg started to hatch was the day I woke up. I know I existed before then, but it was as if my mind lit up the moment I felt my connection to you.' This made Adairia feel a pang of guilt as she reflected on her first reaction to discovering Fia had chosen her from inside her egg. 'I couldn't wait to get out and meet you.' Fia gave one of her toothy dragon smiles, which Adairia found difficult not to return.

'I just wish we knew what were in the documents King Mactire provided the university with along with your egg. They might have given us some clues as to how you were able to survive for so long unhatched, or even contained vital information your companion should know once you'd hatched.' Adairia was starting to panic but she was distracted by the change in Fia's expression. Her teeth ground against one another as she spoke next.

'Who would dare steal my documents from me?' she snarled and Adairia was taken aback by the ferocity of her words. She had not expected Fia to feel so personally scorned by the actions of whomsoever had removed these papers from their place in the archives. Her shock was momentary, however, as she felt Fia's emotions wave over her and experienced the indignation she felt at having her past denied to her. The dragonling was right to be furious Adairia thought. She was too.

'I'm sorry.' Adairia reached out a hand to sooth the agitated dragon. 'You know we'll keep looking, don't you? There are more of us now and we've only just returned. Aliya didn't share

189

this with us for nothing.' Fia calmed at her words.

'How is she, the chancellor?'

'Not well. I believe Ode is with her now. I told Isla I would join them for dinner.'

'The others should be back with ours shortly,' Fia replied. 'Stay with me until then?'

'Of course.'

*

Adairia had waited with Fia until they heard the thud of heavy feet outside, indicating the return of the other three dragons. She bid them farewell as she set off back for the university, wrinkling her nose at the deer carcasses hanging from their jaws. As she walked, she attempted to reassure herself that she would be able to keep her promise to Fia and find answers to their mounting list of questions.

On her return journey Adairia bumped into various familiar faces from around the university, old and young, who were curious to hear about her new life. She smiled and shook hands but attempted to keep her responses short in order to find the people she truly sought. She did stop, however, when she came across the Lady Mirin for the second time that day, this time deep in conversation with Bar. It took the two fairies a moment to notice Adairia approaching, and she could not help but sense the tension between them.

'Ah Adairia. It is good to see you again.' With Bar's back to her it was the Lady Mirin that first spotted Adairia from the corner of her eye.

'Good evening to both of you.' Adairia nodded politely. 'Are you joining us for dinner?' She directed this question to the fae woman.

'Unfortunately not, but please do not let me delay you any

further. Bar, always a pleasure.' With that she turned and headed back up the stairs in the main foyer of the building; she moved with a grace that more closely resembled gliding than walking.

'You know the Lady Mirin?' Adairia asked Bar as they both moved towards the dining room.

'She is an old fae, older than I am, and from an even older family. I don't think there are many of my kind that don't at least know of her... but yes we have met a few times.' Bar was difficult to read, as Adairia had found with all the fairies she had come into contact with, but something about their response felt stiffer than usual.

'You're friends?' She added tentatively only to receive the response she had suspected she might. Bar scoffed loudly, making a sound quite unlike a fairy, but when Adairia looked up at their face they were smiling.

'The Lady Mirin is a follower of the old ways. My people are often more traditional, but many have chosen to move with the times, I like to think I'm included in that. Some, however, have not.'

'By which you mean?' Adairia pressed, intrigued now.

'She does not approve of interspecies relationships. If it were not for the fact that neither Aftab nor I can bear children, I doubt she would deign to speak to me at all.' Adairia was taken aback by this statement. She knew it was true that fairies were often traditionalists but for the Lady Mirin to be so outwardly disapproving of another member of her own people took her aback.

'Yet you speak with her?' she asked hesitantly.

'I wish I could tell you that her opinions are meaningless, but she is a powerful woman. Her family are descendants of the royal line as much as Isla's, and that still holds weight within the fae hierarchy.' Bar's expression was grim as he spoke.

'On that topic I actually have some news you might be interested in learning.' When Bar raised an eyebrow curiously Adairia jumped into detailing what had unfolded this morning, including Fia's own prestigious lineage.

'Well, this I was not expecting. Of course, I knew Fia's egg was presumed lifeless,' they mused making Adairia flinch slightly at their choice of words. 'But still, almost a millennium... interesting. Tarin hatched within ten years of his dam laying her first clutch, although he was the only one of his brothers and sisters to survive.'

'What do you mean *survive*?' Adairia frowned.

'Dragon's rarely lay one egg at a time, there are usually two or three, sometimes four, eggs in a clutch. It is rare, however, for more than one to hatch. Usually, its sibling's eggs will slowly lose their colour and appear nothing more than large rocks to the naked eye. I suppose that is why Fia's supposedly fossilised egg was perceived as so unique, that it retained its colour you know. I have never heard of an egg that waited longer than a century to hatch though. How very interesting.' Adairia simply nodded, processing this new information. 'We'll have plenty to talk about over dinner it seems.' Bar smiled as they approached the open doors leading to the dining room.

As they entered the main hall Adairia caught sight of Calder waving to her from a long table where he sat alongside Morag, Isla, and Ode, all of whom had already poured themselves glasses of wine and were evidently enjoying one another's company as Ode laughed loudly at something Morag had just said. Usually, Adairia would have smiled at such a homely scene, but her thoughts were elsewhere, back in the main hall of the museum as she polished the marble podium on which sat a gleaming, orange dragon's egg.

Extract from An Introduction to Dragons

The lifespan of dragon kind is comparable to that of the fair folk. They may live anywhere from two hundred to two hundred and fifty years on average, although the oldest dragon recorded died at the impressive age of three hundred and nine. Due to their lengthy lifespans those dragons that bond with creatures such as humans, goblins or dwarves tend to outlive their companions and make second or even third connections in their lifetime. Meanwhile, pairings between dragon kind and the fair folk can often survive within a few years of one another. It is said by some that the dragon Cartimandua and Queen Isolde passed away within months of one another their bond was so deep, although there is no official record to corroborate this.

Chapter Twenty-Five
The New Chancellor

During dinner Adairia informed her friends that she planned to spend the evening looking through the library archives for anything that might shed further light on the acquisition of Fia's egg. Morag and Calder had their own work to attend to and Ode and Bar wanted to check in on their dragons, but Isla insisted on accompanying Adairia to the library.

'Two heads are always better than one.' She had winked playfully. So, a few hours after they had eaten, Adairia and Isla found themselves surrounded by seemingly useless papers and straining their eyes to read what felt like the hundredth scroll by candlelight. As night fell, however, the scriptorium had completely emptied out apart from the two women, and they seemed no closer to finding any answers to Adairia's questions.

'Adairia.' A hushed voice tickled her ear. 'Adairia,' this was followed by a gentle hand squeezing her shoulder, 'wake up.' The voice was Isla's.

Adairia opened her eyes blearily and saw the other woman's face inches from her own. She had fallen asleep, head in her arms, slouched over the last volume she had been scanning before her eyes gave out on her. The room was pitch black apart from a tiny flickering flame dancing feebly atop the stub that remained of their candle.

'You nodded off.' Isla smiled. 'You would make a terrible banshee you know.' Adairia smiled back, if a little groggily, and raised herself up from her desk.

'Sorry.' She yawned, stretching her arms out behind her, and shaking her head in an attempt to liven herself up.

'Don't be daft,' Isla replied, reaching over to close the book Adairia had been resting on. 'I think it's time for bed though, don't you?' Adairia nodded reluctantly and made to stand up.

Both women exited the scriptorium quietly and proceeded to ascend the stairs to Adairia's bedchambers. It was no longer a question whether Isla would sleep in separate quarters or not. After freeing herself from her clothes and letting out another loud yawn, Adairia crawled under the sheets first, shortly followed by Isla. She just managed to ease in behind Adairia and wrapped herself around the other woman in a comforting embrace before they both drifted off into dreamless sleep.

*

It was not until a loud series of raps came from behind the heavy wooden door that either of the two women woke up. Adairia was the first to be startled awake by the noise and was disorientated at first to see the light streaming throughout her bedroom from the window where she had forgotten to draw the curtains; she almost never slept this late, even after a long night's studying. It took another noisy hammering at the door before she fully registered what exactly had interrupted her slumber.

'Coming,' she called, feeling Isla stirring behind her. She grabbed her crumpled dress from the floor where she had discarded it the night before and pulled it over her head. 'Isla,' she whispered, urgently throwing the red-head's trousers and blouse to her in the bed.

Isla's only response was to wave her hand silently in acknowledgement before she began pulling on her clothes, her eyes still crusted with sleep. Once the other woman was suitably decent, Adairia finally pulled open the door to her room to reveal Morag standing behind it, fist raised, about to unleash another furious series of bangs on the wood.

'Morag,' Adairia said in surprise, 'what is it?'

'I'm sorry,' Morag responded and Adairia looked more closely at her, taking in the dishevelled state of her clothes and hair.

'What?' she repeated more serious this time.

'It's the chancellor,' Morag continued haltingly, 'she's... she's gone.' For a moment everything was silent. Adairia simply stared at Morag whose face was lined with exhaustion. That was until Isla came up behind her and rested a hand on her lower back.

'She... she died, when?' Stammered Adairia.

'About an hour ago. I was there. Aelish and I were doing our morning drop in, but she wasn't speaking. Her breath... the rattle...' Morag's voice caught in her throat, and she could not get the next words out.

'I'm sorry. Come in, take a seat,' Adairia said, reaching out to take her friend's arm, but she shook her away.

'No, no, I came to take you to her. Cyril said the people who knew her should be allowed a chance to say goodbye, properly.' Once again Adairia was lost for words, but thankfully Isla spoke up for both of them.

'Of course, thank you Morag, we'll come with you now if that's alright with Adairia?' Adairia nodded without looking back at Isla and the two women exited the room to follow Morag back the way she had come.

Adairia felt lightheaded as she stood with her back pressed against one of the walls in the chancellor's bedchambers. Cyril, Ode, and Aelish had already been there when Morag returned with Adairia and Isla in tow. Cyril and Ode sat on either side of Aliya's bed, each one holding one of her limp hands, whilst Aelish pottered around the room. As soon as she spotted the three younger women approaching the open doorway, she gestured for Morag to wait there and shuffled out silently to allow Isla and Adairia more room to enter.

Adairia could not bring herself to get any closer to the chancellor's still form. It was a brutal sight. Her skin was ashy grey and her eyes glassy. The woman who had once held such a commanding, reassuring presence, now seemed so much smaller in death than she had done in life. It was as if something essential had truly vanished the moment she had exhaled her last breath. Finding it impossible to look any longer Adairia turned her attention to Cyril whose face was stained with tears. *Why was she here?* She asked herself. *The chancellor was gone. There was no point in her being in this room with the corpse of a woman whose soul had now abandoned it.*

'I'm sorry.' Adairia stammered and turned on her heels, fleeing the room.

The funeral was held three days later in the University chapel. Sitting in the third row from the front, listening to Cyril talk lovingly of the chancellor, Adairia found her attention distracted by the building itself: its high arched ceiling, supported by heavy wooden beams; the ornate stain-glass windows that cast rainbows across the floor when the sun hit them at the right angle; and the rows upon rows of simple benches overflowing with friends, family, and acquaintances. Sitting there, her eyes roaming the building's interior, she could not help but think back on what the chancellor had said to her about the gods the last time they had spoken. Adairia was unsure of her own feelings on the subject, but this gathering was for more than just Aliya.

After Cyril it was Ode's turn to speak, followed by a few unfamiliar faces who had evidently known Aliya over the years. They then stood to sing two songs apparently chosen by the chancellor herself. First, they sang a song Adairia had never heard before, but the lyrics were provided for them. It was a traditional song about loss from the homeland of the chancellor's parents. It reassured the listener that just as the emotion conjured by the notes of this song would remain once the music had ended, so too would the memory of the person now gone. Adairia found the words surprisingly comforting as she sang them for the first time. Then they sang the Ballad of the Uprising – an adapted folk tune that had become popular after the dismantling of the monarchy; it sang of the revolutionaries and their hopes for freedom and fairness in Albiyon.

After the service itself they moved to the main dining hall in the university. Those younger guests were carted off to bed and everyone else found themselves cracking out the goblets of wine or ale until the room was filled with shouts and laughter as everyone vied to be heard over the din. Adairia was just thinking to herself that she should probably grab herself one of the sandwiches from over in the far corner when a gradual hush spread throughout the room. Turning around to identify the reason why everyone had abandoned their conversations so suddenly, she saw that the Lady Mirin was standing alone at the head of the hall, calmly waiting for everyone's attention.

'I would like to start by thanking everyone for attending today's memorial.' She began. 'I know this is an incredibly difficult time for many of you who were close to our previous chancellor, may she rest in peace. Many of you may also be concerned about the university's future. Aliya oversaw the running of this institution for thirty-four years and worked here for much longer. I myself had the privilege of working alongside her on the university council for the past twenty and I would like to think I knew her as well as anyone could.' Adairia was watching Cyril who was seated closest to the fae woman, with Ode beside him, her arm resting on his back. He seemed to be absorbed in a haze of grief, red-eyed and staring blankly into his lap. She was not sure he could even hear what the Lady Mirin was saying.

'Much has changed at the university under Aliya's leadership. She brought this institution into a new age and opened its doors to new people. These changes have not been without their difficulties, and it has been no small task for the council to manage the university over the past few decades. But I do not want any of you to worry about this bastion of education and culture in our country. I will personally make it my mission not to allow our previous chancellor's passion to go wasted by permitting our standards to slip in her absence. I am, therefore, honoured to announce I will officially be taking on the role of chancellor myself. We, as the council, felt that it would be best for the university that this role was formally filled as soon as possible for the good of everyone here. I hope you will now join me in raising your glasses to the memory of our previous chancellor and to the future of this great institute.'

Adairia raised her goblet with everyone else in the room,

although some cups were raised notably higher than others. Angus alone could be seen venturing up to the front of the room to join Mirin in toasting to the old chancellor and, she supposed, the new. Taking a sip from her own drink Adairia observed her companions: Bar who was staring at the Lady Mirin, eyes narrowed, hands clasped in their lap; Isla who was scratching her chin thoughtfully and Morag who was whispering in Calder's ear beside her.

'Awfully convenient isn't it?' Adairia hissed through gritted teeth.

'If I hadn't been there when Aelish did the examination on the body myself I would find natural causes a little difficult to swallow right now,' Morag replied and Isla nodded.

Morag was right of course. The post-mortem had revealed numerous tumours that no one could have known about pressing on the chancellor's organs. It was not unheard of, although the healers were still surprised at how quickly the deadly growths had overrun Aliya's body. It was Bar, however, who voiced Adairia's own thoughts first.

'You don't have to be the cause of something to take advantage of it.'

They all turned their heads back to watch the Lady Mirin chatting with another scholar across the room, considering Bar's words. Adairia wondered what exactly the Lady Mirin had planned for the future of the university.

Chapter Twenty-Six
A Relaxing Bath

Within days of the chancellor Aliya's funeral, both Bar and Ode rode back to Baile to reunite with the other dragons and their companions. When Isla and Adairia were unable to tell them when they too would be returning to Isla's home, they had to accept that it may be some time before they all saw one another again. Of course, Ode and Bar had their own lives to get back to, Adairia had to remind herself, although it was difficult not to feel another pang of loss at their separation. She, however, was not ready to leave. As much as she had fallen in love with Baile, the university was her home, and she did not feel as if she could leave it during such an upheaval. She was just grateful that Isla had decided to remain at her side.

In the aftermath of the chancellor's death, Adairia had become singly focused on researching the origin of Fia's egg. Her scholar's instincts had kicked in and she spent most of every day and night either in the library or scriptorium poring over various documents. Up until this point, she had been so fixated on researching dragons as a species that she had to admit she had overlooked the specifics of Fia's lineage. Before the dragonling was born she had been such an abstract concept to Adairia the thought had not even occurred to her. A small part of her could not help but feel she had let her companion down and she was determined to make it right.

It was now the dead of winter in Albiyon and the winter solstice had passed with little fanfare, falling only days after Ailya's funeral. Despite the dip in temperature, however, Adairia had still wanted to take Fia to visit her allotment now that the dragonling was older and more able to communicate. It was a place of solace for Adairia, even if there was not much to see or do at this time of year.

'This is where you grow your food?' Fia had asked, a sceptical expression marring her dragon's face. Adairia had been tempted to laugh but quelled the desire.

'Aye, well some of it anyway.' She gazed at the shades of brown and white typical of this time of year and mourned the significant absence of green. 'It's not really the right time of year for a lot of what I like to grow. The soil needs some time off.'

'What about meat? Surely you don't grow that here?' Fia asked giving the earth a curious sniff.

'I don't eat meat Fia,' Adairia smiled.

'Why? It's very tasty,' Fia explained.

'Perhaps,' Adairia laughed, 'but why consume what I don't need. Vegetables can be very tasty too, I promise you.'

'Hmm,' came the dragons reply, 'maybe I'll test your theory some time. But not today.' This made Adairia chuckle harder.

But after that day there had not been much point in visiting her allotment regularly anymore. Instead, she churned through the stacks of seemingly useless information the university had to offer. After one particularly late and frustrating research session, Adairia decided to take herself to the baths and relax her body in the warm water. The bathing rooms were situated in the west wing of the university in an enclosed space where water was fed in from the local reservoir and heated by furnaces in the basement below. There were baths of all different sizes, from small individual basins to large swimming pools carved into the rocky ground.

It had to be past midnight this night, which meant the rooms were entirely empty of anyone else. Steam furled up from the various bodies of water giving the air a misty quality. Adairia stripped out of her clothing and decided to take advantage of the largest pool by swimming a few laps to work out her limbs after hours cramped stationery in the same spot of the library. After a while, however, she settled into a crevasse in the rock and simply allowed the hot water to soothe her muscles.

The world around her felt changed. Even Calder and Morag seemed more tense and less chatty than usual, if not with her at least around each other. Fia meanwhile was growing increasingly frustrated with her inability to fly. She insisted on launching herself off any surface she could climb up onto, flapping her wings to no avail. Adairia knew she should not worry about her; she was a dragon after all. Tearlach certainly seemed to find these repeated attempts at flight hilarious and often pushed Fia from heights himself without any warning. *But who would not feel a pang of fright in their gut watching a child fling itself haphazardly from tall surfaces only to meet the ground each time?* Or maybe it was simply that Adairia was equally concerned about the speed at which Fia was developing. The timeline all seemed so vague. She knew she should just lighten up a little, but damn if that was not hard.

Lost in her thoughts Adairia dipped below the surface of the water, submerging her hair and watching it float above her like sheets of golden hay. When she came back up for air, she was momentarily surprised to see that she was no longer alone. While she had been beneath the water a second figure had joined her in the pool. At first, she could not make out her companion but as the woman moved through the water towards her a shock of red hair broke through the mist like a beacon in the dark.

'Isla?' she whispered.

'It's me.' The other woman smiled, now close enough for Adairia to make out her features. 'I've been looking for you everywhere. You didn't come to bed.'

They were face to face now; Adairia could feel Isla's breath on her skin and she closed her eyes for a moment just to absorb the other woman's physical presence. *Gods,* she thought, *they had only found one another so recently. They had barely had time to be with each other, to relax in each other's company, to enjoy each other.*

'I just needed to relax a little,' Adairia replied, her voice coming out huskier than she had intended.

'Well, it's the perfect time for it. I've never bathed in here when it has been so empty.' Isla smiled.

'I'm glad you came to find me,' responded, Adairia reaching up a hand to cup Isla's cheek.

'Me too,' she whispered back, raising her own hand to cover Adairia's.

Slowly, Adairia moved forward to eclipse the space between them and felt her body press up against Isla's soft flesh beneath the water. It felt a little magical. She leaned in to kiss the other woman who responded with enthusiasm, wrapping her arms around Adairia's waist, and pulling her closer, if that was at all possible. It was invigorating to feel the other woman's body against hers while the water rippled around them and Adairia could not help but whimper aloud.

'We don't do this enough,' sighed Isla between kisses.

205

Adairia could only murmur her agreement; *what was there to say?*

Adairia stroked the backs of her hands along Isla's shoulders and then flipped them over so she could travel further down her back. When she reached low enough beneath the water, she cradled the red-head's backside in her palms; *it was a lovely rear,* she thought, squeezing the flesh a little harder. Isla's mouth twitched in a grin beneath Adairia's mouth, thrilled by the other woman's palpable desire. When she broke their kiss Adairia let out a groan of disappointment and gave Isla the look of a spoiled child whose ice-cream had been confiscated.

Isla laughed but she did not return to the kiss. Instead, she patted the stone behind Adairia, indicating that she should lever herself up ever so slightly so that she was sitting on the edge of the pool. Anticipating what was to come next Adairia did as instructed and pulled herself up so only her calves and feet dangled in the warm water. She did not need to worry about feeling the cold. Adairia's entire body was on fire. She watched mesmerised as Isla's gaze drank her in. As abashed as she felt about being so thoroughly on display, she resisted the temptation to cover herself with her arms. Instead, Adairia took the opportunity to enjoy the sight on display to her. Isla stood, submerged from the waist down, one breast obscured by the brilliant red curls that fell from her head. If there were goddesses surely this is what they must look like, supposed Adairia. She was only made more certain of Isla's divine status when the other woman lowered herself to her knees and continued to kiss Adairia, if only a little lower.

*

'Tell me about your day?' requested Adairia as they lay tangled together in the shallows sometime later.

'Well, I know I'm only a stand-in member of the council, but I can't tell you how glad I'll be when I can leave this new vocation behind,' Isla snorted.

'That bad huh?' Adairia sighed.

'Worse,' nodded Isla.

As a member of parliament Isla had seemed like the obvious choice to stand-in while the council's numbers were so diminished. What with the death of the ex-chancellor Aliya, and the resignation of Tronk, the goblin representative, stability was in short supply and Isla at least knew the protocol. Isla had of course accepted the temporary position, but it was with a certain trepidation. Ever since the Lady Mirin's announcement at Aliya's wake everyone had been on high alert. The fairy representative certainly had some strong opinions on the running of things, and she was perfectly comfortable taking advantage of her new self-appointed position to implement them. It was clear no one had been able to think of an appropriate reason to refuse her the position of chancellor, at least in the interim, given that she was the longest standing member of the council after Aliya, but that did not mean everyone was happy about it.

In the back of everyone's minds were the increasing shortages in grain supply to the surrounding countryside, and how they might eventually impact the university. In light of this, or so she said, Lady Mirin was continuously arguing for the closure of the foundling program.

'The university cannot afford to continue taking in other people's unwanted offspring in these anxious times', were the words Isla parroted back to Adairia, accompanied by a grinding of the teeth that she was sure the Lady Mirin had not mirrored.

207

For the time being, Cyril and Isla had steadfastly fought against this proposition, with the head librarian Angus refusing to participate in the debate. But, as Isla had informed Adairia, the Lady Mirin seemed quite willing to take her proposals to the parliament if she could not get the support she desired from the interim council.

'And I don't think it's only me she wants rid of.' Isla sighed. 'She is constantly at poor Cyril's throat about one thing or another. You would think they would be more amenable to one another after so long, but it seems Aliya truly was the glue that held them all together.'

Adairia wanted to tell Isla not to worry. She wanted Isla to tell her not to worry, that everything would be back to normal any day now. It did not ring quite true though, and neither of them said it. Although, mused Adairia to herself, perhaps it was not the time to worry, perhaps it was the time to act.

Chapter Twenty-Seven
Grain Shortages

The next morning Isla and Adairia reluctantly disentangled themselves from the bed they had eventually relocated to the previous night. Adairia had made Isla promise to rise early so they could eat breakfast with Morag and Calder, a ritual she sorely missed. The four of them were seated lazily around one of the tables in the now mostly empty dining hall, plates and bowls stacked high and warm mugs clasped in their hands. Morag picked distractedly at the remnants on her plate as she read through a pile of parchment sheets covered in complicated diagrams, while Adairia allowed Isla to rest her head groggily on her shoulder as she drunk her tea. They had been occupying a quiet silence for some time when Calder interrupted everyone's reverie.

'I was helping unload the monthly grain supply from the farmers this morning,' he mused.

'Uh huh?' replied Adairia, only half interested in this line of conversation while staring down at her brew.

'I think it'd be generous to say we were sent fifty percent of the usual weight,' he continued.

This got everyone's attention. Adairia set down her mug and was unsurprised to find both Morag and Isla's gaze fixed on Calder when she looked up. Meanwhile, he simply shrugged under the three women's scrutiny.

'Was there some sort of mistake?' Isla asked.

'Doesn't seem that way. One of the other lads asked when the rest would arrive, but the driver said that's all there was coming. Said the *chancellor* was already aware and had signed off the delivery.' He spoke the Lady Mirin's new title with the air of someone who had drunk curdled milk by mistake.

'This wasn't discussed at the council meeting?' Morag asked Isla, clearly knowing what response to expect.

'It most certainly was not. She didn't say anything about this during our last conversation. That is something I most certainly would have remembered.'

'We've all heard about the shortages elsewhere though,' Adairia pointed out.

'There's been no indication it had spread this far south, however. At least not that I've been informed about.' Isla pushed her chair from the table, glowering at her half-finished breakfast. 'I think you'll have to excuse me; I'd like to pay the Lady Mirin a visit this morning.' And with a squeeze of Adairia's shoulder she was gone, leaving the other three to exchange uneasy looks.

Adairia, Morag, and Calder finished their breakfasts in companionable silence. At least, it was companionable for Adairia. She could not help but notice Calder regularly sneaking glances at Morag over his food while she seemed determined not to meet his gaze. She would have to confront them about this if they did not volunteer whatever was going on before long. A lot had happened since Adairia had left the university and returned; some of it she could not help but feel she was not as well informed on as the rest.

When all three of them left the dining hall to set out for their

210

separate activities Adairia hoped she would be able to find Isla before too long, so she could ask how her conversation with the Lady Mirin had gone. What she was not expecting was to find both of them arguing loudly in the main foyer of the university itself. Their raised voices had been muffled by the high ceilings and thick stone walls but now that Adairia, Morag, and Calder were in the chamber with them it was impossible to ignore. In fact, their disagreement had begun to attract a small crowd of onlookers who were exchanging wary glances and whispering amongst themselves.

There was one group of faces that Adairia did not recognise, even from passing, though. This small cluster of figures stood slightly back from the two irate women, huddling amongst themselves. They all looked rather downtrodden, like they had not had a clean change of clothes in weeks now. One little girl looked particularly drawn, the hair that escaped her braid hanging limply around her face as she clung to an older woman's leg who might have been her mother. It did not take long, however, before it was made clear who exactly these people were, or why they were there at least.

'This is an academic institute Lady Isla, not a homeless shelter.' The Lady Mirin's words were firm and steady, but her fury was evident in her expression.

'This academic institute has always opened its doors to those with nowhere else to go, chancellor.' They used one another's titles like barbed insults.

'Not always,' Lady Mirin retorted. 'I think you'll find that development only came about in the last century. That may seem like forever to a human like you, but it is a mere blip in the lifespan of the fae.'

'I will not allow you to turn this family away,' Isla practically snarled. 'You may have appointed yourself chancellor of this university in the wake of Aliya's death, but I sit alongside you as a peer in Albiyon's parliament and you cannot continually do as you please without accounting for your actions.'

'This is rich coming from the one whose peerage is a result of who their grandfather was. I, on the other hand, was chosen by my people to represent them. Who chose to appoint you champion of the homeless and hapless?' Lady Mirin snorted cruelly as she watched Isla's face redden before the gathered onlookers. 'We simply cannot afford to feed any extra mouths. Our supplies will not allow for it.'

'Oh yes, I heard about those diminished supplies this morning. Were you trying to hide it from the rest of us?'

'Hardly. I am not your keeper human girl. If you cannot be bothered to keep abreast of the university's ongoing situation then you are not fit to sit on this council, even as a temporary measure.'

Adairia watched as Isla's hands bunched into fists at her side. Before she could step forward to take Isla's side, however, another figure joined the throngs. This one pushed past the rest of the bodies to the front, clearly on a mission, though uncomfortable about the audience. Adairia quickly recognised him as Derek, one of the regular postal carriers that travelled between the University and the other settlements of Albiyon to transport messages and parcels. Today he clutched in his hands two scrolls bound in black ribbon, which he proffered up to the two women.

'What is it?' snapped the Lady Mirin, finally allowing the full extent of her frustration to show.

'Urgent messages for Ladies Mirin and Isla from the parliament,' Derek mumbled, holding out both scrolls awkwardly. Each woman took the one nearest to them impatiently and unfurled it.

Adairia watched as the two women scanned their documents, jumping edgily from one foot to the other and chewing her lip to stop herself from interrupting Isla's reading process. It was difficult. Finally, it seemed after an age had passed, did the red-head look up from her own letter. She immediately caught Adairia's eyes in the crowd that surrounded them. It was not a comforting look, and Adairia dashed to her side, her concern growing.

'I have to go to parliament. There's been a petition put forward by the community of Verulamium and it needs the whole parliament in session to vote on it.' Isla glanced over at the Lady Mirin who had finished reading her own scroll. 'I'll have to leave today.'

'What could possibly be so important?' Adairia responded in surprise. It was clear from the look on Isla's face that something was upsetting her, in addition to the scene that had already unfolded this morning.

'They want to ban the free movement of Albiyan citizens into their town, effectively putting up a border between themselves and the rest of the realm.' She had lowered her voice significantly and kept glancing around at their spectators. 'I say they, but of course it's just the noisiest group. However, they're big enough, and they're threatening to build a wall if the parliament doesn't enforce the policy on their behalf.'

'What?' Morag exclaimed. 'Where has this come from?'

'Something about limited resources. They haven't provided all of the details in the summons but there's no ignoring it.'

'Yes, well, Lady Isla, time to serve your people,' interjected the Lady Mirin, her own expression significantly less downcast.

213

'I suppose I will see you in parliament.' And with a twirl of her long silver dress, she absconded the entryway, leaving devastation in her wake. Isla meanwhile cast her gaze around for someone and spotted Cyril in the crowd.

'Will you make sure this family have somewhere to sleep and meals in their bellies?' Isla asked. 'I'm not leaving without knowing they'll be safe here.' She scowled back in the direction Lady Mirin had headed.

'Don't worry,' he nodded. 'This is what we do.'

Isla turned back to Adairia.

'I don't know how long I'll be gone.' She took the other woman's hand in her own.

'Just write to me when you get there, let me know that you've arrived,' Adairia reassured her, giving Isla a half-hearted smile.

'At least I'm not the only one who will be gone,' Isla glowered, jerking her head in the direction Lady Mirin had departed.

'We'll take care of her.' Interrupted Calder who had sidled up to them, casually slapping Isla on the back.

Morag rolled her eyes, but Adairia had to confess she was glad Calder was there to dispel the tension that had mounted in the entrance hall.

'I've no doubt you will.' Isla smiled, and it was a real smile this time.

Extract from An Introduction to Dragons

It is a common misconception that all dragons are blessed with the capacity for flight. Depending on wing size and strength some dragons may never fly, while illustrations of pure-bred hydratic dragons usually depict this elusive sub-species with no wings at all. Aetherial dragons are, in fact, the only sub-species that fly in their infancy, endowed with large wings and slight frames from birth. For the pyratic and chthonic dragons, first flights can occur anywhere in the first year. If they remain flightless beyond this, however, it is unlikely they will ever develop an aptitude (although there are always exceptions).

Chapter Twenty-Eight
Teething Problems

Both Fia and Adairia waved farewell from the ground as they watched Isla and Tearlach fly away, not knowing when they would next be together again. Fia, who was equally as forlorn as Adairia at the departure of their friends, had attempted to follow at first, jumping as high as she could and flapping her wings, but to no avail.

'You'll get there,' Adairia reassured her but the young dragon only gave a dissatisfied snort in response.

'Gods, you remind me of a teenager sometimes,' said Adairia, shaking her head.

'What's a teenager?' asked Fia, curiosity rousing her from her sulk.

'It's when humans are not children anymore but nor are they quite adults. It's pretty rough to be honest.' Adairia scratched her head reflecting on her own teenage years. 'Your body changes, your emotions are unpredictable, and no one seems to take you seriously. Makes you pretty impatient in my experience.'

'Hmm,' mused Fia, 'I don't think dragons have teenagers. Tearlach hasn't mentioned anything about them to me.'

'Well, maybe dragons should consider the idea.' Adairia laughed heartily as Fia frowned nonplussed down at her.

Fia had asked if she could spend the night in Adairia's old room now that Isla and Tearlach were gone, but Adairia had to explain that there was no way she could fit in her chambers anymore, let alone squeeze through the university corridors to get there. She understood Fia's desire for company, however, and offered instead to bed down with her in the barn. This seemed to placate the young dragon and when dusk fell on the university grounds they settled in together for the night; Fia curled in the haystacks while Adairia lay at her side and wrapped a thick downy blanket around herself to keep out the cold. It was not long before they were both fast asleep.

*

'Come on, Fia. Get up,' Adairia sighed, scratching the dragon behind one of her ears in a gentle attempt to rouse her. In response, she only opened one eye part of the way while letting out a cavernous yawn and closing it again.

'You're the one who said you wanted to practice flying this morning while it was quiet,' Adairia added.

'Oh fine,' Fia responded after a long pause. She kept her eyes closed but unfurled each leg one at a time and proceeded to stretch her whole body out as long as it would go, forcing Adairia to back away if she wanted to remain standing.

After a few more grumblings and toothy yawns, the two set out from the barn to a large empty field where the ground sloped up at quite a dramatic angle towards the woods. This had become a semi-regular affair now for the two of them, although Adairia knew Fia occasionally came out here with Tearlach as well, when her companion was occupied elsewhere. Neither trainer had been awarded much success as of yet though.

'Start with a run,' encouraged Adairia once she had climbed

217

onto the dragon's back.

Fia knew the score and began jogging on the flat of the field before speeding up to what must have been the dragon equivalent of a sprint and flapping her wings at an increasing pace to match. Although the sensation made Adairia feel as though she were soaring through the sky, Fia's feet never left the ground for more than a couple of seconds at a time. Next, she attempted to use the slope for leverage but, although her jump had her entire body off the ground for a moment or two, she very quickly came back in contact with the earth, much to her annoyance.

'I think you're landing is definitely smoother though!' Adairia cheered. 'I managed to keep my grip that time.' Fia did not look comforted by these words, however. 'I'm sorry Fi,' Adairia added, squeezing the dragon's neck from behind with both arms in an attempt at a hug.

'I've had enough,' Fia stated with finality, sitting down on her haunches so Adairia could clamber back down to the ground.

'We could get some food then try again this afternoon, I'm sure no one will mind.' As the morning had proceeded the sleepy castle had begun to stir and they had started to see various figures making their way between buildings to carry out whatever tasks they had waiting for them that day.

'No,' replied Fia. 'No more today. I'm going hunting.'

Adairia took that to mean that the young dragon wanted to be alone, so she nodded her acquiescence. As much as she wished she could cheer her friend she also wanted to respect Fia's need for space. This was much harder for the dragon than it was for her, she had to constantly remind herself.

'I'll go back up to the university in that case. I'd like to find out what happened to the family from yesterday.' Adairia explained. 'Just call if you need me.' Fia simply snorted and turned towards the woods leaving Adairia to watch as she trudged away.

*

Fia's bad mood was still lingering in the back of Adairia's mind as she set off for the main building, but she instead tried to focus on her own task for the afternoon. It was difficult to articulate her curiosity regarding the family who had arrived yesterday. As a foundling, raised by the university, she had always felt a particular gratitude for this function of the institution. Not only was this where she slept and worked but she was invested in the way it was run, and listening to the Lady Mirin talk so derisively of its role as a refuge the day before had set her blood boiling. She had to admit, a small part of her interest was also motivated by a sense of loyalty she held for Isla. The other woman's passion for her role in government and the wellbeing of Albiyon was infectious, and Adairia did not want to let her down in her absence.

After searching a few different rooms and alcoves Adairia finally tracked down Cyril in the small section of the museum dedicated to goblin history. He was engaged in an animated discussion with one of the few goblin students who had chosen to travel from the mountains in order to study at the university. They were both pouring over some contraption that looked as though it was used for digging based on the part that reminded her of a trowel. The numerous additional appendages were a mystery to Adairia, who knew little to nothing about mining in the practical sense. Goblins, on the other hand, had made some of the most impressive advancements in this area over the centuries and many of their inventions had revolutionised mining practices along with other industries.

'Adairia, lovely to see you,' Cyril exclaimed as he spotted her entering the small chamber. 'What brings you here?'

'I was actually looking for you but can come back later if you're giving a lesson.' She smiled at the young goblin who gave her a toothy grin in return, two baby tusks poking out from the corners of his mouth.

'I think Sticks here is the one teaching me,' Cyril laughed. 'He's quite the engineering prodigy.' The goblin, Sticks, looked a little abashed.

'Thank you, Sir.'

'It's only the truth,' Cyril insisted. 'What do you say Sticks, pick this up later?'

'Absolutely. I've had a few thoughts I'd like to sketch out whilst they're fresh in my mind anyway.'

'Wonderful.' Cyril turned to Adairia as Sticks hurried away clearly focused on whatever inspiration had taken him. 'What can I help you with my dear?'

'I wanted to ask you what happened to the family from yesterday?'

'Ah yes,' nodded Cyril, his face taking on a more serious expression. 'Well, don't worry, we got them settled into one of the family outhouses. I told them to take a little time to readjust but the mother has already volunteered her services as a stable hand and the children seemed quite curious about the school, so hopefully we can get them into some classes later this week.' Adairia found Cyril's words reassuring but she was still concerned with what had brought the family so far from their home in the first place.

'Did you ask them more about what brought them here?'

'Briefly but they were pretty rattled after that scene with the chancellor.' Cyril pursed his lips as if the mere act of referring to the Lady Mirin as chancellor of the university put a sour taste in his mouth. 'I didn't want to press them too much on their first night. From what I can tell they were not the only family in their village considering abandoning their homes or farmsteads. They were just the first to accept they couldn't support themselves on what was coming in anymore. The mother seemed particularly worried about the baby; it did look a little on the scrawny side.'

'Do you think they would mind me paying them a visit?' Adairia asked a little awkwardly. She did not want to sound pushy, but Cyril simply gave her an understanding smile.

'I am quite sure they would welcome your company. The little girl in particular seemed quite enamoured by the idea that there was a dragon living at the university, well, two at the time. I'm sure she would love to chew your ear off.' This made Adairia grin.

After thanking Cyril profusely and receiving specific instructions on which outhouse she could find their new residents in, Adairia bid him farewell and set off from the museum. Although numerous scholars, students, and other workers lived within the walls of the university there were very few suites large enough to accommodate families within the main building. Over the years, therefore, various clusters of outhouses had been built to accommodate those who raised families while on the grounds or came here accompanied by partners and children. It was one of these buildings that Adairia made her way to, breathing in deeply the late morning air and hoping Fia was alright by herself. Eventually she came to a small two-bedroom hut and rapped lightly on the brightly painted yellow door with her fist. Adairia waited patiently for

221

a couple of minutes until finally the door was opened from the inside and she was greeted by the sight of a tall, burly man with long unruly golden hair and a coarse beard, a baby wrapped tightly to his chest in thick swathes of fabric. He smiled when he saw her, but it did nothing to distract from the otherwise harassed expression on his face.

'Hello there, whit can ah dae ye for?'

Chapter Twenty-Nine
Questions and Answers

Ten minutes later, Adairia found herself sitting at a small wooden dining table with a mug full of hot peppermint tea. The man who had answered the door, and who she now knew as Bryce, was sat opposite her, the baby now unwrapped from their swaddling and tugging playfully on their father's beard. Meanwhile a little girl and an even littler boy peered at her from one of the two-bedroom doorways, not quite willing to fully enter the main living area. Coyly Adairia wiggled a few fingers in their direction, but this only made them turn to one another and exchange whispered conversation.

'Adairia, huh, that wid make ye yin o' the dragon companions. Like the lass who stood up fir us yesterday wi' the chancellor,' Bryce mused.

'Aye, although I'm pretty new to that title.' She smiled as she heard a little gasp come from the direction of where the two children stood.

'Ye have a dragon?' The little girl had stepped further into the main room towards Adairia, curiosity clearly overriding fear.

'Well, I'm not sure I *have* Fia, but she is my companion. I can introduce her to you sometime. If your parents don't mind that is.' She glanced back to Bryce who shrugged his consent.

'I'm going to be a dragon companion one day too.' The little girl puffed out her chest.

'No, you're no,' interrupted her brother defiantly. 'There aren't any more dragons who need a companion.' Both children's complexions were darker than their father's, presumably taking after their mother, and while the boy's hair was cropped close to his skull the little girl's was braided neatly in tiny rows down her scalp.

'Well,' mused Adairia diplomatically, 'that doesn't mean there won't be one day, dragons can always lay more eggs. I'm sure you could both be dragon companions if you wanted.'

Adairia had to admit she had not thought much on the subject before now and she wondered why none of the dragons she had met had given birth to their own children over the years. That was something she would have to ask the others when she next saw them, she thought.

'I don't want to be a dragon companion.' Replied the little boy whose father gave him a stern look, but Adairia was not offended.

'In that case, I'm sure you could be whatever you want to be when you grow up,' she smiled.

'I want to be a horse,' was his proud response. Adairia almost spat out her tea, instantly regretting her assurance that the young boy could be whatever he wanted. His father, however, let out a loud guffaw.

'Their mither, my wife Shona, is a horse trainer,' he explained to Adairia. 'Born and raised aroond the creatures, the both o' them.' He rubbed the baby's back thoughtfully. 'Three o' them now, I suppose. The dragon companion is cried Ashleigh, the horse is Chris, and the howler here is wee Jessie.' He nodded his head in the direction of each of his children in turn.

'It is an honour to meet you all.' Adairia replied causing the two older children to turn to one another and start giggling conspiratorially.

'Well, Adairia dragon companion, whit brings ye here?' Bryce interrupted.

'Sorry, yes, of course. I hope you don't mind me visiting but I wanted to learn a little more about what brought you here. What's going on in the rural villages? If it's not too intrusive to ask,' she added.

'Intrusive?' Bryce snorted. 'If only we could get mair people tae listen.'

Adairia, therefore, listened intently as Bryce explained how he and his family's circumstances had reversed in the space of a year. His wife Shona was a well-respected horse trainer who travelled regularly for her work to wherever her skills were in demand. Meanwhile he was responsible for the everyday running of their home and helped supplement their income with a small plot where he grew mostly vegetables; some of which he and his family ate, others he sold at the local market. Listening to Bryce talk about his work made her think of her own garden. She could not help but feel a growing affinity with this imposing giant of a man who clearly tended so diligently to his plants and his children, speaking of them so warmly that there was no doubt in Adairia's mind there was nothing he would rather pass his time doing.

'At first, we thought it was simply a bad winter reaping its rewards, but it didnae get any better. Even the hardiest vegetables werenae taking, and it wasnae jist us either. Naebody could grow anything and if there's nowt tae grow, then there's nout tae trade. We've aw had bad yields in the past, but we also kent we could rely on grains and other surplus being brought

225

in fae elsewhere in the country tae cover the loss. We always made sure tae share whatever extra we'd hud in the past, assuming others would dae the same fir us if the time came. That's how it's supposed tae work.' He sighed heavily.

'But no this time. The grain stopped showing up and when we asked where it wis, we were telt that it was oor responsibility tae feed oorselves, the state couldnae organise oor meals for us. But neither could we.' Bryce glanced in the direction of his children. 'A few faimilies moved oot before we did, traivellin' to stay wi' relatives in other parts of Albiyon but neither my wife or I have any living faimily beside oor bairns. If it wis just the two o' us it might have been different, but we've got three extra mooths tae feed and when the littlest one was born too early, we couldnae get the weight oan her nae matter how hard we tried. So, we finally decided tae pack up the essentials and come here. Didnae quite expect the reception we received, but I suppose tensions are high everywhere.'

At first Adairia could not think what to say and simply sat there chewing her lip. How had she heard nothing about this? True, the village of Understone was rural, and at more than a hundred miles from the University they did not have a lot of unprompted contact. But surely the criers or postal carriages would have brought news of a township going short of food supplies in only the space of a year. Was this an isolated incident? The implication of all these declining grain deliveries, including to the university itself, made her doubt it. In the past few months, it was clear, however, that she had allowed herself to forget about the world beyond her own trials and tribulations.

'I don't know if there is anything I specifically can do to help,' she finally responded.

'You heard oor story. And going by your willingness tae listen am going to hazard a guess that you're also the type tae ask questions. Keep daein tha' and I'll be happy tae cry ye a friend Adairia, dragon companion.' Adairia smiled sadly at the man who sat before her, bouncing his scrawny baby in his arms and nodded.

Adairia.

Adairia's brow furrowed at the sound of her name. The voice had not come from the inside the house itself, though, it had cried out in her mind alone.

Fia? She thought.

Adairia?

The dragon called her name again but there was no hint of fear to her tone, although perhaps a drop of trepidation.

Has something happened? Adairia responded in her head.

I… I'm not sure. Fia's voice sounded uncertain, something Adairia was unfamiliar with. If the dragon was anything, she was usually confident, warranted or not. *Can you come find me?*

Where are you? Adairia replied without hesitation.

The woods.

Adairia stood abruptly from her seat. Looking back down at her still seated host she caught sight of Bryce's own confusion as he stared back at her. A small pang of embarrassment washed over her and she grinned back at him abashedly. He, of course, had heard nothing of her exchange.

'Sorry, it's Fia, my dragon companion, she needs my… assistance.'

'She can communicate wi' ye when yer apart?' He looked surprised but curious all the same.

'Aye, all dragons and their companions can.' Adairia smiled. 'Maybe your daughter will tell you about it someday.' She winked in the direction of the little girl who had been watching intently all this time.

'Mayhap she will.' Bryce chuckled. 'Well please, dinnae delay oan oor account. Go, go.' He stood to accompany her to the door. 'It was a pleasure tae meet ye Adairia. I hope we'll see ye again.'

'Count on it.' She grinned back and hurried from the house.

What could possibly be going on?

Chapter Thirty
In Bloom

It must have taken Adairia at least thirty minutes to walk from the home that Bryce and his family were lodging in to the woods on the other side of the university. In all that time Fia had not communicated anything else through their telepathic connection, leaving Adairia to fret nervously as she sought out her companion. *There is no need to panic,* she continuously assured herself. Fia would have let her know if there was a reason to panic. But Adairia had always been inclined to panic.

Adairia? Finally, she heard Fia's voice in her mind.

Fia! Where are you? she answered in kind.

Just a little further ahead. I can smell you.

This information sped Adairia up so that she began hastily kicking aside leaves and branches that were otherwise slowing her passage. The earth beneath the trees was strewn with pine needles from the hardy firs that had managed to battle out the sharp chill in the air. The same could not be said for all the trees and foliage, but even in the winter the forest was beautiful. What was once lush greens, bright purples, and dazzling yellows, was now dark russets and cool silvers, as though nature had switched her wardrobe for a different ball. As much as Adairia usually missed the spring and summer months, when her allotment required most of her attention, she could hardly complain that winter was not keeping her busy; unlike previous years she had not found herself wishing the time away. Finally, Adairia pushed through a thick wall of gorse bush to see Fia standing stock still in a small clearing.

'There you are,' she said aloud, relieved to finally be reunited.

'Adairia, look!' Fia did not turn around but simply remained staring at the ground beneath her feet.

So, Adairia looked. She followed the dragon's gaze to settle her eyes on an unexpected sight. The patch of ground upon which Fia stood was in stark contrast with the rest of the forest around them. Instead of pine needles and hard earth there were blooms in every colour imaginable; pink tulips, purple crocuses, and yellow daffodils jumped out at Adairia who was momentarily stunned. She considered herself well-versed in seasonal agriculture, but this did not make any sense. What were thriving spring flowers doing growing here, at this time of year?

'That's strange,' she eventually murmured before her neck snapped back up. 'Is it a spell? Some sort of fairy circle? Are you trapped?' The pitch of her voice climbed higher with each question as her anxiety grew.

'No, Adairia, look!' Fia seemed more restless now, as if there were something Adairia was not quite comprehending. To demonstrate she shifted her gait and stretched a foreleg out to settle outside of the miniature wild garden. A few seconds passed before anything happened, but slowly Adairia watched as green shoots began to break free of the earth at Fia's feet. Before her eyes the stems unfurled and opened to reveal pale indigo petals that fanned out like delicate dresses: bluebells, she realised.

'How are you doing that?' Adairia practically yelped.

'I don't know. Adairia, help! I can't control it.' Fia slumped back so she was sitting on her hind legs and let out a pitiful mewl.

'Fia, it's going to be alright.' Adairia had walked around so that she was at the dragon's side and put a hand on her long, scaly neck. The flowers were crushed beneath her feet, but they were undeniably real.

*

Eventually, the two companions trudged back towards the university, leaving Fia's impromptu flowerbed behind as soon as they stepped outside the forest boundaries. Adairia wanted to offer Fia answers, but she had no idea where to find them. Suddenly it hit her how alone they were right then. The chancellor had passed, the rest of the dragons and their companions had returned to their lives, and even Isla and Tearlach had had to leave. Adairia had only turned her studies to dragonlore these past few months and Fia had been a part of this world an even shorter span of time. As her anxiety began to rise some of those feelings must have bubbled over and begun to pour into Fia's own mind.

'Adairia!' she said sharply, hoping to bring the young woman back to the world. 'We're not alone. I've never felt alone my entire life, even if that hasn't been a long one yet. We have each other. We have Calder and Morag. We have the university and all its stores of knowledge at our disposal.' The dragon pondered for a moment. 'Although I think you'll have to bring the books outside to tell me what's inside them because I've definitely outgrown those library stacks.' This made Adairia give a small chuckle that loosened the tension in her stomach ever so slightly.

231

'It's so strange to think that little more than a season ago I had never met you, and now I can't imagine my life without you Fia.' She paused midstride to lean against the dragon's shoulder and let out a deep sigh. Then she laughed for a second time.

'Tearlach did say that dragons bonded to those they felt akin to, even if subconsciously. Maybe you were always destined to be a gardener.'

At these words, Fia let out her own burst of dragon laughter that echoed much further and louder than any sound Adairia could make. They both smiled at each other, basking in their connection for the passing of a heartbeat until Adairia let out a throaty exclamation that took Fia by surprise.

'What is it?' the dragon asked, concern marring her features.

'You're a gardener!' Adairia replied at which Fia's confusion only deepened. 'I mean that's exactly what you are. Your connection to me, my connection to you, our connection to the land, it's what we share at our very core. Like Tearlach and Isla's pursuit of justice.'

'Usually, I'd say we were on the same page Adairia but I admit, you've lost me somewhere along the way.'

'There are four kinds of dragons. Hydratic, aethereal, pyratic, and chthonic. I read all about them in *An Introduction to Dragons*. Think about it, we didn't know what kind you were; until now that is. You're a chthonic dragon Fia, you have to be.' Fia stared at her as Adairia ran with her train of thought. 'Cthonic dragons get their power from the land. They're connected to the earth and what grows there.'

'They can make things grow?' Fia asked, starting to mirror Adairia's excitement.

'They must! That would explain what just happened.'

'So, I'm not a pyratic dragon like Greer?' Fia added. 'Why did no one suggest this before?'

'The book... well, the book said chthonic dragons were extinct. None have been recorded for centuries, maybe even a millennium.'

'Well obviously I'm not extinct,' said Fia, suddenly indignant. She had latched onto the idea that she was a chthonic dragon with gusto and could not help but feel offended at the suggestion that her kind had been dismissed by whoever wrote this *Introduction to Dragons*.

'Your egg had been in the museum for hundreds of years Fia. Maybe you are the last of your kind...' This statement left a silence in its wake that neither friend knew how to respond to at first. Adairia eventually broke the quiet. 'We can't be sure though; we don't even know how to check if you are a chthonic dragon or if that's why you affected the seeds that were hibernating in the forest earlier. First things first, we need to do some more reading and maybe even write to some of our friends. They might be able to help us find the answers even if they don't have them themselves. And in the meantime, there is absolutely no reason to worry.' There was a certainty to Adairia's tone that she was not sure she felt but Fia simply nodded in return.

'No reason to worry.'

*

'Cthonic dragons?' Morag mused aloud.

'Always knew there was something special about ye wee yin,' Calder chuckled and patted Fia on her rather-larger-than-wee shoulder.

'We all knew she was special Calder, it wasn't exactly a well-kept secret,' Morag scolded, but Calder simply stuck out his tongue and continued to smile proudly.

'Well, it seems to fit,' interrupted Adairia.

All four friends were sitting huddled in a covered courtyard, the humans wrapped in their heaviest coats and scarves while clutching warm mugs of tea that were cooling quickly. It was not exactly the weather for leisurely sunbathing, but Fia's bulk had long exceeded the capacity of any rooms inside the university. While the barn that Tearlach had occupied for so many months usually suited their needs, no one was supposed to take any of the library books out of the immediate university grounds and this square, cloistered between various official buildings, seemed to skirt well enough within the rules.

'Look here.' Adairia held up the slightly mouldering leather-bound book in her hand and pointed a finger at the open page. 'It says that Cthonic dragons have close ties to the land. They can fertilize soil by simply touching it and even heal dying plants. I suppose that's how you made the flowers in the woods bloom earlier Fia. The potential was already there but you just… sped it up.'

'But I didn't mean to,' Fia frowned.

'Maybe it starts sporadically at first?' Calder ruminated. 'Pyratic dragons start burping flames without any control over it when they reach a certain maturity, so I guess the same could be true of this.'

'Makes sense,' Nodded Morag. 'They just wouldn't know to write it down in the dragon texts because there hasn't been a chthonic dragon to study in living memory.'

'Well, it also explains why you've been having trouble flying Fia,' Adairia continued. 'It says here that cthonic dragons have more difficulty learning to fly because of their strong attachment to the ground. Aetherial dragons fly from their first

234

month and pyratic dragons find it relatively easy to learn, but it it's harder for cthonic and hydratic dragons. Some hydratic dragons aren't even born with wings apparently.'

'But I will be able to fly, won't I?' Fia sounded slightly desperate and Adairia's heart strained against her chest.

'I shouldn't see why not. It doesn't say you won't learn eventually, you might just be a late bloomer.' She stroked the dragon under the chin soothingly.

'This is really exciting though Fia,' Calder jumped in. 'You're the only dragon alive who can do what you can do! You're unique.'

'I suppose you're right.' Responded Fia. She lifted her head higher as if trying on a little pride for size.

'Damn right I'm right. Imagine what you can do with those powers. We depend on the land for food. You could help so many people.'

'There's an interesting thought.' Morag ruminated; her eyes focused intently on the contents of her mug. 'There's been one or two grain shortages recently...'

'See!' Calder exclaimed. 'You might be able to help the farmers whose harvests aren't yielding.'

'I wonder if that's exactly what someone else thought.' Morag replied, her tone less excited than Calder's.

'What do you mean?' asked Adairia.

'We know someone, or someones, has put Fia's life in danger at least once now. What if the two things are connected? What if said someone doesn't want Fia interfering in whatever is causing the grain shortages?'

'How would they have even known she was a chthonic dragon?' Calder scowled.

'We don't know what they know, do we? The documents

that were missing from the archive, the one's that should have accompanied Fia's egg, they could have said anything.'

No one knew quite what to say to that.

Extract from an Introduction to Dragons

Dragons are typically a carnivorous species. There is nothing to prevent them from consuming vegetation and they have been known to survive off it when nothing else is available. It is not their preferred diet, however. Their size, strength, and intelligence make them excellent hunters, ideally suited to the wild. The pyratic, aethereal and presumably chthonic dragon species prefer red meat such as deer or cattle, whereas the hydratic dragon typically favours fish. While in the past disputes have been documented between the owners of livestock and dragons who have helped themselves, the dragons are generally respectful of such social boundaries.

Chapter Thirty-One
Cthonic

Dear Isla,

I know you've only been gone four days, but your absence has been felt, as has Tearlach's. I confess, I never thought I'd notice another person's absence so fiercely after such a short time, but then I never thought I'd feel anything so strongly before I met you. It's been less than a year and you are already so much a part of my life that I keep turning to tell you things, but you're not there. I could hardly write a new letter for every passing thought, or you would have been receiving post every few hours since you departed. So here I am, finally, sat down to write to you and everything I wanted to say has vanished. How can I explain everything that we've discovered since you left without being able to see your reactions and talk them over with you immediately? How can I wait for your responses in a letter? Well, I guess I'll just have to.

I know the reasons for your leaving were important, and I can only hope you and the other members of parliament are finding some resolution to the realm's problems. Here we have uncovered some more information regarding Fia's origins. When we were in the forest the other day Fia made a surprising discovery – she was able to bring forth the spring blooms that should have continued to sleep for months yet, with simply her touch. She cannot do it at will, but we are almost certain this can only mean one thing, Fia must be a cthonic dragon. All the books I have read suggest that the cthonic dragons died out centuries ago but there doesn't appear to be any other explanation for what happened. Perhaps you can ask Tearlach for his thoughts?

As strange a discovery as it is, I think it would have been a reassuring one if it were not for Morag's observation. She thinks there may be some connection between Fia's abilities and the attempt on her life. I can't help but wonder now, if that also explains the day she called out to me from her egg when we thought someone might have broken into my room? But there is no way of proving that, failing travelling back in time. If there is someone at the university with a vested interest in making certain that Fia's powers are not tested, surely they know something about the increasingly infertile land across Albiyon that we have been hearing of more and more even over the past few days. It seems too coincidental if not. I wonder if you have learnt anymore of what is going on with our farmlands since your trip to parliament?

I wish we could discuss all of this in person, but I realise you have obligations that must be fulfilled. Please know I miss both you and Tearlach, as does Fia. If either of you know of anything else that might shine a light on what we've learned, then we would greatly appreciate your counsel. In the meantime, we will see what we can discover with the help of Morag and Calder, and wait patiently for your reply.

Yours always,
Adairia

Dear Adairia,

I would be lying if I said that I was not shocked by your and Fia's

239

revelation. Neither Tearlach nor I suspected that she might be a cthonic dragon, although we agree there is surely no other explanation for what you reported in your letter. Tearlach wishes he could offer more insight into the situation, but he has never met another cthonic dragon, or known anyone who has. Like you we both feel this is cause for celebration, however, or would if it were not for the anxieties you shared with us.

I think you may be right. There is something insidious at play in our realm that none of my fellow parliament members or I can quite identify. The grain shortages stretch much further than we first suspected. The entire west coast is barren, and it has affected all crops as far as we can tell. Seeminly the only arable land left is in the east but what exists can hardly keep up with demand. As you know there has been ill-feeling spreading amongst certain communities whose fears have spiralled. Some have demanded an end to trading between villages in order to preserve their own stocks, effectively shutting themselves in and turning those that have abandoned their infertile homes away; some have even been accused of carrying a plague that may spread to their fields in turn. There is no evidence of this of course but fear is hard to reckon with, especially when we have yet to identify the cause of their problems. Our problems too it would seem.

I suspect it will be some time yet before I am able to return to the university and speak to you in person. I hope you know what pain that this causes me. If it were not absolutely necessary for us to remain here at parliament, I would hop on Tearlach's back and be with you within the day. I miss you more than words can say.

Yours forever,
Isla

*

'Come on Fia, you can do it!' Calder cheered from the side lines.

Adairia, Fia, Morag, and Calder had all congregated in the currently deserted university allotments. Calder had taken down a long line of wooden fencing that bordered Adairia's own plot, with the promise that he could put it back up just as it had been before. The reason for the deconstruction was to stop Fia from trekking across anyone else's allotment in order to reach the tilled earth in Adairia's. None of them much wanted to incur the wrath of some angry gardeners. Physical obstacles out of the way, Fia now had both her front paws immersed in mud and her eyes squeezed tightly shut.

'I can't look. Did it work?' she groaned.

'Nothing yet,' Adairia consoled, rubbing the dragon's back leg encouragingly. 'Keep trying.'

'Feel the life in the soil,' Morag urged.

'I can feel the soil between my teeth. I don't think that's the problem,' Fia growled back.

'Not like that. Deeper. Reach down deeper with your mind, like when you connect with Adairia. Feel the seeds and bulbs that are buried there and speak to them. Draw them out.' Morag was the only one of the three friends with any practical knowledge of magic, so Adairia and Calder were inclined to listen to her.

'Do as Morag says,' cheered Adairia.

'Talk to those vegetables,' shouted Calder.

'I can't!' Fia finally howled, sitting back on her haunches, a look of defeat spreading across her features. 'I can't fly and now I can't even do this. What kind of excuse for a dragon am I?' The last sentence came out as a mewl that almost brought tears to Adairia's eyes. But she refused to let Fia give up.

'Nothing worth doing is easy. Morag has spent years studying alchemy. I didn't just wake up one day with a green

241

thumb, I worked on it. Calder may have been born with an affinity to animals, I don't know about that, he's close enough to one himself.'

'Oi,' yelled Calder although he continued to smile.

'What I'm trying to say is that everything takes time. You're so young and we've barely started Fia. You just have to keep trying. Even if we don't succeed today, we'll be one step closer to succeeding tomorrow,' Adairia hoped her words had filtered through to Fia but it was difficult to tell. The dragon did drag her tail from where it lay on the flattened earth and stand back up on all fours, which was something.

'I'm tired and I'm hungry,' she scowled stomping her front feet like a stroppy child. That was when Adairia spotted it. A few gangly shoots had sprung up between Fia's claws, and leaves were beginning to sprout from their stems.

'Fia! Look at your feet,' Adairia squealed in delight, also turning Morag and Calder's attention to the plant that was now rising rapidly from the ground.

'What is that?' Fia asked in awe as Adairia clambered round her bulky form to stare more closely at their visitor.

'I think…' Adairia knelt down to push the leaves aside, 'yes, it's a courgette,' at which she leant back to look up at Fia, a wide grin spreading across her face. 'You've grown a courgette.'

'Can you eat it?' Fia asked studying the courgette.

'You can indeed, makes a braw soup,' Calder chuckled. Without a second thought Fia bent down and ripped the entire plant from the earth, swallowing it in one fell swoop.

'That's disgusting.' She grimaced. 'How do you humans eat this watery mush? I'll take meat over that any day.'

'Well, we don't usually eat it raw,' replied Adairia and all three friends burst into fits of delirious giggles.

242

Adairia had to admit that Fia was progressing quicker when it came to harnessing her cthonic powers than when it came to conquering flight. Over the next day they established a routine, which they repeated come rain or shine. Breakfast was followed by some wing exercises that Asha had detailed for them in a letter transcribed by Ode; Adairia had been incredibly grateful for their missive when she had received it. Fia spent her mornings stretching her wings out as far as she could before snapping them back in again, in repetitions of fifty. She would then beat her outstretched wings for a count of one hundred without lifting a single claw from the ground. Something about the exercises seemed to be working as Adairia could clearly feel the definition in Fia's wing muscles increasing when she massaged the aching dragon each night.

Then they would spend the hours before lunch working on Adairia's allotment. Adairia tilled the earth and prepared the ground like she would usually do, while teaching Fia the names of all the different fruits and vegetables she usually planted. This knowledge seemed to aid Fia in rooting each plant out beneath the soil and drawing it forward with more ease. Gradually the plot began to resemble what Adairia would have expected in early spring not mid-winter. The energy Fia expended during each session, however, left her exhausted and ravenous. The dragon was eating twice as much as she usually would every afternoon. But, regardless of how she attempted to keep her strength up, they were no further forward when it came to flight.

Each afternoon without fail Fia would try everything she could think of to lift her ginormous dragon's body from the ground with her wings. She ran at it, jumped into it, even attempting to sneak up on it, but nothing worked. Adairia tried to stay upbeat for Fia's sake but the inevitable look of heartbreak on the dragon's face each evening was hard not to be affected by.

'Look how much stronger your wings are Fia,' she reassured the dragon one night. 'The exercises Asha sent you are definitely doing something.' But Fia merely snorted in response rolling onto her side so she faced away from Adairia.

'Do you want me to sleep in here with you?' Adairia asked gently, hoping to comfort her companion.

'No, go back to the university. I'm done for today,' Fia mumbled in response and Adairia decided not to press her. She had been spending her own evenings mostly cooped up in the library, when Fia was no longer interested in their sessions. She could not help but feel as if she would never be able to learn enough about dragons, but that did not mean she was about to give up trying.

Chapter Thirty-Two
The Chancellor Returns

Adairia took her usual seat in one of the quieter library reading rooms and set about taking notes on her most recent choice of tome. She nodded at a couple of fellow residents poring over their own books and waved when she caught sight of the young goblin Sticks walking past with a precarious pile of scrolls bundled in his arms. He smiled back, unable to free his hands and shuffled off to one of the larger tables in the centre of the room set up especially for rolling out large maps or diagrams that one might want to examine in more detail.

It was an amenable environment to work in. Everyone with their heads down concentrating on their own work, only the occasionally whispered exchange between two passing colleagues or the rustle of papers to disrupt the silence. Over the past few days, Adairia had been stopped by a number of people in the corridors remarking on her flourishing allotment. Each time she had provided an increasingly abridged summary of Fia's involvement. It was not exactly natural to see courgettes and carrots springing up with frost on the ground and snow on the horizon.

Of course, everything they had successfully grown together to maturity Adairia had taken straight to the kitchens where they could put the ingredients to good use in feeding the university residents. It was not much though; especially when anxiety seemed to be increasing steadily around the declining grain and produce deliveries from outside the university. They had never been entirely dependent on outside sources of food, with plenty of workers available to tend the land around the campus itself, but there were lots of mouths to feed and everything they did manage to grow had always been supplemented by farms further afield, who seemed to have less and less to offer these days. It was difficult not to be affected by the general air of nervousness.

'Adairia.' She felt as much as heard the voice whisper sharply at her ear and almost jumped out of her seat entirely. Turning to glance over her shoulder she discovered that Morag had snuck up behind her and was now crouched beside her chair, a worried expression marring her features.

'What's wrong?' Adairia asked, frowning.

'She's back,' Morag answered dryly. At first Adairia's heart sped up thinking that her friend meant Isla but then she wondered why this news would lead Morag to look so sullen. She had to mean someone else.

'Whose back?' She whispered in turn.

'The Lady Mirin. I just saw her in the hallway when I was coming back from,' Morag blushed, 'well never mind. She's here. I wonder what this means; have you heard anything from Isla?'

'Nothing new in the past few days. Her last letter didn't mention anything about the parliament concluding this week, in fact it sounded to me as if they'd be in session for quite a while yet. I wonder why Lady Mirin has left already?'

'Only one way to find out,' replied Morag.

'I'll write to Isla immediately,' nodded Adairia.

It turned out there was more than one way to find out why the new chancellor had returned so soon. As she had promised, Adairia had composed a short letter to Isla that very night and sent it out with the morning post. While she expected to wait a couple of days before receiving any response to her missive, answers were in fact much quicker to come. Morag, Calder, and Adairia were all eating breakfast in the common dining room when Cyril bustled over to their table and put a hand on Adairia's shoulder to catch her attention.

'Good morning my dear, sorry to disturb you but I don't suppose you're done eating?' he asked kindly.

'Good morning Cyril. No worries at all, I'm full to bursting. What can I help you with?' Adairia responded jovially.

'The chancellor would like to see you in her office whenever you're ready,' Cyril explained.

It still sounded wrong to hear Cyril refer to the Lady Mirin as the chancellor, and even more so to hear the tower suite referred to as 'her chambers'. He and chancellor Aliya had always been particularly close and there was a sadness in his eyes that had refused to dissipate since her death.

'Of course. I'll head there now. Thank you, Cyril.' The older man nodded before hurrying off to take care of his own duties for the day.

'I wonder what she wants to speak to you about?' Calder piped up, knitting his eyebrows together while Morag stared pensively after Cyril.

'No idea, but I guess I'm about to find out.' Adairia shrugged standing up from her bench. 'I'll see you both later then.'

'We'll be waiting,' Morag responded sombrely, and Adairia

headed off to find out what the Lady Mirin had in store for her.

*

Adairia climbed the winding stairs up the tower that led to the chancellor's rooms. A small part of her still expected to be greeted by Aliya when she reached the landing, although she knew very well that was no longer the case. She was trying very hard not to speculate on why the Lady Mirin had requested her presence the first morning she was back at the university, but one tends to have very little control over one's own thoughts. *Was it something to do with Adairia herself? Or was it about Fia or Isla?* Even the possibility that it might be regarding the late chancellor herself crossed her mind, but none of her trains of thought led her anywhere solid. Eventually, she found herself standing outside the solid-wood door that separated her from the new chancellor's office.

'Come in,' came a melodic voice from inside.

Adairia had barely lifted her fist to knock so the sound of Lady Mirin calling out made her jump. No turning back now, she thought before shaking her head admonishingly and pushing open the door.

'Adairia, thank you for coming.' The Lady Mirin did not look up from whatever she was doing but waved a hand to indicate that Adairia should proceed. The new chancellor was sat at the large desk on the far side of the room, quill in hand, purposefully penning something in her elegant looping script.

Unsure of whether she should speak Adairia simply walked up to the desk and stood there, trying very hard not to shuffle backwards and forward on her feet and appear impatient. Even if that was exactly how she was feeling. As Adairia looked on, the Lady Mirin signed her letter with a flourish and began to fold the piece of paper neatly between her fingers. Finally, she

248

secured the missive with a waxen seal and raised her eyes to Adairia who hoped she did not look as nervous as she felt. When the chancellor did not speak immediately, however, she could not help blurting out the first thought that crossed her mind.

'Do you have news from Isla?'

'Isla?' The Lady Mirin smiled delicately. 'No, no. I wanted to speak to you on my own behalf.'

'I see,' Adairia replied, not seeing anything at all. She stood there uncomfortably waiting for the chancellor to continue but she seemed to be in no rush. 'How can I help?'

'That's what I've been wondering myself,' the Lady Mirin replied leaning back in her chair and placing her hands regally in her lap.

'Oh?'

'I heard some interesting news while I was away, about your dragon.' She paused briefly before carrying on. 'You have made some discoveries regarding her breed have you not?'

'Well, yes,' responded Adairia, struggling to keep her puzzlement from showing on her face.

'She is cthonic in fact?'

'Yes.' Adairia nodded.

'How rare. Her parents' child more than any of us realised it would seem. And you have been developing her powers in the allotments I hear?'

'Well, yes, they could be incredibly useful.'

'Indeed, and she is coming along, is she?'

'I suppose so.' Adairia had no idea where this conversation was going but the Lady Mirin had a way of making her feel exceedingly uncomfortable and she wished that she would get to the point, whatever it was.

'You think she can help with some of Albiyon's produce shortages?' This point-blank question surprised Adairia who had spent very little time in conversation with the Lady Mirin up until this point.

'Um, I think she's a long way off that.' Then adding a little defensively, 'she's still a child really.'

'Of course,' Mirin nodded. 'Well, I would very much appreciate it if you were to keep me abreast of the situation Adairia. As I'm sure you can understand I have a vested interest in the wellbeing of both this university and the rest of our land. What with my various titles these days.'

'I will do my best.' Adairia replied warily. She doubted very much that the Lady Mirin required Adairia's updates on Fia's progress; she seemed pretty well informed without them.

'Please do. And Adairia do feel free to call on me should you need any assistance yourself. I understand my predecessor was attempting to support you through this change in situation. I can only imagine how you feel now that she has gone, and I would like to think, as her successor, I can perhaps fill in somewhat.' The Lady Mirin gave her a sympathetic smile that made Adairia wince. 'Unfortunately, the previous chancellor was not much for paperwork so I may be a little bit behind. Do you know if she was any further forward in uncovering answers concerning Fia's illness a few months ago?' To which Adairia could only shake her head.

'Oh well,' Mirin nodded, 'do bear my offer in mind.' She returned her gaze to her desk and drew another sheet of paper from a drawer before dipping her quill back in its inkwell. Adairia hesitated for a moment longer but quickly concluded that she had, in effect, been dismissed. *Well*, Adairia thought, *she was not one to linger where she clearly was not wanted.*

'That was all she dragged you up there for?' Calder exclaimed indignantly on Adairia's behalf. 'What was the point in that?'

'What was the point indeed?' Morag mused a little more thoughtfully. 'I wonder why she's so interested in Fia?'

'I wonder what she meant by her parents' daughter?' Adairia added ominously.

'Well, I suppose it's natural to assume that at least one of Fia's parents must also have been a chthonic dragon,' Morag pointed out.

'She talks as if she knows who they were? We don't even know who they both were. And the one we do know about wasn't a chthonic dragon either. According to the books I've been reading Cartimandua was a pyratic dragon.'

'Isla or the old chancellor could have told her who Fia's mother was?' suggested Calder.

'I can't see Isla telling her much and Aliya didn't seem to be spreading the information around either. She was pretty secretive when she gave me that ledger.'

'It was public record though, that was the whole point of the ledger, wasn't it?' Morag tried to explain.

'A public record that is half missing,' Adairia responded, a dark look coming over her face.

'You think the Lady Mirin has something to do with the missing archive material?' Calder gasped, slamming a hand against the low table they sat round. The noise, as well as the pitch of his voice, was little louder than intended, and a couple of the other people sat reading in the common area turned to glare at him admonishingly. He grinned sheepishly at Morag who meanwhile was rolling her eyes at the disturbance.

'We can't be certain that whatever information the ledger

was referencing was taken purposefully,' Morag reminded them. 'It's an old university with huge archives. Things have been known to go missing on occasion.'

'Missing documents are one thing,' Adairia conceded. 'But missing documents, someone disturbing my things, and let us not forget, a blatant attempt to poison Fia are quite another. Illness indeed,' she harrumphed, recalling the Lady Mirin's words.

'Don't forget the grain shortages and the villages in uproar,' Calder continued enthusiastically, getting into the speculation.

'We're sure this is all connected, are we?' Morag asked a little less convinced.

'You were the one who made the connection in the first place?' Adairia's tone was a little sharper than she intended.

'You're a scholar too Adairia,' Morag rebuked, raising an eyebrow. 'All I'm suggesting is that any speculation without evidence is just that, speculation.'

'Where are we supposed to get evidence from?' Calder responded leaning back into the sofa he was perched on.

'I just wish there was a book that could give us the answers,' Adairia grumbled. 'This isn't exactly your typical research project.

'No,' Morag mused, glancing around at the rest of the room's occupants to check none of them were listening in. 'This sort of job requires an entirely different skillset. This requires a spy.'

Chapter Thirty-three
The Plan

Lady Mirin was the youngest member of a family tree that could be traced back more than a millennium. Still, she was often the oldest person in the room. Fairies tended to live into their late hundreds, even two-hundreds, which made the lifespans of most other creatures seem fleeting. Apart from an older brother, who had not been seen in decades, she was also the last of her line.

Mirin's grandfather had served as the last fae advisor to the Albiyan royal family before the role was struck off along with that of monarch. The position had been the closest thing the fae had had to their own sovereign and whoever had filled it had held incomparable power over their kind. Now the fae had twenty seats in the Albiyan parliament and Mirin had to fight every five years to hold her own, begging for votes as if she was not descended from the oldest and purest fairy family in the known realm.

Not that the Lady Mirin had ever come close to losing her membership to the parliament. Among the other ancestral fae families she was well respected. Unlike the younger fae who had interbred and diluted their lineage, there were enough of them who still valued the old ways. The first queen of Albiyon had been a fairy after all, even if she had polluted her offspring's blood when she married her human husband.

Without those like her in the parliament, Albiyon would have collapsed under mob rule long before now. Watering down aid-parcels and blocking new taxations on the wealthiest citizens when she could, however, had never been enough. Those who considered themselves progressives may not have a care for the realm's coffers, but she certainly was not about to have her lineage dragged into the gutter with the squealing masses. In a world where magic was free to all and any street urchin could learn how to brew a potion, however, she and those who shared her views had struggled to retain their power. Wealth. Magic. Power. It was all one and the same. Control one, you controlled the rest.

*

Dear Adairia,

I'm glad you wrote. Tearlach and I were thrilled to hear that Fia is making progress in learning to control her powers. Cartimandua would have been proud, I'm sure. Please be careful though. I'll admit that the Lady Mirin's comments were suspicious, but she is not one to accuse lightly. She is a powerful woman, Adairia.

I have been away from parliament myself these past few days. This is why my response has been delayed. A contingent of us have been traversing the barren farmlands in the west with members of the magician's council. They have conducted a survey of the land and identified some sort of poison deep within the soil. What it is or where it comes from is something none of them could answer. No one had recognised it, but what they did say was that it seems to be coming from the ground itself.

Without any clear cause none of our experts can settle on a recourse for tackling the problem. Parliament itself is fracturing. As

I'm sure you would agree, I'm desperate to find some sort of way to heal the land but in the meantime I am convinced we need to do everything in our power to support the citizens of Albiyon and distribute what food we do have as evenly as possible. The traditionalist faction of parliament has taken this opportunity to vie for much harsher measures, however. They are convinced that the realm is overcrowded, and the land is lashing out. They wish us to close our borders while some are even suggesting that those who are the first generation in their family to settle here should be denied any 'hand-outs', as they call them, if they refuse to leave our realm. It may not surprise you to hear that one of the most vocal members of this group is our mutual friend, the Lady Mirin.

These voices have always existed, but they grow stronger every day. Our parliament is all about open debate, but I cannot help but think that these ideas go against everything my great grandparents fought for. Even Tearlach has started to show his age. The frustration that he cannot uphold Bayrd's hopes for Albiyon has struck him at his very core and I have never seen him look so distraught in all our years together.

But let me reiterate. Do not do anything foolish. Do not bait the Lady Mirin. She has insisted that she requires time to fulfil her duties as chancellor despite the ongoing situation, but it is difficult to be entirely sure of her motives right now. Do not draw more of her attention to yourself and Fia than is unavoidable. Promise me, Adairia. I worry.

Yours forever,
Isla

*

Adairia folded Isla's letter and tucked it securely in the leather purse attached to her belt. She had already read these words four times since the post had arrived that morning, each time more bittersweet. Seeing Isla's handwriting on the page, reading her name in Isla's script, it all filled her heart with joy. But then there were the words themselves. If she had expected reassurance from Isla, then she had been sorely disappointed. If anything, the tangled web that were her emotions had grown more scrambled since she first opened the letter. She had not shared the letter's contents with her friends yet and she was reluctant to do so. It would not change anything; it would only make them more anxious. And they had a plan to enact.

Adairia, Morag, and Calder had discussed it in detail over the past six days. They were going to conduct a raid. A small raid, but a raid, nonetheless. Adairia could not believe how fortunate she was to have friends like these when they sat huddled together in a private alcove discussing their scheme. Calder had taken to the art of plotting with gusto and Morag had offered her practical input at every turn. It was moments like these when Adairia was reminded of just how cunning her oldest friend could be. She hoped she would never get on the wrong side of Morag or she was sure she would come out the worse for wear.

It was reasonably straightforward; what Adairia wanted was some uninterrupted time alone in the chancellor's office to do a little bit of snooping. There were a few things standing in her way, however. The chancellor's personal chambers were connected to her study and only accessible through a single door. That made sneaking in during the night an impossibility unless they wished to unleash the wrath of a sleeping fairy. During the day, however, the chancellor was in and out of her study, with no predictable routine. Adairia needed to be sure that both rooms would be unoccupied for at least an hour to be on the safe side. The three friends needed to arrange for someone or something to keep the Lady Mirin busy and out of the way. And if the chancellor were to leave her office without the intention of coming straight back, she would likely lock it up behind her. Adairia was therefore relying on Calder living up to his claims to be a lock picker extraordinaire. This put Morag on distraction duty; not that she seemed to mind.

Adairia had decided not to involve Fia in their plans. Despite the dragon's strength and size, she could not help but still think of her as a child. Not to mention the threat that she felt lingered over her companion's back, putting her in more danger than any of them. Keeping things from Fia was not easy, however, due to the connection they shared. That was why they needed to act on their plans as quickly as possible, and then share anything they found with Fia after it was done.

'You're sure this will work?' Calder asked for the hundredth time, snapping Adairia out of her reverie. He sounded equally nervous and excited.

'As long as you don't get caught.' Morag eyed them both sternly. 'But we know for certain that there is one thing the Lady Mirin is going to want to see with her own eyes right now and that's anything claiming to have solved the grain crisis. If I can convince Aelish that I've come up with something real then the chancellor will have to listen to her, she's the highest-ranking alchemist south of the mountains.'

'And you think your potion can convince her?' Adairia pressed.

'I think it will have her seriously considering it at least,' Morag nodded.

'I still dinnae fully understand how this magic is supposed to work,' Calder mused. 'If it's that convincing then why can't it really be used to heal the earth? That'd solve a lot of our problems.'

'It's an illusion Calder. We've got samples of the infertile soil that we've been testing for poisons, but we've not come up with anything. We can't heal the ailment if we don't know what the cause is. What I can do is make it look as if it's recovering with a glamour. It won't really be healthy, and a glamour can't last more than an hour or so. They're easy enough to create with the right ingredients though. What I'm more concerned about is convincing Aelish I've found something I genuinely think can draw out the toxin. We're lucky I've got such a good reputation.'

'Nothing lucky about it.' Calder winked and Morag gave him a coy smile in return.

'What you two are going to need to do is make yourself comfortable somewhere you can keep an eye on the staircase to the Lady Mirin's rooms. I can't tell you when Aelish will fetch her but I'm sure that when she does, I'll be able to keep them both distracted long enough for you both to sneak in and out without getting caught.'

'Thank you, Morag, I don't know what we would do without you.' Adairia clasped one of Morag's hands in her own and gave it a heart-felt squeeze.

'Flounder purposelessly, I'm sure,' she grinned, giving Adairia's hand a squeeze in turn.

'Braw!' proclaimed Calder pushing his chest out and wrapping an arm around each woman. 'I never felt like we broke the rules enough when we were younger. Why not start by breaking into the study of the most powerful person in this place and rifling through her things? We should have done it sooner.'

Chapter Thirty-Four
The Heist

'Could you try and not breath so loudly!' Adairia hissed.

'We're no invisible Ads,' Calder retorted. 'Try and keep it together alright?'

'Sorry, I'm just...' *Bubbling out of her own skin,* thought Adairia; crawling with insects; grinding her teeth into oblivion; digging her fingernails into her thigh through the thick wool of her dress. If there was a nervous habit she had picked up over the years, she was exercising it now, and she had no idea how to rein it in. Calder, meanwhile, remained inexplicably calm. He was reclining in an overstuffed armchair, his feet propped up on a well-worn footstool and his eyes only very occasionally flitting to the archway that led to the tower's winding staircase. 'I don't know how you can be so relaxed?'

'It's an art,' Calder grinned, to which Adairia could only sigh and return to scanning the room for their signal.

'Well, you might want to look like you're doing some actual reading there,' she nodded, pointing at the stack of books between them that they had drawn down from the library shelves to disguise their true purpose in the hall. Calder shrugged, picking up the first volume to hand and glancing at the title.

'Advanced Techniques in the Art of Love. Alright, this'll do.'

He grinned.

'It does not say that.' Adairia insisted, covering her mouth to stop a giggle escaping.

Finally, after what felt like ten hours, but could barely have been one, she spotted Morag's tutor Aelish hurrying towards the aforementioned archway. She turned to catch Calder's attention, but it was clear from where his eyes were trained that he had spotted her too. Not long now, Adairia reassured herself. Morag had promised them an hour and she had to believe her friend. If she could rely on anyone to make good on their word it was Morag.

Approximately ten minutes later they heard two sets of footsteps dashing down the circular staircase hidden behind the walls and out came Aelish, quickly followed by the Lady Mirin. Aelish looked flustered but it was the look on the chancellor's visage that most unnerved Adairia. The usually calm and collected woman had screwed up her entire face so her lips had formed a thin line, and even from a distance Adairia could have sworn she saw the chancellor's jaw pulsating. Nothing about her demeanour implied excitement, and everything about it suggested apprehension. What mattered to them, however, was that she seemed entirely focused on following Aelish, as opposed to surveying the room as they passed through.

Once the two women had disappeared from sight, Adairia expected the knot in her chest to loosen but if anything, she felt more anxious than she had sixty seconds ago. Come on, she mouthed to Calder beckoning him towards the archway with a wave of her hand. She could not bring herself to break their silence in case the words she released came out as a yell.

Once she had assured herself that no one was paying any particular attention to their movements, Adairia proceeded to trudge up the stairs with Calder close on her heels. The noise her timeworn boots made on the stone steps caused her to physically wince with every step. *This was ridiculous,* she scolded herself, *they were not even doing anything wrong, yet.* When they arrived in the short corridor between the staircase and the chancellor's study door, she paused for a moment, collecting herself. As Adairia stood there and steadied her breathing Calder squeezed past her purposefully. Now, here was a man on a mission.

Adairia watched as Calder first tried the knob only to confirm that it was locked and then proceed to crouch down in front of the keyhole on the balls of his feet. From the pocket of his waistcoat, he drew out a small cloth pouch that he opened to reveal two thin pieces of metal before returning the fabric to his pocket again. With a quick glance behind him to check that Adairia was still there, and presumably had no objections at that time, he turned his attention on the lock. Jamming them inside Calder gave the metal tools a few deft wiggles and flicks that resulted in a small clicking noise from inside the door itself.

'Is that it?' Adairia gasped aloud, forgetting to keep her voice down in her awe.

'Should be,' shrugged Calder standing up and putting his hand on the handle. 'Would you rather do the honours?'

'You knock yourself out.' Adairia responded with a grin and a shake of her head.

Calder smiled back at her and proceeded to turn the previously stiff door handle. They both heard a second click before the door swung open, allowing them their first glean of the room within.

'We're in!' Calder opened his arms widely and gave Adairia

a little self-congratulatory bow. *To be fair*, she thought, *he deserved it.*

One by one the two friends crept into the room. There was no real need for their silence. They were too high up for anyone to hear them below, and if the Lady Mirin were to return unexpectedly then there was not exactly anywhere for them to go anyway. There was only one way in and out of the tower. Being heard would be the least of their worries if they had nowhere to hide. For a moment they both stood there staring at one another aimlessly before Adairia remembered that this was her mission. It was time to take the lead.

'Why don't you look in that cabinet and I'll start on the desk?'

'Sounds good to me.' Calder nodded and headed straight for the dark mahogany dresser that sat beside the door.

Adairia watched Calder as he perused the contents of the cabinet for a few seconds before remembering that she had some searching of her own to do. Marching over to the imposing desk she began slowly to leaf through the various papers in her line of sight, trying her hardest to make sure everything she touched returned to the same place once she was done scanning it. They both continued like this for the better part of half an hour. Neither of them said a word as they moved methodically through the books, letters, and documents stored in the chancellor's study. Occasionally one would have to revisit a title or paragraph their mind had glossed over in the haze of breaking and entering, but as the minutes ticked by they continued to make steady progress.

Adairia struggled to focus as she poured over a ledger detailing varying amounts of a metal called kriatine that the Lady Mirin was apparently involved in trading. She was about to replace the book back inside the drawer she had found it in, and move on the to the next one, when she spotted what had lain beneath it. It was a yellowed envelope addressed only with the words 'my child' on the front. At first Adairia assumed it was a personal missive from one of the chancellor's parents, nevertheless, something compelled her to pick it up and turn it over. The envelope and presumably the letter within were aged conspicuously. It had clearly been read before as the wax seal was already broken. *She recognised that seal,* thought Adairia, *but not because it was the crest of one of the old fae families. That was the royal seal. Isla's family. What was the Lady Mirin doing with a letter sealed with an antique crest belonging to a family she had no relation to?*

After a moment's hesitation Adairia carefully slipped the letter from its confines and unfolded it gingerly. She knew how important it was to handle ageing parchment with the utmost care and anything that bore the royal seal had to be more than one hundred years old at this point. Her eyes scanned the first few lines of the text and her heart immediately jumped in her chest. Two words in particular made her catch her breath: unhatched egg.

While I dictate this message, you are still but an unhatched egg.

She must have been staring open-mouthed at the letter for a noticeable pause because she eventually heard Calder's voice break through the fog.

'Did ye find something?'

Silently Adairia held the letter and envelope out to him, unable to articulate her confusion. Calder took it from her gingerly and flicked his eyes up and down its length in a matter of seconds before turning the envelope over in his other hand.

'It says here this is from the dragon Cartimandua. I'll bet my good looks she isnae the Lady Mirin's mother though.'

'Calder it's got to be the missing document the ledger referred to. But why does she have it? Why would she take something like this from the university archives?' Adairia could hear the increasing pitch in her own voice and winced.

'Ah dinnae ken, but I think we should get out o' here. Times running short and we've got to give this some proper thought.'

Adairia nodded taking the letter back from his outstretched hand.

'I'm not leaving this here.'

'Ah ken,' he agreed. 'But come on, now's no the time to dither.'

Adairia slid the ledger back into the drawer before closing it and together she and Calder hurried to the door, giving the room one final glance to be certain it looked as it had done when they arrived. Hearts pounding, Calder closed the door behind them and they hastily followed one another down the staircase and out of the tower. Without voicing it aloud they both knew where they were heading: to Fia.

Chapter Thirty-Five
My Dearest Child

My dearest child,

While I dictate this message, you are still but an unhatched egg, the last of your brothers and sisters to experience everything the world has to offer our kind. I fear, however, that when your time comes, I will not be here to welcome you to this glorious realm. I feel your presence in my mind; your life force is strong, but your slumber is deep. Perhaps you are waiting for a day I cannot yet predict. I trust you will know when your time comes as I myself did so many years ago.

I asked my companion to write this letter so you would know that your mother loved you; that I did everything I could to protect you. I am sorry therefore to place so much responsibility on your shoulders. For you, my child, are the last of your kind. Your father, rest his soul, was my final mate. I will not lay any more eggs now; I am too old.

Your father too was like you. He drew his lifeforce from the earth and soil as you do even now. I sense this connection in my mind, although I have never experienced it myself, for I am irrevocably linked to the heat of fire. His kind are old, from a land much further away than even mine, and their numbers have long dwindled. Now he has passed on from this world and you were his only hatchling to share his affinity.

You may be one of a kind, but do not forget that you are part of a whole. The world needs you to complete the series. Each dragon has a part to play in the ecosystem: air, fire, earth, and water. We are these elements and without us they are unstable, susceptible to injury. Together our kind can restore balance but only if the circle is complete. Through one another we are linked to each corner of nature.

This is why you must survive. You must one day be born into this world although it may look quite different from it does to me now. You must join your brothers and sisters because the earth needs you. For now, however, sleep. Rest my child, while you can. For you will recognise when you are needed. Just know this, your mother loved you more than life itself.

Your mother,
Cartimandua

It was difficult for an onlooker to read Fia's expression, but Adairia could feel the waves of longing muddled with bewilderment deep in her soul. Her heart ached as she read the words aloud and her frustration grew as she thought how the Lady Mirin had denied Fia this for so long, this connection to her kin. Adairia knew herself the pain of never knowing one's parents, of never having heard a father's praise or felt a mother's embrace. Not that she had ever felt alone. Her family was the university, her friends, and now Fia. But nothing could entirely eradicate that niggling sense of the unknown at the back of her mind. It was part of the reason she had strived so hard to find Fia any answers she could to her own history. And now that search had led them here: to this letter.

'Is that everything?' Fia asked tentatively. Although she could see herself there was no second sheet of paper that did not suppress the hope.

'It is, Fia. I'm sorry,' Adairia responded softly folding the letter back up and sliding it delicately into its envelope. The paper was thin and brittle, which was unsurprising now that they knew how old it really was.

'There is nothing to be sorry for. I never expected to have even this much,' Fia assured her companion. It was clear she was trying to be what she considered fair and mature about the situation, but her eyes were full of pain. It was as if she had been given a taste of the sweetest fruit imaginable only to be told she would never again be able to sample its juices. Love was like that.

'Ye ken what I dinnae understand,' Calder interjected, 'what our enigmatic new chancellor was doing with this letter in her desk drawer in the first place?'

'I suppose it was the previous chancellor's desk beforehand?' Adairia offered up. 'Perhaps she put it in there without even realising it?'

'But the seal was broken,' interjected Morag.

Morag had caught up with both Adairia and Calder as they exited the main university building on their way to visit Fia. With the revelation of the letter, they had not yet had a chance to hear exactly how Morag's part in the plan had gone; the fact that she had not been far behind them, however, made Adairia certain they had been right to leave the Lady Mirin's study when they did. She and Calder may very well have only narrowly avoided being caught rummaging through her things.

'I can't imagine the chancellor Aliya could have opened and read that letter then simply forgotten about it,' Morag continued. 'To even open a letter clearly not addressed to her when the correct recipient was ostensibly at hand seems out of character. She was the most respectful person I have ever met and as committed to finding out more about Fia's past as any of us. Which is more than I can say about some other staff members at this place.' Morag scowled and Calder nodded emphatically.

'Wishful thinking, I guess,' Adairia sighed.

'Why would the new chancellor try to hide my letter from me though?' Growled Fia, allowing a few plumes of smoke to spiral from her inflated nostrils. She made for an intimidating sight.

'It must be something in the letter itself.' Morag pondered. 'As much as I dislike her, I don't see the Lady Mirin doing something like this just to be vindictive. She barely even knows you, either of you. I'm sure she doesn't do anything without what she considers a very good reason. Not to mention how strangely she was behaving this morning as well.'

'What? What did she do?' Adairia pressed, her curiosity peaked by Morag's words.

'She kept asking me how I had figured out what was poisoning the fields.'

'What's strange about that?' Interjected Calder. 'Surely they'd want to know what was causing the problem so that they could prevent it from happening again.'

'But she kept pressing me. All she seemed to care about was whether I knew the cause or not. She didn't even seem particularly excited at the prospect of a cure, just fretful. It wasn't until I admitted that I had no idea what the cause was that she relaxed. And then she barely paid my sample of supposedly cured soil any attention before dismissing it and storming off again. Aelish looked pretty flustered after the whole encounter, but I don't think she blames me so that's something at least.'

'That's cause yer her star pupil.' Calder smiled giving her a playful shove with his shoulder. Morag batted him away with one hand, but she was not able to entirely suppress her own smile in return.

'And the letter was just stuffed in a drawer?' Morag asked.

'Aye, I didn't even notice it at first. It was lying underneath some accounting ledgers,' Adairia thought back on the contents of the drawer where she had discovered the letter. 'Kriatine, why does that sound familiar?' Calder shrugged but Morag's eyes widened.

'Kriatine? What about kriatine?'

'That's what the accounting ledgers were for, kriatine.' Then it hit Adairia like a sledgehammer. 'Kriatine is a banned substance. I've read about it in the historical trading laws. I'm pretty sure it was a big money maker, but the crown outlawed any mining of it in Albiyon more than three centuries ago.'

'I've never even heard of kriatine. Why was it banned?' Calder mused.

'I can't remember,' Adairia replied and both turned instead to look at Morag, whose expression was grim.

'It repels magic. Worse than that, any creature that comes in contact with it has their natural magic blocked. Not so bad for humans but there are some who it's incredibly dangerous to be around. A lot of creatures depend on their natural magic to live.' Morag paused again, clearly mulling this new information over. 'Did these ledgers look recent? Or could they have been from the archives?'

'The dates were current.'

'But the Lady Mirin's a fairy. What would she want with something that supresses magic?' Fia piped up, her brow furrowed.

269

'Good question,' replied Adairia darkly. But none of the friends had an answer for it.

Extract from A Dirty History of Mining in Albiyon

In the twelfth year of his reign, King Domnal IV issued a decree that outlawed all commercial mining of the substance kriatine. The edict came after many years of campaigning against the use of the metal by certain magical subgroups in the kingdom, and met with general popularity amongst the rest of the citizenry. Previously kriatine mining had been tightly controlled since the metal was so scarce, and under the Precious Metal Diktat of King Leith no natural resource should be depleted to negligible quantities until untapped deposits were identified.

Before the ban came into place, kriatine mines were concentrated in the west of Albiyon. King Domnal's decree, however, mandated that all proprietors safely shut down their pits or else they would face severe sanctions from the crown. Any colliers who were employed in kriatine mines were offered severance payments from the royal coffers and promised placements in alternative mining and quarrying industries. Those, who up until King Domnal's decree, profited from the kriatine trade, meanwhile, were vocally displeased with the measures taken. Many years of strong lobbying in opposition to those calling for a ban on the substance had suppressed the edict up until this point, but they were finally defeated.

Kriatine has a number of desirable properties. It is much stronger than its light weight implies, and particularly malleable making it ideal for use in delicate metalwork. The substance by all accounts appears to replenish its natural deposits, which are found on average between seventy and one hundred metres beneath the topsoil layers; although this process takes hundreds of years. One of its most controversial qualities, however, is its repulsion of magic. Similar to

271

the magnetic properties of metals such as iron and cobalt, kriatine creates an opposing force to organic magic. As far as magic practitioners can ascertain, the inability for organic magic to physically leave its hosts body forces it inwards, suppressing natural abilities and weakening the affected creature.

Chapter Thirty-Six

Fire

Adairia was furious. She did not think she had ever been this angry in her entire life. The rage heated her from the inside so that her whole body felt as if it were aflame; the fury threatening at any moment to engulf her. The largest part of her ire was directed firmly in the direction of the Lady Mirin, who seemed to be the root of so many of their problems. A tiny part of that anger had turned inwards, however, towards the small thought that niggled at the back of her mind: *this time last year her life had been so much simpler, so much easier,* it lamented. But how could she mourn a time when she had not had Fia, when she had not known Isla or Tearlach, or any of the other dragons and their companions. Her chaotic feelings resulted in an internal struggle that she knew she must relay back where it belonged: to the woman who knew more than she had ever admit to.

Adairia had been the first to voice what they were all thinking out loud. Perhaps it was because she was growing less and less surprised with the turns her life was taking, or simply a result of the intense fear for Fia's safety that had rooted itself deep within her from the moment the dragon hatched. Morag and Calder had approached her conclusion more cautiously, but it was evident that they could come up with no alternative theory that fitted the facts. The Lady Mirin had to be involved in whatever had led to the grain crisis somehow, or she at the very least knew who was. And what was she doing involved in the trade of a substance that had been banned in Albiyon for three hundred years? These things had to be connected.

The chancellor was also keeping a close eye on Fia, seeking out information, and hiding knowledge from the dragon herself. It seemed impossible to imagine that Fia's mother could have predicted their current circumstances, but she had certainly imagined a time in which the realm would need the assistance of dragons, including her unhatched daughter. There were too many coincidences. The earth was failing and Fia was the first dragon in a millennium to have access to the magic that could communicate with the soil. If the Lady Mirin was responsible for the poison that had taken root, then it would follow that she viewed Fia in particular as a threat. Who else could it be?

Without Fia the other dragons were incomplete. There was still one problem with her theory, however, and it was a significant one. Fia may have taken after her father but there were four dragon breeds. From what Adairia could discern, no one had seen or heard from an hydratic dragon for centuries, which meant that the circle Cartimandua had spoken of in her letter remained incomplete, as far as they knew. But she was starting to wonder what any of them really knew at this point.

*

Adairia expected falling asleep to be a struggle that evening after she had returned to her chambers. Often these can be the times that sleep sneaks up on the unsuspecting mind with the most unyielding ferocity, however, and within minutes of stretching out on top of her quilt, Adairia was fully under; still dressed in everything but her leather boots. Her dreams, meanwhile, kept her thoughts alert. She was searching the Lady Mirin's study, but this time she was entirely alone. It was dark outside, and her skin felt icy cold. When she glanced down at her feet, she realised they were bare against the marble flagstones. *Where had the rug gone?* She wondered.

Then her dream-self remembered why she was there. She was looking for something. There it was on top of the tallest cabinet in the room, higher up than she could reach on her own. Scanning the room she spotted the armchair by the window and slowly began to drag it across the floor towards her quarry. Once she had the improvised stool in place, she hitched up her skirts and placed first one, then the other, of her bare feet on the plush upholstery. With her hands stretched out as far as they would extend, she was just tall enough to grab the cumbersome object that sat atop the cabinet and gently lift it down.

It was lighter than she had anticipated, lighter than she remembered. Intently, Adairia stared at the impressive egg in her hands, the smooth orange surface shot through with veins of gold that reflected the light from a nearby candle. The same colour as Fia's scales. *Fia*, she thought, *where was Fia?* Gently she shook the egg and then tapped her index finger against the shell. It was hollow. In her shock she lost her grip and the egg slipped from between her fingers. It fell to the hard-stone floor smashing open loudly upon impact and making Adairia wince. Her suspicion had been correct. The egg was empty, except for… *what was that, mist? Or was it smoke?* Wispy tendrils were winding their way up from the mess of shattered eggshells and towards her frozen limbs. As they climbed higher, Adairia inhaled deeply only to breath in a lungful of suffocating smog that made her choke painfully. She tried to move but all she could do was double over while coughs wracked her body.

275

There was nowhere to go. Everything had gone black. And then she woke up.

But was she awake? Adairia wondered for a split second. She could still smell the acrid scent of something burning, although this time it seemed further away. She was also positively freezing, she realised. Her quilt lay beneath her and, when she cracked an eye open, she realised, her window was also ajar. She had forgotten to close it before falling asleep and it was allowing a cold draught into her room, along with something else. That smell was not just in her dream. It was coming from outside. Smoke. And smoke could only mean one thing: fire.

Fire! Adairia jumped from her bed suddenly wide awake. She rushed to her window, almost slipping on the cool floor in her bare feet. When she shoved the window wide open her nostrils were hit by the true intensity of the smell. Glancing furiously outside she could not see any flames that might account for the swirling smoke that was visible across the portion of grounds that could be observed from her room. *The fire,* she thought, *must be somewhere outside of her field of view. And if the smoke was travelling this far it must be big.*

Desperately, Adairia shoved her feet into the brown leather boots that she had discarded earlier that night and knotted them up with more haste than care. Abandoning her open window, she gripped the handle of her door with all her might as she wrenched it open and ran out into the corridor. She was immediately aware of numerous muffled voices travelling up the stairs from the floors below and sped downwards to seek them out. Once on the ground floor landing, she found a group of bleary-eyed residents in a jumble, each as confused as the last.

'Is that smoke I can smell?' asked one dwarf still dressed in her floor-length nightgown and hair standing on end.

'What's going on?' came another voice from an unidentifiable source.

None of these questions seemed to be addressed to anyone in particular, and instead of joining in with them Adairia decided that it would be better to push on. Out of the corner of her eye, she spotted a broad-shouldered figure pulling open one half of the large entryway doors and sped up to meet them.

'Do you know what's going on?' she panted when she had caught up with the figure on the path leading out from the entrance. As she looked up into their face, she realised it was the librarian Angus, worry painted thickly across his usually calm features.

'Adairia?' he replied in surprise. 'No, not a clue. But if there's a fire somewhere on the grounds of the university we better find out where. Come on!' He marched ahead and Adairia trotted to keep up with him as they turned to the right, in the direction from which the smoke appeared to originate.

As they rounded one last corner that allowed them to have an unobstructed view beyond the main building, they finally saw the flames. The dancing inferno spiralled angrily upwards in the distance, marring the night sky. A thick wall of yellow and orange had interrupted the line of outbuildings dotted across the nearby fields that backed onto the woodlands. And with a sinking feeling in the pit of her stomach Adairia recognised straight away which building was its source.

No, no, no, no, she screamed internally. She could not force the words out, feeling as though she had been punched hard in the gut by a stone golem.

'Is that?' Angus started before turning to look at Adairia directly and receiving all the confirmation he needed. 'Quickly,

quickly girl, you can't freeze up now. We need to ring the alarm.'

Just as Angus spoke those words, however, they both heard the loud clanging of a bell reverberate throughout the grounds, signalling to anyone still asleep that there was a fire in the university. It seemed as though they were not the first to spot the catastrophe, a fact which gave Adairia the invigoration she needed. Leaving Angus to follow in her wake, she began sprinting towards the blaze; towards the barn where she could only pray Fia was not trapped inside, or worse…

Chapter Thirty-Seven
Trapped

'Fia!' Adairia screamed, the sound tearing through her throat and vanishing into the commotion.

All around them figures were swarming. By some small grace, the nearest well to the barn was not far; two short lines had formed so that helpers could pass overflowing pails of water between themselves and get them to those at the front as quickly as possible while maintaining momentum. To the right of the building two fairies, a young man and a woman Adairia recognised from the university halls but could not put names to, were attempting to suppress the fire with magic. They each had one arm stretched out whilst gripping the other fairy's free hand in their own. Their eyes were closed, and they were desperately muttering words that Adairia could not make out over the din. Despite the haze of magic that caused the air around them to shimmer, their spell seemed to be having little effect on the fire itself.

Fia! Adairia cried again but this time for no one other than the dragon herself. She reached across the distance between them with her mind as if it were no more than a foot or two long, begging Fia to respond.

Adairia? There it was. The voice in her mind that was not hers but may as well have been. *Trapped! Fire!* Fia communicated in single words, stressing the fear she was experiencing. And then: *Got Calder.*

Calder? Adairia thought, her panic rising. *Calder was in there too? I'm here Fia! I'm here! We're going to get you both out.*

Adairia ran frantically to the front of the crowd where she now realised Cyril was conducting the lines passing bucket of water after bucket of water between them. Angus had hurried ahead of her and Cyril was explaining something to the larger man with perceptible haste. When he spotted Adairia he paused only briefly so that he could wave her over.

'Is Fia inside?' Cyril asked franticly.

'Yes, and Calder too,' she nodded.

'Calder? Anyone else?' Angus frowned but Adairia shook her head.

'Can you still communicate with Fia?' Cyril continued.

'Yes, yes, what can I do?' she practically begged.

'Right, this fire is burning too wild and strong. We can't put it out fast enough. We need to get them out by force, clear a path by knocking down one of the walls, but we need to be sure they won't be hit by the debris. Can you help with that?'

'Of course.' Adairia nodded and turned to face the barn, focussing all of her attention on her connection with the dragon. *Fia? I need to know where you are?*

Beneath the hayloft. Fia responded.

That was on the right-hand side of the barn, thought Adairia.

'Where do you need them?' she asked Cyril. Angus had moved away to organise the increasing numbers of university residents who were flocking to the scene.

'The fire is thickest at the front. We need to knock in the back wall, so out of the way but near enough that we can get to them as soon as there's a path.'

Fia, listen to me. They're going to have to try and knock through the barn to get you out. Get as far from the back wall as you need to in order to avoid any falling planks and beams but stay near enough that you can still get out.

Adairia felt the dragon acknowledge her instructions wordlessly and then her mind drifted out of reach while she focused on her task. *This plan seemed risky,* thought Adairia, but she certainly did not have an alternative. Despite the attempts to extinguish them, the flames just seemed to be growing fiercer by the second, engulfing every visible inch of the barn. The heat was claustrophobic even from the outside; Adairia did not like to imagine what it was like for anyone inside there. Fia's hide was thick and able to withstand temperatures higher than any human she knew – but she was no more impervious to fire than any other living creature. And then there was Calder. She could not dwell on it. Action was what was needed of her now.

Adairia followed the rest of the volunteers Angus had gathered and headed to the spot that Cyril had indicated. Extraordinarily quickly they had collected ropes and one particularly impressive caber that Adairia assumed was intended to be used as a battering ram. One of the fairies she had seen moments ago at the front of the outhouse had accompanied them to the back of the barn, and when their group was in place, she stopped at Adairia's side.

'I'll try to keep the flames round this side under control as best I can, to make it easier for you all.'

'Thank you.' Adairia nodded before turning to take the rope that Angus was holding out to her.

'Try to loop it over any protruding planks and pull,' he instructed her before moving on to the next person with the same instructions.

281

Just as she was watching four figures heave the caber onto their shoulders in order to distribute the weight evenly, Adairia felt another hand on her shoulder and turned to see Morag's anguished features.

'Adairia, I was in the basement, I hadn't realised, is she in there? What can I do? Have you seen Calder?' she was flustered and the words were streaming out of her without pause for breath.

'They're both in there,' Adairia explained and then held up her rope. 'Grab one.'

'Both?' Morag panted and then, without waiting for an answer, dived on a discarded rope and began to unravel it.

Adairia could not hear a thing for the next few minutes. She could see that Angus' mouth was open and he was shouting something at the log bearers. She could even feel her own breath coming thick and fast from her chest as she raised her arm to throw the rope as high as it would reach. The fairy woman beside her had raised her hands again and was murmuring an incantation but Adairia's ears were full of a static buzzing that muted the rest of the world. She was focused entirely on her task and although it took several tries, she finally looped the rope around a projecting beam and began to pull. To her right Morag had done the same and on her left, the figures that held the caber were running at the wall with their bludgeon. Together, they began to bring pieces of wood and other debris down as the barn lost its battle against the double fronted attack from both the fire and the rescuers. Meanwhile the fairy woman's spell seemingly kept the fire from spreading as quickly as it otherwise would have, so that the opening they were creating remained free of flames.

Adairia, I can see a gap, came Fia's eager voice in her mind.

We're coming, Adairia replied desperately as she pulled with all her might. And then the worst thing possible happened. Just as Adairia had dreaded, the fire had gained control and eaten through the overhanging barn roof. Before anyone could even yell out in surprise the right-hand side of the ceiling had collapsed inwards, right in the path of their escape route. Beams came crashing down and the noise suddenly swamped Adairia causing her to stumble backwards. Smoke curled up from the collapsed section of the building where the fire had abandoned its assault at last, victorious.

'No, no, no, no!' screamed Adairia making to dive forward but feeling herself instead pulled back by two strong sets of hands. She turned and saw both Cyril and the fairy whose name she still did not know grasping at her dress, preventing her from running any further forward. Glancing to the side she saw that Morag had collapsed onto her knees and was clutching at her stomach wide-eyed in horror.

'Fia!' Adairia screeched, first out loud and then in her mind, where she could usually always reach her companion. But no response came. She heard and felt nothing.

Angus was shouting something at the men and women who had previously carried the log or held the ropes, and who were now regrouping, their tools abandoned. Cyril was trying to say something to Adairia who could only hear the deafening sound of falling wood replaying over and over again in her mind. In her peripheral vision others were still attempting to quench the fire with water and magic; *but what was the point now*, she found herself wondering absently. That was, until she saw something move.

Through the smoke and shimmering air Adairia saw the pile of rubble shift. It could be the fire eating the caved-in roof from beneath but wait, no. She could feel something at the back of her mind. Something alive. As Adairia stared on, the wreckage bulged and then exploded. Wood and stone flew in every direction as onlookers dove for cover or coiled into balls on the ground. Adairia, however, could not tear her eyes away. From the flames and rubble burst an enormous shape. A dragon, its wings outstretched, one bent at an awkward angle but flapping furiously, lifting the creature, and the bundle it held in its claws, aloft.

Fia's first flight did not last long. Whatever strength that had fuelled her escape was quickly fading as she faltered in the air. Her wings continued to flap, and she sputtered forward, over the heads of those who had circled the back of the building and towards the woods. But not for long. Less than twenty metres from Adairia herself, Fia began to plummet to the ground, her only saving grace the fact that she had not gained a great deal of height in the first place. Before she could land, however, Adairia watched as the dragon turned on her side so that she crashed to the ground on her already damaged-looking wing.

Without another moment's hesitation Adairia sprinted in her companion's direction, simultaneously overjoyed and terrified, confused as to why Fia had rolled in the air at the very last minute. That was until she could see the dragon's heaving body more closely. The bundle she had noted in Fia's claws moments before, which now lay discarded beside the splayed-out beast, was not a bundle at all – it was Calder.

Chapter Thirty-Eight
Calder

Morag was quicker on her feet. Adairia lagged behind as the other woman almost tripped over herself to sprint in Fia and Calder's direction. The dragon having now released her bundle was lying prone on the ground, her injured wing crushed beneath her. Calder's body meanwhile was strewn beside her but remained eerily still. Adairia could see that even in her awkward position Fia's chest was visibly rising and falling against the moonlit sky. She could not help her heart from giving a leap of joy when it was clear the dragon was still breathing that was immediately suppressed again by guilt that Calder on the other hand showed no signs of life.

'Calder!' Morag's ear-splitting shriek hung in the air even as she fell to the ground at his side.

Adairia caught up to them but hesitated for a moment standing between the dragon and the human, unsure of where to turn. It was Fia that made up her mind. *I will survive.* She heard the rumbling assurance in her head. For all it comforted Adairia that Fia was out of peril her mind immediately latched on to one thought: *did that mean that Calder's survival was in question?*

Adairia slumped to her knees beside Morag who was leaning over the inert body. She had one hand pressed against his right wrist and the other to his neck. Between Morag's figure and the darkness, much of Calder frame was obscured but she had already gleaned a flash of his face before she knelt. His skin was a fierce shade of pink that practically glowed in the dim light. Adairia was not sure how much of him had come in contact with the flames, but it was clear that at least some of his skin had been badly burned. The extent of his wounds became more apparent when Morag leaned back and turned to face Adairia. The pink skin was actually the least worrying. All across his right cheek, jaw and neck the skin was destroyed and blood wept from his face. The clothing on the right side of his body was equally distressed and Adairia feared the wounds stretched further than she could ascertain at a glance.

'He's breathing,' Morag's voice broke through Adairia's reverie; tears were cascading down her face. 'He's breathing Adairia.' The pitch of her voice was barely audible it was so high but Adairia nodded reassuringly, gripping her friend's shoulder tightly; she would need to be the calm one right now.

They were no longer alone. Everyone surrounding the barn had seen Fia burst from the wreckage, and plenty had followed in Morag and Adairia's footsteps. When a hand fell on her shoulder Adairia turned to see Cyril looking down at her.

'There's a stretcher coming. We'll get him to a healer inside.'

'The fire?' Adairia croaked back.

'It's under control now, they're managing to smother it.'

Just as Cyril had promised a couple of figures soon pushed past the crowds, a stretcher carried between them. Morag reluctantly stood back as they loaded Calder's prone body onto the long stretch of canvas, unable to contain the loud hiccupping sobs that wracked her body. Adairia watched as they all hurried purposefully towards the University making sure to keep Calder steady as they marched. Adairia, however, did not follow them. There was nothing she could do for Calder right now and Fia also needed her.

As soon as the group accompanying Calder and Morag were out of sight, Adairia jumped towards Fia. She placed a hand delicately on the dragon's snout and watched as one of her previously closed eyes fluttered open. *Where does it hurt?* She murmured soothingly in her mind. Rather than scramble for words, however, the dragon opened up to her companion completely. Adairia stumbled back as the wave of pain engulfed her and she was able to fully appreciate the extent of Fia's injuries. Her face and back prickled with dozens of tiny cuts and bruises, while a searing burn spread across one of her back legs and up her tail, although it looked superficial to the naked eye. But none if this was anything in comparison to the agony of her right wing. The limb was an intricate web of tiny bones and at least a third of them must have been broken. The outer rim had bent back painfully on itself, and the joint twisted awkwardly where the wing met her torso. Adairia was all the more astonished that the dragon had been able to fly even the short distance she had, now that she understood exactly how extensive her wounds were.

'I don't suppose you've got a dragon sized stretcher stashed away somewhere?' Adairia called to Cyril in a falsely light tone, her eyes filling with tears. The older man shook his head and stroked his fingers delicately across Fia's damaged wing.

'Can you walk?' He addressed his question to the dragon herself, who snorted in assent.

Slowly, Fia shuffled first onto her stomach and then pulled herself into a kneeling position. Then leg by individual leg, she stood until she reached the burnt back leg and yelped painfully

287

when she attempted to put her weight down on it. Balancing on three legs, she wobbled slightly but she was nevertheless upright and Adairia smiled grimly in encouragement.

'You don't want to stay here. If you can make it to the courtyard at the rear of the university, we'll settle you in and get you looked over,' Cyril explained calmly.

Fia grunted again but did not speak. She was clearly exerting all her remaining energy on remaining balanced on her three good legs. Then without looking down she fixed herself determinedly in the direction of the university and began her steady journey through the night.

*

Adairia watched on as two healers and their assistants tended to Fia. Although it was frustrating to have no physical contribution to make, she could sense that her presence kept the dragon calm while these strangers poked and prodded at her. Despite their limited experience with creatures quite so large, the healers' pragmatism was impressive. They had cleaned her wounds from head to toe, treated the burn on her leg with a medicinal poultice, and fashioned a contraption of fabric and wooden dowels to keep her wing straight while it healed. The older of the two had also brought Fia a bucket of some unidentified amber liquid to sip on through the rest of the night, which she sniffed at suspiciously before plunging her face in nose first.

'Whiskey.' The healer winked at Adairia who almost choked on her own glass of water in shock before cracking up laughing.

'Do you know how Calder is doing,' she asked, 'the man who was caught in the fire?'

'They were tending his wounds last I heard, pretty extensive burns there.' The healer grimaced. 'He's in one of the medical suites in the east tower if you want to go look in on him though.'

'Thank you,' Adairia nodded, stroking a hand absently-mindedly along Fia's good wing. *Will you be alright?* She asked the dragon silently who did not raise her head from her trough to reply. *Go, check on our friend, I'll be here.* So, she did.

*

It was eerily silent in the medical tower; very little movement could be overheard and Adairia wondered if everyone had returned to bed. *What did that mean for Calder?* She peered around three separate doors into empty rooms before she found what she was looking for. There, highlighted by the dim light of a lone flickering candle, was Morag sat in a simple wooden chair. She was bent over an occupied bed that had to contain Calder. Sure enough, when Adairia crept further in she could make out his face through the shadows, what was uncovered of it, that was.

The greater part of Calder's exposed right half was coated in a thick, muddy green paste that Adairia recognised as the same poultice they had used to treat Fia's burns. He was shirtless, the blanket only covering his lower half, and someone had applied the ointment thickly from his face to his torso. Adairia tried not to flinch but the pain he must have felt was unbearable to even consider let alone experience. *Thank goodness he was asleep now,* was all she could think. Hopefully they had been able to give him something to numb the discomfort.

'Adairia?' Croaked Morag from her position at his bedside. Adairia had assumed she was asleep, and she may very well have been, but her eyes were now half-open and bloodshot as she looked round at her friend.

'I'm here.' Adairia reassured her, crossing the rest of the room in one long stride. 'I'm here.'

289

'They said he's stable, but the burns are severe. They're concerned he might yet be overcome by them, so they wanted someone to stay with him through the night. I volunteered.' Adairia could not see another chair so instead she knelt on the ground next to Morag's and took her friend's hand in her own.

'How are you doing?' she asked a little pointlessly she felt, but what else could they say. Morag clearly agreed, however, because she ignored the question.

'I love him so much,' she sniffed, new tears trickling down her cheek.

'I know, so do I,' Adairia cajoled rubbing the back of Morag's hand in circular motions.

'But I'm in love with him, Adairia.' It was not exactly a huge revelation. Adairia had realised long ago that this thing between Morag and Calder had grown beyond friendship, but neither of them had admitted it to it out loud, at least not to her, so she had not pushed it. She had been so busy, so overwhelmed by everything happening in her own life. She felt a small stab of guilt.

'Well, he's a very lucky man then Morag,' she managed to reply, attempting a small smile. 'He's got a lot to look forward to when he wakes up.'

'Thank you,' murmured Morag in return. 'How's Fia?'

'She'll be alright.' Adairia felt Morag squeeze her hand back and she counted her lucky stars to have such wonderful friends; such a wonderful family. She hoped that she would not lose anyone yet.

*

The next three days were the worst Adairia had ever experienced. The healers repeatedly informed them that Calder's condition was in no way worsening but nor were there

290

any indications of improvement as he remained fast asleep. Adairia eventually convinced Morag that she had to leave his bedside at least to get a few hours of sleep in a proper bed and not propped up on an uncomfortable chair. Otherwise, Morag ate all her meals in his sick room and abandoned her usual activities while Adairia split her time between both patients. By a stroke of luck, however, both women were sat beside one another watching over their friend on the evening of the third day.

Calder, who had thus far lain entirely still, turned his head to the side in his sleep. The small movement made Morag jump in her seat, and smack Adairia painfully on the arm to make sure she had seen. She had. His eyes remained shut but his dry and cracked lips parted just enough to allow a whisper of sound to escape.

'Morag,' he murmured before repeating the name again, 'Morag.'

It was Adairia's turn to slap Morag's arm as a wide grin spread across her face. Morag however simply let out a strangled cry and fell to her knees. She stretched across the bed and took hold of Calder's undamaged hand in both of her own.

'I'm here Calder. I'm here,' she sobbed burrowing her head in his bed sheets. Calder did not wake or utter another sound, but Adairia could not help but feel the first kindling of relief burning in her chest that evening.

Chapter Thirty-Nine
Isla Returns

Fia's mending had been more straightforward than Calder's. After she had passed out on the first night, she woke the next day feeling weary but very much alive. Her bandages had been changed, her wounds checked for infection, and all appeared well. Even the fractures to her wings the healers were optimistic would heal quickly. They were all clean breaks and, thanks to their diligent attendance, had been set cleanly and safely in good time. With Fia's dragonish ability to heal much faster than most other creatures it seemed there was little to worry about, apart from the origin of the fire itself.

An investigation, headed by Cyril and a group of senior scholars, had been undertaken the very next morning, after the last of the flames had dwindled down to leave a burnt-out shell in their wake. The surrounding greenery had shrivelled to an unnatural brown ten metres in every direction and the acrid scent of smoke continued to hang in the air. No source could be identified for the fire itself, however.

Adairia was exhausted. Her sleep had been sporadic and insubstantial over the preceding days and nights, while dark semicircles had become a permanent feature on her otherwise pale complexion. When she had failed to convince Morag to return to her own chambers after Calder's brief moment of lucidity, she had left her two friends alone together for the night. The journey between the medical tower and her own room felt like one of the most challenging she had ever traversed. Her groggy eyes blowing every step wildly out of proportion. When she finally reached her own bed, she collapsed on the sheets fully dressed, just as she had done three fateful nights ago.

*

Knock, knock!

There it was again.

Knock, knock!

'Adairia! Are you in there?'

Adairia attempted to flip onto her back, but she was cocooned in thick layers of quilt and instead rolled right off the edge of her bed, which she had apparently been precariously straddling.

'Ugh,' she groaned, extricating her right arm from the fabric and rubbing her head where it had hit the wooden floorboards.

'What was that?' came the voice again. 'Are you alright?' She recognised that voice, Adairia thought deliriously.

'Coming,' she croaked from her position sprawled out on the floor, and the knocking immediately ceased.

After a brief battle with tightly-wrapped bedding, Adairia freed herself from its hold and pushed herself up onto her knees before finally stretching to her full height on wobbly legs. That remaining grogginess did not last long when it fully hit her who had so rudely awoken her. With renewed vigour she leapt towards the door to unlock it, and practically pulled it off its hinges to get it open. There, standing framed in the wooden doorway, was an unmistakable freckly face and fiery mass of ginger curls. Isla was back. Adairia found she was lost for words when she tried to open her mouth and speak, instead

293

emitting only a small squeak of surprise.

'Good morning sleeping beauty.'

'Isla you're back,' Adairia finally exclaimed, flinging her arms around the new arrival's neck. Isla responded in kind by wrapping her arms around Adairia's waist and burrowing her head in her neck.

'Gods, I missed you,' Isla groaned bringing her face back up and planting an enthusiastic kiss on the other woman's lips. Adairia responded enthusiastically and they remained locked together in that position for what was probably longer than either of them would have liked to admit.

'Oh, Isla I'm so glad you're here, I had no idea you were coming back.' Without any pre-emptive warning, Adairia realised there were tears sliding down her cheeks as she remained clutching Isla tightly.

'I'm sorry to turn up out of the blue, it was a pretty spontaneous decision and once we'd made it there was no point delaying to send word ahead.' Isla smiled, bringing two thumbs up to wipe away the tears from beneath Adairia's eyes.

'Were you not still traveling with the magicians?' Adairia asked, sniffing but unable to refrain from grinning.

'I was, but I'm no alchemist. They can manage quite well without me peering over their shoulder for a short while, and I was needed here.' Her face fell at these words. 'I got your letter. Adairia I'm so sorry about Fia, and Calder especially. Has there been any change in his condition?'

'That may actually be looking a little more positive since yesterday, he started talking in his sleep.'

'That does sound promising,' Isla sighed, stroking a hand absently down the back of Adairia's hair. 'Do they know what happened yet to cause the fire?'

Adairia just shook her head in response before burying her face in the other woman's chest once more. She inhaled deeply, revelling in the physical presence of her friend and lover. The full force of her longing hit her hard in the chest now that the subject of it had appeared as if by magic, and she was reluctant to let her go, less she vanish like a mirage that her delirious mind had conjured up. Isla did not seem to mind either and the two stood there silently wrapped in each other's arms for some time before separating.

'And Tearlach?'

'He's with Fia.' Isla grinned sheepishly. 'We may have stopped in on her on our way here.' Adairia feigned offence, letting out a loud gasp and clutching her hand to her chest.

'I was not the first person you ran to find upon your return?"

'Got to keep you on your toes you know.' Isla stuck out her tongue teasingly and Adairia chuckled. *It was nice to laugh*, she thought.

'Can we see him?' Isla finally asked, and it was obvious who she meant. It warmed Adairia's heart to know that not only had she found such a strong connection with Isla since they first met, but she too, had come to care for her friends as they in turn did for her.

'Of course. He would be glad to know you're here,' Adairia nodded. It turned out she was more correct than she could have anticipated.

*

'Adairia, Isla, you're here.' A hoarse but joyful voice greeted them upon entering Calder's sickroom.

'Calder! You're awake,' Adairia squealed, wincing at the pitch her own voice reached.

'Aye and about time it sounds like,' he grinned, although it was a gentler one than his usual wide smile. 'Morag tells me I've been out of it for four days. I'm surprised I was allowed to get away with slacking off work for so long, but I guess people are willing to give you a little bit of leeway when you're almost toasted alive.' Adairia grimaced at Calder's dark attempt at humour, but Isla chuckled.

'It's good to see you friend. Sounds like I missed all the drama while I was away.'

'Alright for some isn't it,' Calder responded jovially. Adairia meanwhile turned to Morag who was slumped in the chair she had occupied for the past few days and saw that she was fast asleep.

'Does she know you're awake?' Adairia asked.

'Aye, you should have heard her, never known Morag to be so openly emotional. Turns out all it took was being trapped in a burning building to turn her into mush. Thought she deserved a rest after all the greetin so was just letting her sleep.' Calder's gaze settled softly on Morag's face. She was drooling slightly.

'You gave us all a scare,' Adairia responded seriously. 'What were you even doing in the barn? Fia said she couldn't hear anything over the flames, but you came running in waving your hands and then got knocked unconscious by a falling beam. She was frightened it had killed you.'

'That's my moment of bravery for you isn't it. I was trying to warn Fia about the fire, but the way Morag told it she saved my life,' Calder replied sombrely. 'I owe her more than a thank you, but I'd like to give her one nevertheless.'

'You spotted the fire first?' Isla chimed in. Calder nodded.

'A mare had given birth that night and I was just settling the foal in before heading back to bed when I smelled the smoke. I went to have a look and saw the flames starting to take hold of the outhouse. I knew Fia was inside, so I sprinted over to warn her, but the fire was spreading more quickly than any I've ever seen. I never expected to get trapped inside. I'd seen Angus running from the barn back to the university to get help but I couldn't just leave Fia there alone. Little use I turned out to be though.'

'What do you mean you saw Angus running to get help?' Adairia snapped, startled by his words.

'Well, there wasn't exactly time to stop and have a blether, but I saw him running in the direction of the university fast as anything. The smoke was already forming, and he was a few metres away so I'm not sure he spotted me, but I assumed it was him who sounded the alarm.' Both Calder and Isla stared at Adairia questioningly, looking for confirmation.

'He did no such thing,' she responded indignantly. 'I saw him in the entrance hall when I came downstairs to investigate the smell. He'd just woken up.'

'I know I hit my head, and a few other parts,' Calder winced, 'but it was definitely Angus, Adairia. There isnae any other ginger giants roaming the university to my knowledge.'

'But, but,' Adairia spluttered, 'he made it seem as if he'd only just been alerted to the fire at the same time as I had. He came to help put it out, but he certainly wasn't the one to sound the alarm. There was already a tonne of people there when we arrived.'

'Well, that doesnae make any sense.' Calder frowned but Adairia began to wonder if it did.

'Did you see anyone else Calder?' Isla asked.

'Nah, the grounds were empty apart from me and the animals,' he confirmed.

'Angus set the fire,' stated Adairia, her tone ominous.

'What are you haivering on about?' chocked Calder.

'No one knows how the fire ignited but they're pretty sure it wasn't natural causes, not when it accelerated that quickly and was that difficult to put out.'

'That doesn't mean...' Calder trailed off.

'That's exactly what it means.' Adairia was practically shouting now. She did not know when her volume had started to rise but she had evidently reached a level that even Morag could not sleep through, and the slumbering woman started awake in her chair.

'What's going on?' she slurred, peering blearily through half opened eyelids.

'Angus tried to kill Fia,' Adairia stated matter-of-factly, at which Morag's eyes flew open and she sat bolt upright.

'Huh, what?' She swivelled to look around the room and spotted Isla standing on the other side of Calder's bed. 'Isla you're back?'

'I am,' she nodded but did not smile this time around.

'Do you know who sounded the alarm?' Adairia asked Morag, redirecting her attention back to the topic of hand.

'Cyril, I'm pretty sure. He was among the first few on the scene and he started delegating immediately from what I'm told.

'Not the chancellor?' interjected Isla.

'No. No one saw her outside until after we'd freed Fia and Calder from the building. But it was the dead of night.' Morag turned her head back to face Adairia. 'But Adairia, Angus was there with us. He was helping.'

'Tell her what you just told us.' Adairia nodded at Calder.

'Angus was there before even I arrived. I saw him hurrying

from the barn towards the university as I was running towards it.'

'This doesn't make any sense,' Morag groaned, looking between the three other occupants in the room in turn with confusion.

Adairia, on the other hand, felt like she could finally see clearly. The anger and fear that had been quietly bubbling up inside her over the past few days, since she had almost lost two of the people that she loved most in the entire world now had a focus. Before she could say anything else, however, Isla spoke up.

'It certainly bares some explanation. Whether Angus is responsible or not it does seem a little strange that Calder should see him there just as the fire was kindled and then from the sounds of it pretend that he knew nothing of it when the entire university was woken up shortly after.'

'More than a little strange,' growled Adairia.

'But Ads, we've known Angus our entire lives. He's a librarian!' Calder objected.

'Isla's right though,' offered Morag. 'We should ask him at the very least. If Angus had nothing to do with the fire, then I'm sure he'll have a perfectly good explanation for what you saw Calder.'

'This is no casual query,' Isla ruminated aloud. 'I don't think we can just approach Angus ourselves.'

'Then what do you suggest?' asked Adairia, her frustration growing.

'I hate to say it as much as you will dislike hearing it, but I think we are going to have to take this to the Lady Mirin, along with the rest of the university council.'

Isla was right. Adairia did not much like the prospect of

seeking assistance from the Lady Mirin but she was the chancellor now. This was not something to be treated lightly and as personal as it felt it concerned the whole university. Luckily, they were all in agreement. Calder was of course still too fragile to leave his bed let alone march up to the chancellor's study and make accusations, as much as he would have liked to; Morag meanwhile was reluctant to leave him alone even despite his insistence that he would be fine. Adairia could see how anxious Morag remained and had no desire to drag her away either. As Isla pointed out the council would presumably want to speak with Calder later to receive his account first-hand anyway, so they both may as well stay where they were. In the meantime, they both insisted that two messengers were more than enough. And so, the two women found themselves climbing that winding staircase together once again, hands clasped in each other's.

Chapter Forty
Revelation

Once the two women had reached the landing, they paused for a few tense moments and exchanged nervous glances. Neither of them said anything out loud but there was a silent understanding that passed between their shared looks. It was Isla that knocked on the door; firmly, she rapped her fist twice against the heavy wood, the noise making Adairia cringe. They only had to wait a split second before they both heard a melodic voice call out to them from inside the room.

'Come in, it's open.'

Without further hesitation Isla turned the handle and pushed the door open into the room. The red-head entered first with Adairia following close behind, letting the door swing shut behind her. It only took a quick scan of the chamber to fully appreciate its range of occupants. The Lady Mirin was not alone. In fact, it appeared that the entire council was present. Cyril sat in the comfortable armchair while Angus occupied the well-worn settee. Even Tronk was there, standing with his back to the fireplace, hands stretched out behind him to absorb its heat. The goblin must have returned as recently as Isla, and probably for the same the reason. Meanwhile, the Lady Mirin held court, standing framed by the window, clearly the sole focus of attention prior to their arrival.

'Lady Isla, I was hoping you would stop by. I was already informed that your dragon was on campus a short while ago.' Her eyes flicked over Adairia. 'And Adairia, welcome. To what do I owe your visit this afternoon?'

'Good afternoon chancellor,' replied Isla, a little more hesitantly. 'We had hoped to speak to you in private. It's regarding the recent fire.'

'What luck, that was exactly what we were meeting to discuss. Please, join us. It does concern the whole university after all.'

'Yes, but it is a sensitive matter we have to disclose.'

'Anything you would like to share with me can be shared with the entire council.' Isla looked uncomfortably from the Lady Mirin, to Angus, and then Adairia who had, personally, had quite enough.

'We've heard from a witness who saw Angus fleeing the scene of the fire before anyone else was aware it had ignited.' Declared Adairia. She glared at the librarian through every word and watched as his pallor turned from a ruddy red to sickly grey before her very eyes.

While Angus remained silent, the rest of the room was not quite so peaceful. There was a cry of 'How dare you!' from the place where Tronk stood, and Cyril gasped so violently that it sent him into a fit of coughing. Even Isla muttered Adairia's name in a hushed but clipped tone as if to reel her back in before she started a physical fight.

'What exactly is it that you are suggesting?' responded the Lady Mirin calmly turning her gaze on Adairia, one neat eyebrow quirked dubiously.

'We're suggesting that Angus had something to do with what happened to the barn, to Fia and Calder.' Adairia was about to stride up to Angus and confront him herself, but she was beaten to it. Cyril had overcome his outburst and drawn himself up to a standing position. In one long stride he positioned himself in front of Angus, who remained seated, and stared down at the younger man with a look of utter horror on his face.

'Is this true Angus? You were at the scene of the blaze before anyone else, before myself and the other first responders? Tell me this is a mistake. Because I saw you arrive with Adairia myself when the building was fully alight, as shocked as any of us by what you found, and both cannot be true.' Cyril's expression seemed torn between tears and full-blown fury.

Adairia expected the large man she had known for most of her life, who she had spent so much time searching bookcases and discussing the merit of various translators' styles with to refute her claims. She expected him to tell Cyril no, that there must have been a misunderstanding and he had no idea what they were talking about. She even expected him to turn on her, spitting fire and accuse her of having malicious intentions. But he did none of those things. His mouth opened and closed repeatedly but no words came out as he looked up wide eyed at his friend and colleague.

'I… I…' he finally began to splutter. As Adairia watched on, however, his eyes flicked from Cyril's face to the Lady Mirin who was staring back at him intently, her own countenance eerily calm. Within the passing of a split second the look of pained confusion disappeared from his features and was replaced by something far more disturbing – complete expressionlessness. His face went blank, and he turned back to Cyril. 'Yes. It was me. I started the fire.'

'But why?' cried Cyril, his voice catching on the last word.

'I started the fire,' Angus repeated.

'Yes, we heard you the first time. Now explain yourself,' growled Tronk who had taken two steps forward from his previous position.

'I started the fire.' There was something unnerving about the glazed look on Angus face that in her anger Adairia could not fully comprehend. He was not even really looking at Cyril, not directly anymore. His eyes were glassy and directed instead to an unidentified point somewhere above the older man's left shoulder.

'Why do you just keep repeating yourself man?' Cyril was beginning to sound more aggravated as he raised his own voice.

'Is he under some kind of spell?' Demanded Tronk from no one in particular.

'That or he has completely lost his mind.' It was the Lady Mirin that offered up this insight. Her face was impassive, but she had swung her body round to focus fully on Angus. She was twisting her hands over and over again in what appeared to be agitation, something Adairia had never associated with the fae.

'Snap out of it!' Cyril reached a hand-out and clasped Angus' shoulder firmly, but nothing changed. 'None of this makes any sense. Why would you do something like this?'

'I started the fire,' he repeated for the fourth time.

'Well, there's no refuting your witness now ladies,' Lady Mirin said lightly. 'Our head librarian has confessed.'

'He was fine ten minutes ago,' Tronk pointed out, eyeing Angus sceptically but Lady Mirin ignored him.

'If you would leave us Lady Isla, Adairia, I think this a matter for the council to handle and possibly a healer. Neither of which you are.' Her voice was calm and even her wrists had ceased gesticulating. *This was not right*, thought Adairia. *None of this right.*

'You did this,' Adairia hissed.

'I did what?' Lady Mirin's voice took on a sharp edge that had not been there before.

'Angus, the fire, you're involved in all of this somehow.'

'Adairia!' exclaimed Cyril spinning round in shock at the young woman's accusations. Isla reached her hand out and grabbed Adairia's arm, firing a questioning look at her with those sparkling green eyes. The Lady Mirin, however, merely smirked.

'This isn't madness, it's magic.' Adairia wanted to scream but she attempted to keep her voice level.

'That I can agree with,' nodded Tronk, his expression difficult to read.

'And what possible reason could I have for setting a barn in my own university alight?'

'You've got something against Fia. I know you have,' Adairia pushed. 'If not, why were you hiding a letter from her mother in your desk?' This was the wrong thing to say, however.

'Am I to believe that you have broken into my study in my absence?' Lady Mirin's tone was surprised but her expression did not mirror it. 'And based on the absence of said letter, stolen from me as well?'

'It wasn't yours to keep,' Adairia barked.

'If you must know child, I found that letter amongst the previous chancellor's things only the day before you must have snuck in here uninvited. It had been my intention to present it to your dragon at the first opportunity until I discovered it had vanished.'

'I don't believe you.' Adairia's voice was growing steadily louder and even though she could feel Isla tugging at her sleeve pleadingly, she could not stop the words escaping her mouth.

'Got any proof of this girl?' Tronk asked. From the look on his face, he would have very much liked for Adairia to offer up such proof, but she had nothing. Her silence said everything.

'I think Adairia is quite aware that she has no proof whatsoever and I for one am tired of having accusations flung at me in my own chambers.' She paused long enough to run her eyes around the room and sigh as if pondering what to do. 'In fact, I'm afraid I'm going to have to rescind your welcome to this entire institution.' Adairia's mouth fell open.

'You're throwing her out?' cried Isla, horrified.

'You can't do that. This is my home!' Adairia whelped.

'Chancellor, don't you think we should discuss this,' Cyril piped up but the Lady Mirin dismissed them all with a flick of her wrist.

'This university does not tolerate thieves. You live here on our good faith. Faith which I can no longer extend to you given what has just transpired. You have three hours to collect your belongings and then I expect you to vacate the grounds. I will not tell you twice.'

Chapter Forty-One
Together

The chancellor was true to her word. Both Isla and Cyril attempted to plead her case, but Adairia could only stand there agog, unable to pick out any of their words as her ears filled with a thick buzzing sound. Angus remained inert and Tronk watched on with a keen eye but said nothing. *What could they say?* The Lady Mirin had made up her mind and as chancellor it was her prerogative to extend or rescind any invitation to stay at the university. With Adairia's confession hanging in the air she had all the ammunition she needed to enact her will.

Adairia was barely aware of her own feet as Isla gently led her from the room, their arms linked together with Isla's hand on Adairia's elbow to guide her. Eventually they arrived at her room. Or what had been her room, Adairia realised. It would be someone else's room soon. Isla pushed open the door and held it open while Adairia walked over the threshold for what was presumably the last time. For a few overwrought moments both women stood silently side by side and took in the space around them before Isla broke their reverie.

'Adairia, you'll come back to Baile with Tearlach and I. You and Fia. You have a home with us, you must know that.'

Adairia turned to look Isla directly in the eyes and saw the sincerity there. It was this that finally broke her. She let out a heart-breaking wail and slumped to her knees on the cold wooden floor. Once the dam was broken the tears would not stop coming and they began to streak down her face and neck as if participating in a mad race to some unknown destination. This was her home. This was where she had grown up. This was where her friends and makeshift family were; where she did her research; where she tended her garden. This was where she had broken her first bone, falling from an old oak tree that Calder had convinced her to climb, of course; where she had had her first sloppy kiss in a dark corner of the building during their Yuletide celebrations; where she had met Isla and found Fia. How could she leave?

'Isla,' she sobbed, unable to find words to express her misery. The other woman did not need them to understand, however, and wrapped her arms around Adairia's body, pulling her in close to her chest and murmuring soothing sounds in her ear.

'I know it doesn't seem that way, but it's all going to be alright. We'll make it alright.'

'I need to tell Fia in person,' Adairia hiccupped.

'She'll be fine.'

'And Morag and Calder,' Adairia wailed again, her tears falling with renewed vigour.

'We'll go to them as soon as we've packed your things.'

And so, they did.

*

It did not take long to pack Adairia's belongings up. Most of the books in her room were the property of the university; a fact that had never before made Adairia feel as though she was handling someone else's tomes. In all reality her most prized possessions were buried deep within the soil over in her vegetable plot; none of which could come with her. So, in the end her life whittled down to two overstuffed leather duffle bags, one of which filled by her various dresses and skirts and the other holding her small selection of personal books and trinkets.

Once they had completed that task Adairia felt it was only fair to speak with Fia first. This university had been her home even longer than it had been Adairia's, even if the dragon had been asleep in her egg for all but a fraction of it. Something that made all the difference apparently. Fia was saddened to hear their news but more so, it seemed, in sympathy with Adairia's own sense of loss than her own. She did not like to leave Morag and Calder, she explained, but she also felt as much at home at Baile as she did here.

'Home is wherever we are caraid bheag, together.' These words sent Adairia into renewed floods of tears that Fia found surprisingly alarming.

'You're leaking. Why are you leaking? Isla! What is wrong with her?' she barked fearfully. Rather than elicit concern, however, this simply sent Isla into fits of giggles that she managed to eventually stammer an explanation through.

'I can't believe you've never seen me cry before.' Adairia eventually sighed, managing to conjure a small smile as she wiped a sleeve across her damp face.

'We will have to walk at least part of the way to Baile,' Tearlach interrupted. He had been at Fia's side ever since that morning when he and Isla had arrived. 'Fia's wing is not fully healed, and she is too large now for me to carry on my back along with both of you.'

'You're right, Tearlach. Adairia, why don't I go gather us

some provisions for the journey and allow you some time alone with Calder and Morag. I'll come and find you when we need to leave.' To which Adairia nodded sadly and squeezed Isla's hand in a gesture that could do nothing to fully express her gratitude.

*

'She can't do this!' Calder repeated for the umpteenth time. But she could, and they all knew it. The Lady Mirin could do whatever she wanted. His protests were involuntary exclamations at this point.

Morag must have been more exhausted than even Adairia had realised because when she had first told them both the news her oldest friend's eyes had filled with her own silent tears and she had jumped on Adairia with a fierce hug. Evidently, things had been getting to her too. The sight of her usually so stoic friend breaking down in front of her had sent Adairia into her own fits of sobs and when she and Morag had separated, she had been able to see that Calder too, was teary eyed in his sickbed, staring at them both.

'You can come visit Baile when you're fully healed,' she told Calder who grimaced rather than smiled.

'That might be a little while yet but when I've stopped erratically bleeding through my bandages you can count on it.'

'We'll be there,' Morag concurred, nodding her head fervently. 'And in the meantime, I'm going to be watching her every move.' They all knew that the 'her' Morag referred to was the Lady Mirin. If there had been anything she could have done to cement herself as their enemy, it was this. What exactly three twenty-something nobodies could do in the face of one of Albiyon's most influential citizens was an entirely different, and less appealing topic for discussion.

310

After thirty minutes or so, a knock came at the door and upon being invited in by Morag, Isla entered. She had a bulging satchel slung across her shoulder, which was presumably full of food for their journey. It was not going to be a day's long trip this time around. After Isla had hugged both Morag and Calder, although more gingerly, in turn she took Adairia's hand in hers.

'We have to go,' she said softly and Adairia nodded.

'Soon,' Morag whispered giving Adairia one last kiss goodbye on the forehead.

The two women then exited the room hand in hand, refraining from looking back or else Adairia knew she would start crying again. She felt reassured by the solid presence of Isla beside her, their hips occasionally brushing against one another as they made steady progress to the open fields at the back of the university. There, waiting for them were Fia and Tearlach, luggage strapped firmly to their backs and Fia's wing newly dressed.

'There are spare bandages and poultices in one of the bags for Fia,' Isla assured her as they approached. 'And the healer I spoke to was confident she'd be right as rain in a few days. Perhaps even ready to give flying another shot.'

'Thank you.' Adairia smiled pausing to press a gentle kiss on the other woman's lips.

'Of course, Adairia. Anything.' Isla hesitated before continuing. 'I love you.' There it was, in a moment of utter darkness, the light that Adairia had needed.

'I love you too,' she responded confidently and watched with pleasure as Isla's nervous smile transformed into a grin wider than anything she had seen before. They both carried on till they reached their companions' sides and, united, the four of them set off together.

THE END, FOR NOW.

Afterword

Where do I start? Thank you so much for reading *The Flames of Albiyon* and following along on Adairia's adventure, so far. This novel has been my passion project for the last three years and it has been a nerve-racking experience deciding to put it out into the world. This book is more than a story to me and I'm not even sure I can articulate all the ways in which writing it has brought me joy and catharsis. The themes of love and grief that are touched upon in these chapters are very much real, as opposed to fantastical. As are the political ideas explored in the realm of Albiyon.

Nothing about this book is subtle and I realise that, but that's exactly what I wanted. I wanted to write about a fantasy world where monarchy was a thing of the past and where the people actively participated in the running of their home. As much as I would have liked to imagine the socialist utopia of my dreams, however, it was important to me to explore the ways in which, even when it seems that equality and fairness are the status quo, there are always those who oppose these ideals; those who seek to dominate, impose hierarchy, and profit from others. Just as they do in our own world.

At its core, however, *The Flames of Albiyon* is a story of hope. It is about a young woman whose life has been turned upside down but finds solace in her friends and found family. And

313

that's not to mention the love story that runs parallel to this journey. My own coming out story has been a rocky one and, it seems, a never ending one. So, to imagine a world where Adairia and Isla could fall in love without comment, or sanction, without second thought or explanation, has been an important part of my own liberation, which I hope others can find solace in too.

I could probably write another eighty thousand words just about how much this story and these characters mean to me, but I'll be my own editor here and say enough is enough. If you'd like to learn more about my other books as well as the realm of Albiyon, you can visit my website www.jeanmenzies.com or come say hi on social media, where I usually go by @jeansthought.

Before I go though, I do want to express my gratitude to all of the friends and family who have supported me through the process of writing and releasing this novel. This book is for Jill, who read every chapter as I wrote them, and helped bring each character to life through our conversations. It is for Chris, proof-reader extraordinaire, who didn't let the fact that I am his girlfriend get in the way of giving me honest feedback. It is for my mum, Fiona, who despite decades of work as a graphic designer had never drawn a dragon but learnt to do so just for this cover. It is for Grace who used her magical speed-reading abilities to read this novel in one evening and give me her thoughts when I needed them most. It is for Lorna who came to the rescue in the final weeks before *The Flames of Albiyon* was published and reminded me why I love this story. It is for Ashleigh and Lianne, who listened to me rant and rave at every step of this journey and, without whom, I might never have published this book in the first place. It is for my dad, John, who passed away the year before I first began writing this novel and without whom I would never have written it at all. It is for them, and all the people who have supported and encouraged my writing, of whom there are too many to name. I love you all.

Made in the USA
Middletown, DE
18 October 2021